WHEN HE SAVED ME

MELODY CLAIRE

For my mom, who gave me my love of books.
I miss you.

Also, Fuck Cancer.

TRIGGER WARNING

Your mental health should be your first priority! Take care of yourself!

This book contains the following subjects which may be triggering for some readers. For a more specific list of triggers (may contain spoilers) please visit my website. Questions may also be directed to melodyclaireauthor@ gmail.com.

***

Grief, homophobia, cancer, parental abandonment

CHAPTER 1

FINN

"PLEASE COME WITH US TONIGHT!"

"No."

"Come on, I really want you there."

"Carmen, I said no, and I meant it."

"Ugh. You never come out with us."

"That's not true." Though it wasn't because I hadn't tried. My best friend could be really, really stubborn when she wanted something. Tonight, she wanted me to come to a Halloween party with her and her bitchy girlfriend. "I went out with you guys on Tuesday." *And spent half the night watching your girlfriend flirt with some dude while you acted like you didn't notice.*

I turned and walked away from her, heading into the back room to grab straws and napkins to finish my closing duties and get out of there. Despite the fact she didn't actually work in the coffee shop, Carmen hopped off the counter where she'd been sitting and followed me to the back, just as I'd known she would.

"It's Halloween. On a Saturday. Halloween hardly ever

falls on a Saturday, and this party is going to be epic. It's my favorite holiday, and I want you there with me."

"What about Amy? Does *she* want me there?" I was pretty sure Amy hated me. Which was fine since the feeling was mutual. I carried the straws and napkins back to the front and began restocking the containers.

"Of course Amy wants you there. I don't know why you'd think she wouldn't." Carmen didn't take bullshit off anyone except those she chose to date. She had a blind spot when it came to her love life, and it didn't matter when I pointed out that she allowed her girlfriends to treat her like shit. She always found a way to justify their behavior. It made me crazy because she deserved better, but that was something she needed to figure out for herself.

I sighed and turned to look at her where she stood with her arms crossed and her eyebrow raised. "You know I hate people," I said. "I've peopled here at the shop for the last six hours. I've peopled here five of the last seven days and played gigs at Ivory three of those. I just want to go home and chill in peace."

There was a knock on the window at the front of the shop, and we both turned to see an annoyed Amy staring us down. Carmen rushed to open the door and let her in before locking it again behind her. "You ready?" Amy asked Carmen without so much as a glance in my direction. They had a whispered exchange that sounded more like an argument than a conversation before Carmen finally called out, "Are you sure you won't come?"

"I'm sure. Go. Have fun!"

"Come on, Carmen." Her tone petulant, Amy tugged at Carmen's sleeve. "Let's go."

Carmen shrugged out of her grasp and darted over to where I stood, surprisingly light on her feet, despite her Doc

Martins. She leaned up and pressed a kiss to my cheek. "Call me if you change your mind."

"I will." We both knew I wouldn't.

She locked eyes with me, but at Amy's not-so-subtle sigh, she turned, and they both left.

I finished stocking straws and napkins, then began putting chairs on the tables so the night crew could clean. With that task done and the drawers counted and locked in the safe, I shut off the lights, locked up, and headed home.

AN INCESSANT BUZZING WOKE ME. I reached over to my nightstand, blindly feeling around for my phone in the dark. I unplugged the charging cord, seeing Carmen's name lighting up the screen. Noting the time as two thirty-two a.m., I swiped to answer. "Carmen, what the fuck? It's two-thirty in the morning."

"Finn. I need you to come get me." Her voice was low and muffled, and I sat up in bed, instantly alert.

"Where are you? Are you okay?"

She choked back a sob. "Just come get me, okay. I'll send you my location." Before I could ask for more, the call disconnected.

I hopped out of bed, grabbing the same jeans and T-shirt I'd worn to work earlier that night. My phone pinged with an address in what I knew to be an affluent neighborhood, and I blew out a breath as I swiped my keys and wallet off the dresser and headed out.

Fifteen minutes later, I pulled up in front of a perfectly manicured lawn with a long, winding driveway leading to a mansion set back from the road. I'd like to say the size of the house was a shock, but Carmen and I had been brought up in this world.

Since graduating from our elite, private prep school, Carmen tended to bounce between my tiny one-bedroom apartment and the home of whichever girl she was dating at the moment, but that wasn't because of a lack of funds. Her wealthy parents still gave her a hefty allowance to cover living expenses and groceries. She just hated living in solitude.

I, on the other hand, had been unceremoniously kicked out of my house at eighteen. Therefore, I hadn't had the luxury of choosing my accommodations. I worked for every penny to provide for myself, which meant I resided in a small apartment on the third floor of a walk-up in a shabby part of Kansas City.

The life I'd been raised in seemed like a lifetime ago as I stared at the mansion before me. My memories of that world, of those people, weren't rosy. The Jeep my parents had given me for my sixteenth birthday was the only thing I still held on to from that life. Mostly because I couldn't afford a car on my own.

Carmen, however, had never quite been able to cut herself off from it. She simultaneously scoffed at the excesses of that lifestyle, shunning all they stood for, while still seeking acceptance from the very people she showed disdain for.

The property in front of me was huge. The driveway was lined with cars, and I could hear the pump of bass coming from the house, so I assumed the party was still in full swing. If Carmen was in there, it'd be nearly impossible to find her. Remembering the sound of her panicked voice on the phone, I pulled out my phone and sent her a text.

> I'm here. Where are you?

CICI

Don't come in. I'll come to you

> Are you sure? Are you ok? I can come in
> and get you...

CICI

Just wait there. I'll explain when I get in
the car

> Ok

As I waited for her to reach my side, I contemplated what might have prompted her to call me at such a late hour and why she didn't want me to come inside. And what about Amy? They'd come here together, so where was she now?

In the dark, I made out her form coming toward me in the shadows. She was still wearing her pin-up girl Halloween costume, but as she got closer, I could see her smudged mascara and messy long dark hair. She began to run as soon as she spotted me, throwing herself into my arms, shaking with silent sobs.

I pulled her around to the other side of the Jeep, away from the view of the house, and held her as sobs wracked her body. Once her tears began to subside, I walked her around to the passenger door and helped her into my Jeep.

After several minutes of driving, I broke the silence. "What happened?"

"I don't want to talk about it," she responded, her voice uncharacteristically soft.

"Carmen...I need to know what happened. I need to know you're okay."

"I'm okay."

I stopped at a red light and turned to look at her. I couldn't see her face because she'd turned away from me to look out the window. "Are you really?"

Her only response was a one-shouldered shrug.

"What happened? Where's Amy?"

She shrugged her shoulders again, turning her attention to a snag in her fishnets. She picked at it repeatedly, and I watched as she slowly made a hole that got wider and wider.

The stoplight turned green, but I didn't move to drive. At three a.m., there wasn't another soul on the road anyway. "Honey, where's Amy?" I asked more gently. I had a bad feeling Amy was at the root of this situation.

"She cheated on me," she whispered as a tear slid down her cheek. "I went out to the kitchen to get another round of drinks for us, and when I came back, she was sitting in some guy's lap with her tongue down his throat."

I felt my blood pressure rise. I wanted to kick Amy's ass. I reached out and laid my hand over hers, attempting to offer some comfort. My free hand clenched around the steering wheel, my knuckles white with rage. Despite my anger, I kept my tone gentle as I said, "I'm so sorry, honey. You deserve so much better."

Carmen tried to speak, but the words failed to come. She cleared her throat and tried again, her voice a little stronger this time. "Why? Why can't I see this shit coming?" With her free hand, she swiped at her tear-streaked cheeks. Before I could respond, she continued, "You know what, don't answer that. Can I come home with you? I don't want to be alone tonight."

"Of course." I didn't trust myself to say more, so I turned and resumed our drive, holding her hand the rest of the way.

I awoke wrapped in a sweaty pile of sheets with Carmen curled into my side. Her face was relaxed in sleep, a contrast to her usual animated features or, even worse, the panicked state she was in last night. I didn't want to wake her, but she was a human furnace, and I feared I might combust. Carefully, I extricated myself from her grasp and made my way to the bathroom, pulling on a pair of sweats as I went. Morning needs taken care of, I moved to the kitchen to make a pot of coffee.

Knowing Carmen, she'd probably sleep for several more hours, so I pulled out my notebook and began to write. I lost track of time as I immersed myself in the formation of words and phrases. Sentences and paragraphs.

Writing was where I felt my truest sense of self. There was something so satisfying in selecting the perfect combination of words to elicit a feeling from the reader. I lived to capture a thought or emotion on the page in the most perfect way, weaving letters into words and sentences, bending them to my will until they captured my thoughts perfectly. Verbally, I could express myself relatively well, but on the page, I could delve much deeper and speak far more eloquently.

I wrote poetry and short stories, mostly. Some of my poetry became the lyrics to my music, but mostly they were just musings and observations of the life that seemed to pass me by.

Others were fully immersed in their daily existence while I was on the outside, watching life move on around me. I woke, I worked, I ate, I slept. I survived. I didn't seek joy, nor did it find me. I had Carmen. When I really needed it, I had the occasional fuck with a random stranger. This was my life. It just...was.

I didn't have time for additional friendships and all the drama they entailed. People were demanding. They had expectations. And they always, always disappointed you.

No, thank you. I had Carmen, and that was enough. She pushed and pulled me, and while our friendship did make demands of me, she also accepted me. She didn't understand me, but she didn't try to change me. What more did I need?

Movement from the bedroom caught my attention, so I closed my notebook, laid the pen on top, and picked up my cold coffee to take it into the kitchen to warm it up.

Carmen entered wearing a pair of my sweats and a T-shirt. She'd pulled her long, dark hair into a messy knot on top of her head and had mascara smeared under both eyes. There were shadows there that I hated to see, as I knew they came from her experience last night. We hadn't gone to bed until four a.m., and while a quick check of the clock on the microwave told me it was a little after noon, I knew her sleep had been restless. She'd woken me several times as she'd squirmed and thrashed in her sleep, tossing and turning in the midst of whatever dream had a hold of her. Each time, I'd run my hands down her back, stroked her shoulders and hair, and held her until she'd settled. She probably wouldn't even remember those moments, but they would be burned into my mind for a long time to come.

She moved toward the coffee, grabbing a mug from the cabinet above, her eyes not quite meeting mine. I came up behind her, wrapping my arms around her, hoping to offer some comfort and reassurance.

She stiffened momentarily but then relaxed into my hold, leaning her head back against my chest. We stood like that, our breaths synchronized, as we sought comfort from each other. At length, she sighed and pulled away from me, reaching forward to pour her cup.

"I'm okay," she said, staring into her cup without taking a drink.

"Are you?" I asked.

"I am." She turned toward me, looking me in the eye for the first time. Something seemed to shift behind her eyes, a spark of the fire and determination I was used to. "I'm okay, Finn."

A burning anger followed on the tails of my relief at seeing her spirit begin to return, a frustration that she'd once again allowed herself to be in a relationship with someone who didn't treat her the way she deserved.

"You're going to break up with her, right?"

"Finn, don't start."

"Why, CiCi? What possible reason could you have for staying with that bitch?"

Fire flashed behind her eyes. "I didn't say I was staying with her," she fired back.

"You didn't say you weren't either." I ran my hand roughly through my already messy hair and stepped away from her, putting some space between us. "Jesus, CiCi. She *cheated* on you. Right under your nose. When are you going to stand up for yourself? This probably isn't even the first time. I just don't—"

"Enough!" Carmen shouted, slamming her coffee cup on the counter, the contents sloshing over the side. "This is *my* life. She did this to *me*, and *I* will be the one to decide what happens. Not you." I stumbled back in shock as she pushed past me into the living room.

"I just don't want to see you hurt again," I said, following her into the tiny room. We stood facing each other, arms crossed like we were in a showdown. "It kills me every time one of your girlfriends treats you like shit. And yet, you always go back. If not to the same girl, then another one just like her. And who's left picking up the pieces?"

"Fuck you, Finn! I didn't ask for any of this to happen. And I sure as shit don't need you pointing out all the ways I suck at choosing a girlfriend. Certainly not from someone like you. At least I put myself out there."

I threw my hands up in disgust. "What's that supposed to mean? 'Someone like me?'"

"Nothing. Just drop it." She walked a couple of steps over to the couch and threw herself onto it, refusing to look at me.

"No. I'm not dropping anything. If you had the balls to say it, you can fucking explain it."

She sighed, some of the anger deflating out of her, and raised her eyes to mine. "You're not exactly a relationship guy, Finn. It's not really fair of you to criticize my relationships when you won't even try to be in one."

"I don't need or want a relationship. Not everyone's built for that shit."

"I know that. And while I don't agree that you're not built for it, I understand why you feel that way. But that doesn't mean you're exactly qualified to give me dating advice either." She pulled her legs onto the couch, tucking her feet underneath her. "I just need you to be my friend."

I let out a frustrated sigh and plopped down on the couch next to her. "Are friends supposed to just sit by and watch the people they care about get hurt over and over again?"

"Sometimes, yeah." She pulled her legs out from under her and scooted herself next to me so she could throw them across my lap and lean her head on my chest. I wrapped my arm around her, pulling her closer and tucking her head under my chin. "You know what else friends do?"

"What?"

"They go with their bestie to pick up her stuff from her ex's apartment."

I sighed again. It was equal parts relief she was breaking up with Amy and annoyance that I had to deal with this shit. I wouldn't have done it for anyone other than Carmen. "Yeah, okay. When do you want to go?"

"Not today," she murmured, her voice muffled against my chest. "Maybe later in the week. I'm not strong enough today."

"You're the strongest person I know," I said.

She was quiet for a long time, and I thought maybe she'd fallen asleep, but then I heard her say in a small voice, "I love you, Finn."

I pressed a kiss to the top of her head. "I love you too."

I WALKED into The Daily Grind, hoping there wouldn't be a line. I would probably be late to my Adolescent Psych class, but coffee was an absolute necessity this morning and was worth risking a little tardiness for.

By some miracle, there were only two customers ahead of me at the counter, and I pulled out my phone, checking my email once more. Seeing nothing new, I put my phone back in my pocket with a sigh, reminding myself that it had only been twenty-four hours since I'd submitted my application.

A raised voice caught my attention at the counter to the left, where customers' drinks were distributed.

"How hard is it to get a fucking coffee order right?" a gentleman sneered at the barista in front of him.

"I'm sorry, sir. I'll remake that for you," the barista responded, taking the drink from the man and turning to make a fresh one. I watched him as he strode over to one of the machines, admiring the way his Henley stretched across his shoulders, his movements efficient as he remade the drink. The customer stood with his arms crossed, body tense, radiating asshole energy. I hoped he scalded his tongue.

The customer ahead of me stepped to the side to await her order, and I stepped forward to place my order for a dark roast coffee with an added shot of espresso. I moved to the side to wait for my drink, once again pulling out my phone, this time to scroll through my socials.

"Jamie!" someone called from the coffee counter.

I pocketed my phone and stepped up to grab my drink, getting an unobstructed view of the barista who'd dealt with the asshole customer. His dark hair was shorter on the sides and a little shaggy on top, his jaw angular, lips full, and his piercing blue eyes held mine as he pushed my drink forward.

I noted the name on his name tag. "Thank you, Finn," I said, my lips curving in a smile.

"You're welcome," he said, our eyes holding for a moment before he turned back to make the next drink.

"Excuse me," a woman said as she stepped past me to get her drink. I realized I was standing in the way, my feet rooted to the spot. Shaking my head at my reaction to the dark-haired barista, I turned and left the shop.

As IF PULLED by some magnetic force, I returned to the coffee shop after my one o'clock class. I didn't even know if he—Finn—would still be there, but I hadn't been able to get him out of my head all morning. Those piercing blue eyes had intrigued me, and I'd found myself wanting to see him again, even if just to catch a glimpse.

That was some stalker shit right there.

Yet, I didn't pause to consider the impulse that led me back here. I simply rolled with it.

I entered The Daily Grind for the second time that day, immediately noticing there was a different energy at this time of day. Rather than a line of frazzled commuters, the tables were littered with textbooks and laptops as students took advantage of the free Wi-Fi while consuming their caffeine.

I made my way to the counter, my eyes surveying the employees bustling about, dismissing each one in turn until I'd eliminated all of them. Finn wasn't there.

I already knew I'd be back again tomorrow, looking for a glimpse of the mysterious barista, but in the meantime, I ordered a coffee, deciding I might as well find a table and get some work done while I was there.

Grabbing my coffee, I made my way to a two-person table tucked away in the back. It wasn't until I'd sat and pulled out my laptop that I realized my mysterious barista was sitting at the table adjacent to mine.

He was just a bit ahead of me and off to the left, giving me the perfect angle to observe him unnoticed. His head was bent as he furiously wrote in a notebook. I couldn't make out the words from this angle, but I could see that despite his frantic pace, his words were neatly scrawled across the page.

What was he writing? Was it a journal? Poetry? The next Great American Novel? I desperately wanted to know.

I sipped my coffee as I watched, eagerly noting every detail. The curve of his ear. The mole on the back of his neck, just a little to the left of his spine. The stud he wore in his ear. The ring he fiddled with on the index finger of his left hand. The exact angle he tilted his head as he wrote. I consumed it all, filing it away for safekeeping.

As if sensing he was being watched, he turned, and before I could look away, I was held captive by those piercing blue eyes. He raised an eyebrow in question, and I felt my cheeks heat at being caught staring. But I didn't back down. That wasn't my style. Usually, when I wanted something, I went after it.

I wanted *him*.

"Are you a writer?" I asked.

He glanced at his notebook before turning back to me. "Of sorts," he responded, then turned away, effectively dismissing me.

I smiled, though he couldn't see it. Picking up my coffee, I stood and pulled out the chair opposite him. "What does that mean? 'Of sorts.'"

He paused, the point of his pen still resting on the page, mid-word. He finished the rest of the sentence, then let out a resigned sigh before clicking the pen, closing the notebook, and sitting back in his chair to eye me with a mixture of irritation and suspicion.

"Why do you want to know?"

I shrugged. "I don't know. Curiosity, I guess."

"You don't even know me."

"What if I want to?"

He eyed me, likely trying to determine my sanity, before letting out a humorless chuckle. "You're not my type. And I gotta get back to work." He swept up his notebook and pen and walked away without looking back.

"Mom!" I called out, catching the door before it slammed behind me. I dropped my backpack in the mudroom, removed my shoes, and hung up my coat before heading into the kitchen. Aunt Cathy, my mom's sister, stood at the stove, stirring something in a large pot. I came up behind her, peering over her shoulder to see what she was making, and pressed a kiss to her cheek. "Mmm. Potato Soup. My favorite!"

"I know," she said with a wink before reaching into the cabinet to fetch some bowls.

"Here, let me help you," I said as I reached above her, easily pulling them off the second shelf. My six-three frame towered above her. Both Aunt Cathy and my mom were small in stature. I'd inherited my height and broad build from my dad.

"Thank you, sweetie," she said as she began ladling soup into two bowls.

"Are you not joining us?" I asked.

"No. I've got to run and pick up Cody from swim practice, but there's a warm loaf of beer bread on the counter and honey butter and toppings for the soup in the fridge."

She moved past me, sliding her arms into her coat and picking up her purse.

"I could have picked Cody up on my way and saved you a trip."

"No worries, honey. You just enjoy some quality time with your mom."

I hugged her and then pulled back, asking, "How is she today?"

I saw the tightness in her expression, just a flash and then gone, before she replaced it with a reassuring smile. "She's slept quite a bit today, but that's to be expected after having treatment yesterday."

I nodded, swallowing past the lump in my throat. "Thanks for all your help. You know she—we—appreciate you."

"I know," she said softly. "You're a good kid." She patted my cheek and then exited through the garage.

I returned to the kitchen, shoving the somber mood down while I prepared a tray with soup, bread, and a cup of Mom's favorite herbal tea. Sometimes her treatments made her nauseous, but it was important she at least try to eat in order to keep her strength up.

I headed down the hall to the guest bedroom she'd moved into about a month ago when going up and down the stairs to the primary had become too taxing for her. I'd also moved into a room on this floor so I was more accessible if she needed anything. Her door was closed but not latched, so I nudged it gently with my toe and entered quietly.

The bedside lamp cast a soft glow across her features, making her skin appear rosy, though I knew that was just a trick of the light. It had been a while since I'd seen anything resembling a rosy glow in her features. I carefully set the tray on the bedside table and perched a hip on the edge of the bed, taking her hand.

"Mom," I said softly, wanting to wake her but not startle her. Her eyes fluttered open, clear and bright, and her lips curved in a smile.

"Jamie," she croaked, and I quickly reached for her water bottle, always nearby. She took a sip, cleared her throat, and started again. "Hey, sweet boy. How were your classes?"

"I was a few minutes late to Ad Psych today, but thankfully I snuck into the back and the professor didn't notice. And I got my paper back in my Women in Lit course and got an A!"

"Oh baby, that's awesome! I know how hard you worked on that one."

I preened at her praise. My mom had been a teacher for

over thirty years before she had to take a leave of absence due to her illness, and I wanted to follow in her footsteps. Her praise meant a lot to me. I had always thrived on it.

"Yep, and I'm closing in on the last half of the semester before I student teach. I'm so ready to be in the classroom."

"You're going to do great. Did you hear back on that application?" I'd submitted my request to student teach at my mom's old school, and while it wasn't the end of the world if I didn't get assigned there, I was really hoping they'd have a spot for me. Once upon a time, I'd been a student there, and I knew that Swope Middle School had been a home for her in many ways, having taught there for thirty-odd years. As a result, I knew several of the staff and felt like it would be a good fit for me. I was hoping that student teaching there might lead to a permanent position the following year since there were a couple of English teachers due to retire.

"I haven't heard back yet, but I just submitted it yesterday, so there's still time."

"Well, no matter what happens, any school will be lucky to have you."

I grinned at her. "You're supposed to say that."

"Damn right, I am. But in this case, it's not just because I'm your mother. You have a way with kids."

I blushed at the praise. The truth was, I liked working with kids. In high school, I'd worked summer camps and had given swim lessons at the Y. I'd always had a knack for speaking to kids and had patience with them. While I appreciated the compliment, I didn't think I did anything all that special. "Okay, enough about that. How was your day? How are you feeling?"

She sighed. "I'm okay. Pretty tired, but hanging in there."

"Are you hungry? Aunt Cathy made some soup."

"I could eat." I helped her sit up, adjusting the pillows so she could sit comfortably, and began feeding her small spoonfuls. I knew she hated that she had to be helped this way, but the chemo left her weak and shaky, and attempting to feed herself would have resulted in more soup in her lap than her mouth. And as much as I hated to see her like this, I enjoyed spending time with her. Between her teaching and my athletics and school, life had been hectic growing up, especially after my dad passed, but now, it was nice to slow down and enjoy these moments with her.

She managed half a bowl of soup and most of her tea before signaling she was done. Her eyelids were starting to droop, so I set the dishes back on the tray, pulled up the covers, and pressed a kiss to her forehead, turning the lamp down low and retreating to the kitchen.

After cleaning up the dishes, I made my way back to my room, making sure to move quietly so as not to disturb Mom. I changed into joggers and a long-sleeved T-shirt before settling on my bed to do a little homework. When I opened my backpack to pull my laptop out, my fingers brushed against a piece of paper I'd tucked away earlier.

I smiled as I pulled it out, remembering my discovery at the coffee shop. After Finn had gone back to work, I'd noticed a loose scrap of paper on the floor underneath the table where he'd been sitting. The handwriting was similar to what I'd seen in his notebook, so I knew it was something he'd written. I'd debated returning it to him but couldn't bring myself to do so. The paper held just two lines, but they captivated me.

Darkness falls on my descent into madness
The flavor of him lingers on my lips

Was this autobiographical? About a lover, perhaps? And what about the descent into madness? Was that something he was dealing with? Or was it figurative language and imagery?

I loved words. I loved the way they felt on the tongue and the way they looked on the page. I loved the endless ways you could combine them to invoke a mood or feeling, describe an object, or recount an event. I loved all the myriad ways you could use them. The possibilities were endless.

It was why I wanted to be an English teacher. It wasn't just because that's what my mom taught or because I was good with kids, though I couldn't discount those reasons held some weight, but in a world that seemed ever destined to consolidate thoughts and feelings into bite-sized snippets shared on social media, I wanted the next generation to see how much words mattered. How the study and use of words and all their endless possibilities could change and shape the way we think, feel, and interact with the world.

The fact that Finn was a wordsmith made him infinitely more intriguing. If I'd thought I'd been attracted to him before, reading his words had turned that spark into an inferno. I was half-hard just reading those two lines again.

I adjusted myself in my sweatpants and deliberately set the paper aside. I had work to do, and as much as I wanted to solve the puzzle of Finn, I couldn't afford the distraction right now. This close to student teaching, I needed to focus on finishing the semester strong. With my mom's illness and my class load, I had enough on my plate without adding a broody barista.

Still, when I set my laptop on the charger a couple of hours later and settled into bed, it was Finn's face that appeared in my mind's eye as I fell asleep.

WHEN I WAS FOUR, I started preschool at a very exclusive academy just a few blocks from our Mission Hills home. My mother didn't work, so there wasn't a need for me to have childcare. It wasn't to help me socialize and play with other children since I was an only child. It was simply what people in our social circles did. Children were enrolled in the most exclusive private schools so they could get a leg up on their education and lord it over those less fortunate later in life.

I was miserable.

I didn't mind the work with letters and numbers. I had a quick mind that soaked up new information like a sponge, so I picked up new skills rather quickly. But it was the social structures I couldn't figure out. Even at the age of fucking four years old, I had begun to figure out I was different. I liked to run and play like the rest of the kids, but I liked music more. While the other boys pushed and shoved and played dirty and rough, I preferred the quiet, often finding ways of amusing myself and avoiding the larger groups of children.

I was an introvert in a world wired for extroverts.

Shortly after the Thanksgiving holiday, a boy named Shane joined our class. He had blond hair and round cheeks and was quiet, just like me.

We began to sit together at recess, not always talking, mostly just observing the other kids at play. At snack time, he always offered to share his fruit snacks with me, and I shared my crackers.

He was my first friend.

I had noticed that sometimes the girls in my class would hold hands with their friends as they played on the playground, so one day, I reached for Shane's hand. He was my friend, after all.

Shane looked at our clasped hands and then smiled at me. It was the most beautiful thing I'd ever seen. We stayed like that for the rest of recess.

This became part of our routine. While little girls skipped around the playground hand-in-hand and the boys chased each other over and around the play equipment, Shane and I sat on the bench, hands clasped, and watched the other children play.

I was happy.

Christmas break arrived, and we were out of school for two weeks. I was glad to be home, away from the noisy classroom, but I missed Shane. I asked Mom every day if I could see him, and every day she made some excuse or another for why we couldn't. Eventually, I stopped asking.

The day we were to go back to school, I woke up extra early, excited that I would get to see my friend again, only when I arrived at school, he wasn't there.

He wasn't there the next day or the day after that, and when I finally asked one of my teachers where he was, she gave me a sad smile and explained that Shane's parents had decided to enroll him in a different school.

I was heartbroken.

When Mom picked me up that afternoon, I sobbed in the car, telling her how sad I was that my friend wasn't going to my school anymore. She remained quiet, lips pressed together, all the way home.

After dinner that evening, my father took me into his study, sat me on the chair in front of his desk, and explained very clearly that boys don't cry and mustn't ever hold hands.

CHAPTER 4

FINN

I WATCHED as snow fell quietly out the front window of the shop. It was a light powder that swirled in curlicues along the asphalt and sidewalks, coating the piles of recently fallen leaves in a dusting of white.

The Daily Grind was full of bustling college students, sprinkled with the occasional harried mom with toddlers in tow. A colorful array of winter coats hung on the backs of chairs while beanies and gloves were tossed aside on the tabletops. Some students worked solo, curled over laptops, furiously typing away. Others laughed in groups clustered near the fireplace or stuffed into booths, taking a break from the stresses of college life or working on group projects.

I could have been one of those working solitary at a table, coffee at hand, writing away for some class or other. I would have been in my senior year.

Instead, I was on the other side of the counter, serving coffee to those college students. And while I sometimes resented that fact, the truth was that when my father cut me off, in many ways, he set me free. I was no longer obligated to pursue a medical degree I didn't want, and while I didn't think I wanted to be a barista for the rest of my life, it was still my choice.

Would be damn nice to not be living paycheck to paycheck while working multiple jobs though.

While the shop was bustling with customers, no new orders had come in for the last ten minutes, so I poured myself a cup of coffee and leaned back against the back counter, taking a sip. I'd long ago established myself as a loner, so the other employees joked around farther down the counter, leaving me alone with my thoughts.

Almost against my will, my gaze was drawn to the guy in the back corner. He'd come in so often over the last couple of weeks that I'd learned his name was Jamie and he was a college student, but I didn't know anything else about him. He'd come in several times a week, always by himself and always with a huge smile. I'd never known anyone so smiley, and for some reason, it put my back up. How could anyone go through life so happy?

His dirty-blond hair was pulled into a man bun, and I watched as he tucked a loose strand behind his ear before continuing to type on his laptop. I couldn't see his eyes from here, but I knew they were green, the color of moss as it clings to the side of a tree on a fresh spring day. He paused and picked up his phone, frowning at the screen.

I didn't like it. I didn't like the frown that was so out of place on his face. And I didn't like that I was wondering what put it there.

The bell above the door rang, and a large group of teenagers burst through, chattering away. I rolled my eyes and got back to work.

By the time I'd finished making the lattes and macchiatos with extra pumps of syrup and whip for the high school crowd that had come in from the private school down the block, Jamie was gone.

JAMIE DIDN'T COME into the shop for the next three days, five if you counted the weekend. It wasn't unusual for him to skip a day here and there, and I'd never seen him on the weekends, but since he'd started coming in several weeks ago, this was the first time he'd missed three weekdays in a row.

I was worried. Which was stupid. I didn't know him. I didn't want to know him.

As if summoned by my thoughts alone, the door chimed and Jamie walked into the shop. His eyes found mine and his face lit up in a gorgeous smile, which, for some reason, irritated the fuck out of me, so I turned around and busied myself with wiping down the counters. I could have been making his order—he ordered the same damn thing every time—but I didn't want him to know that any piece of him occupied my mind, even his damn coffee order.

Sarah called his order out from the register, and I turned toward the back counter to make it. My back to the rest of the shop, I heard his voice behind me. "Hey, Finn. How's it going?"

"It's fine," I said without turning to look at him. I took an inordinately long time to make his order considering it was a simple dark roast with no add-ons, but after spending so much time thinking about him the last several days, now that he was here, I suddenly found myself...what? Nervous?

It was fucking weird.

Disgusted with myself, I turned and set his coffee on the counter harder than intended. Hard enough, in fact, that some of the hot liquid sloshed out through the opening in the lid, landing on my hand. I pulled my hand back with a hiss, shaking it at the pain.

"Are you okay?" Jamie asked, voice laced with concern.

I stopped shaking my hand so I could inspect it for burns. There were a couple of small, red splotches, but nothing too serious, thankfully.

"It's fine," I said, responding to Jamie's question, feeling like an idiot. I really wished he would just go. Something about him made me itchy in my own skin, self-conscious and uncomfortable in a way I usually wasn't with most people. With most people, I just didn't give a damn.

Before I could turn away again, to find some excuse to be busily working and effectively excuse myself from this interaction, he grabbed my hand gently so as not to touch the burns. I was so stunned at the gesture that I didn't pull away.

The feel of his smooth palm against mine sent a hum of sensation vibrating just under the surface of my skin. It wasn't an unpleasant feeling, though not altogether comfortable either. I watched his face as he inspected my hand, eyebrows drawn up in concern before he brought his gaze back to mine. "It doesn't look too bad, but you should probably run it under cold water for a few minutes. It will help keep it from blistering."

"What are you? Pre-med?" I couldn't figure out why he would care so much. Unless maybe he was studying to be a doctor and was eager to use some bit of newfound knowledge.

He chuckled, the sound warm and rich as it washed over me. "No, secondary education. I'm studying to be an English teacher."

He was still holding my hand.

He was still holding my hand, and I was letting him.

Abruptly, I pulled it away. I hated how it tingled at the loss of contact, and without thinking, I rubbed it against my jeans as if I could wipe off the feel of his touch. His eyes tracked the movement, but he didn't comment.

"I should get back to work," I said, desperate to escape this conversation.

"Yeah, okay." He picked up his coffee, and I started to turn away, thankful for an exit, but pulled up short when he said my name.

He said it softly like I was a frightened animal he didn't want to scare away. I wanted to pretend I hadn't heard him, but there was some part of me, maybe the part that had worried over him the last five days, that wanted to see what he had to say. I turned back to him, an eyebrow raised in question.

"Go out with me, Finn." He hadn't asked a question, just tossed out his request with the confidence of a man who was rarely rejected. And for good reason. He was gorgeous. And though dressed casually in jeans and a fitted sweater, he had the air of someone who wasn't used to doing without. I'd been surrounded by guys like him my whole life. Cocky, rich assholes who thought they were God's gift to the world and felt like everyone owed them something.

"Nah, man. You're not my type."

"Yeah?" He leaned forward on the counter, a gleam of mischief in his eye. "What *is* your type?"

I snorted. "Not rich, pretty boys like you."

"Is that all you see when you look at me?" he asked. He didn't seem offended, just genuinely curious, which surprised me.

This conversation was exhausting.

"Look, man. I don't want to play games, all right. Whatever you think you see in me, just forget about it. Just accept that I'm not interested and move on."

"All right, fair enough." He reached over and grabbed a napkin, then pulled a pen out of his backpack. He quickly jotted down his number and handed it to me. "If you change your mind..." And without waiting for a response, he turned and headed for the door.

I looked down at the napkin, studying the neat handwriting for a moment, before shaking my head and tossing it in the trash.

I walked into my apartment around five that evening to find Carmen sitting on my couch, books and papers spread out in front of her, staring into space. She hadn't even heard me come in.

I'd been worried about her. Ever since her breakup, she'd been...not exactly withdrawn, more...muted. The week after the Halloween party, we'd gone over to Amy's to pick up her stuff, which had been incredibly awkward but, thankfully, otherwise uneventful. Since then, she hadn't been going out to her usual bars and parties. She hadn't even gone out for dinner with friends, which was so contrary to her extroverted personality. Whereas I loathed being around people, Carmen thrived in a crowd. She fed off the energy of others.

Now, she was wilting, and I didn't know what to do about it.

"Hey, CiCi," I said as I tossed my keys on the table by the front door and peeled off my coat and scarf. At my greeting, she turned to look at me, a soft smile lighting her face. It wasn't the wide grin she usually blessed me with, but I'd take it nonetheless. "How was class?" I asked.

She shrugged, pushing aside the notebook in her lap and standing to stretch. "It was all right. The usual. I've got a bunch of stuff due before the end of the week since we're out for Thanksgiving next week." She moved into the kitchen and started a kettle for tea. "How was your day?"

"Eh. It was all right. Another day in the life." I strode toward my bedroom at the back of the apartment to change before heading back out for my gig at Ivory. Carmen had stayed with me since the breakup, and the evidence was littered about my room. A pair of heels lay half underneath the corner chair where she'd kicked them off after a presentation last week. A cardigan and a pair of skinny jeans were tossed across the same chair, and a pair of pajama bottoms and an oversized T-shirt were tossed on the unmade double bed. I strode past all of it to the tiny closet, pulled out the black slacks and button-down I typically wore for my piano gigs, and laid them out on the bed.

I stopped in the bathroom to take a piss, washing my hands while trying not to knock her makeup off the tiny sink, then moved back to the bedroom to dress.

As much as I preferred solitude, I didn't mind Carmen's presence in my space. It was what she needed, so I didn't question it.

I pulled on my pants and shirt, making efficient work of the buttons. I only had twenty minutes before needing to leave for Ivory, so I didn't have time to fuck around. Carmen strolled in behind me, a steaming mug of tea in hand. "Did Jamie come in today?"

I paused on the last button before finishing it and reaching for my belt. I'd mentioned Jamie yesterday in the midst of my worry and had regretted opening my mouth immediately. Since Carmen was living a more solitary life at the moment, she'd diverted her attention to my social life, which I so rarely had use for. She was like a cat who'd caught a mouse, and I didn't like being under her scrutiny. I couldn't hide anything from her. She knew me too well.

"Um, yeah," I said, chancing a glance at her before moving to the closet to grab my black dress shoes and pull socks from my dresser. She didn't even bother to hide her smirk behind her mug.

"So? Did you talk to him?" she asked.

"Yeah."

I didn't have to look at her to know she'd rolled her eyes. "What did he say?"

I sighed and sat down on the edge of the bed to put on my shoes. She wasn't going to let this go. "He asked me out. I said no."

"I knew he had a thing for you! Why'd you say no?"

Finished with my socks and shoes, I turned to look at her. She was sitting in the corner chair with her legs tucked under her. She held her tea as if about to take a sip but was looking at me with confusion.

Exasperated, I responded, "He's not my type."

"Not all rich kids are assholes."

I raised one eyebrow.

"Okay, some of them are. You, for example, but not all of them."

"I'm not an asshole because I grew up rich. I'm an asshole because I don't like people." I got up, tossed the clothes I'd changed out of into the hamper, then walked over to Carmen and kissed the top of her head. "I've gotta go."

As I turned to go, she reached out and grabbed my

hand, stopping me. I looked back at her, eyebrows raised in question.

"Don't miss out on a chance at love because you think you don't deserve it."

"Love?" I scoffed. "He asked me out on a date, CiCi. Probably because he likes a challenge. It wasn't a marriage proposal. And you know I don't do relationships."

"Why?"

"Why, what?"

"Why don't you do relationships?"

I tried to tug my hand out of hers, but she just held on tighter. "I don't have time for this, CiCi. I have to go."

"Just answer the question. Why don't you do relationships?"

"You know why," I said, exasperated. Why was she doing this now?

"Tell me."

"Because I've spent my entire life taking care of myself. I don't know how to do anything else. To *be* with anyone else. I'm just...better off alone."

She squeezed my hand, this time a gesture of comfort. "You're not really alone, you know. You have me."

I softened my features. "I know." I didn't know why, but from the time she'd stumbled into my life, she'd been by my side. She'd been the only one who'd stuck.

"I love you, Finn."

"Love you too." I cleared my throat. "I really do have to go."

She let go of my hand, and I turned to walk out of the room, but her voice made me pause.

"Just...think about giving him a chance, okay?"

I nodded once and walked out the door.

CHAPTER 5

JAMIE

WHEN I WAS SEVEN, I was sent to the principal's office. In all my school years, it was the one and only time. I was devastated. And terrified.

I'd always been taught to be respectful of others, especially teachers since my mom was one and I was terrified of how they would react.

It was a Tuesday in December, and there was a buzz in the air. Winter break was just days away and you could almost taste the excitement of the children in my classroom.

I arrived at the classroom, hung my coat and backpack on hook number 18, and made my way to my desk to begin my bell-ringer activity. I loved school. I loved reading and writing, and while math wasn't my favorite, I was decent at it. Art, Music, PE, recess...I loved all of it. I was friends with most everyone in my classroom, and as an only child, I loved having others to play with.

But on this Tuesday, I pulled up short. A new desk had been added next to mine in our pod, and a boy was sitting in the seat. I looked at the name printed neatly across the name tag on the upper left corner of his desk: Asher. Excitement burst through me at the prospect of making a new friend.

I approached him, pulling out my chair and sitting down. "Hello," I said with a smile. "I'm Jamie. Well, it's actually James, but everyone calls me Jamie."

I frowned when he didn't respond. Thinking maybe he hadn't heard me, I reached out to tap his shoulder, attempting to get his attention that way, but he shrugged me off, scooting his chair farther away.

I was baffled. I'd never had someone react this way to me. I'd always made friends easily. People liked me. It...hurt.

I got to work on my bell ringer, but I kept peeking at him out of the corner of my eye. Asher had dark curly hair that he kept brushing out of his eyes, and I noticed his red hoodie was stained and dirty with frayed edges on his cuffs. Just above the collar of the T-shirt underneath his hoodie, I could see a bruise peeking out, and I wondered how he got a bruise in such an odd place. I got bruises all the time, but I'd never had one on my neck.

The morning proceeded as usual, and pretty soon, I was immersed in our studies. We started with calendar, then reading and math, and then it was time for lunch. Asher had ignored me all morning, but I was determined to make him my friend. Standing behind him in the hot lunch line, I tapped him once again, intending to ask him to sit at my table. Startled, he turned and shoved me backward, causing me to bump into Charlie and Amanda, who were a grade higher and had joined the line after our class.

"Hey!" I exclaimed, surprised by the shove.

"Don't touch me!" he said, his voice laced with anger.

"I was just trying to invite you to sit with me," I fired

back. My blood was pumping with adrenaline, and I didn't like how it felt, but I couldn't help it. I was so mad.

"Stop trying to be my friend. I don't need you."

My jaw dropped. My eyes burned with tears. No one had ever spoken to me that way.

"Everybody needs a friend."

"Well, I don't."

The line moved forward, and we both got our lunches and made our way to the tables. My stomach dropped when I realized there were only two seats left at our grade-level table, one across from the other. At this point, I no longer wanted anything to do with Asher, and not only would I be forced to sit near him, but I'd have to look at his stupid face while I did it.

We crossed over to the table and sat down. One of my friends tried to talk to me, but I wasn't in the mood, so I turned my body away from the table, facing away from my classmates. I nibbled at my food but wasn't really hungry. My stomach was knotted with anxiety.

One of the cafeteria supervisors began dismissing tables to head outside for recess. Asher's side of the table was dismissed first. He stood and gathered his tray, making his way over to the trashcans, but because of the way I had angled my body into the aisle, his foot caught on mine, and he tripped.

I watched in horror as he hit the ground, his tray landing underneath him as he fell. He sat up, and we both looked down at where he was covered in ketchup. A few other kids started laughing, and his eyes filled with tears. "You tripped me!" he shouted at me.

My eyes widened, and I shook my head. "No! It was an accident."

"No, it wasn't. You did it on purpose!" He stood and

approached me, hands clenched in rage, angry tears running down his red face.

My own eyes flooded with tears at the accusation. "I swear I didn't. It was an accident!"

Ms. Nelson, one of the cafeteria supervisors, came over with a stern expression. "Boys! What happened here? What's going on?"

We both began speaking at once, Asher accusing me of tripping him while I vehemently denied it. "Come on, you two. Let's head to the office where Mrs. Brewer can sort this out."

By one-thirty, both of us were being sent home. Neither of us had eaten lunch, but I wasn't hungry anyway. My stomach roiled at the thought of disappointing my parents.

My dad arrived, still dressed in his suit from work, and after having a few words with Mrs. Brewer, I was escorted out to the car. He said nothing on the way home, but I could feel the weight of his disappointment settle on my shoulders.

He pulled into the driveway, and we both sat for a moment, the heavy silence permeating every inch of the space between us. He sighed deeply and then got out of the car. I scrambled to follow, not wanting to disappoint him further.

We went in through the mudroom, stripped out of our coats, and I hung my backpack on my hook. I followed him to the kitchen but was brought up short when he disappeared into the pantry, returning shortly with an unopened package of Oreos. He grabbed the milk from the fridge and two glasses from the cabinet before sitting at the island. He pulled out a stool, taking another for himself, and invited me to sit.

"Tell me what happened."

I remember many things about my father, but the thing that will forever stand out in my mind, the characteristic that I will always strive to model myself after, was his kindness. When I finally met his eyes that day, I didn't see disappointment or anger, only compassion.

The whole story came tumbling out of me in a mess of tears and snot. How I'd tried to make friends, not once, but twice, and how the tripping incident had been an accident. And after it all was done, I will never forget the words he spoke.

"Some people will make it difficult to know them. Some will bristle at kindness and brush away our attempts at friendship. Those are the people who perhaps need it the most."

He poured two cups of milk, then opened the cookies, offering me one.

"But why, Dad? Doesn't everyone want a friend?"

"Sometimes people get hurt in here." He gestured to the area right in the center of his chest. "And they lash out to protect themselves from it happening again."

I thought about that, trying to puzzle out what he meant. "Like when someone is mean and it makes you feel sad, so you don't want to play with them anymore?"

"Something like that. I think maybe someone made Asher feel very, very sad and now he's scared other people might make him feel sad too."

"Asher didn't seem sad, Dad. He was just really mad."

"I think maybe his sadness is hiding underneath his anger. He's trying to make sure you don't hurt him."

"I would never hurt him!"

"Yes, but he doesn't know that," he said gently.

"I guess I'll just have to try harder."

Dad smiled at me. "I know you will, kiddo. Just be patient with him, okay?"

"I can try."

CHAPTER 6
JAMIE

I'D LOST track of the days as I sat in Mom's hospital room and watched her sleep. A nurse came in, checked some readings on the machines, and then changed out her IV bag and left. I barely noticed him.

I held Mom's hand as if it was a lifeline anchoring her from the next life to this one. I wasn't ready to let her go. Not yet. I wasn't ready to be an orphan.

Late last week, while I'd been working on some homework at The Daily Grind, I'd gotten a call from Aunt Cathy. Mom had been admitted to the hospital with a high fever and suspected dehydration. I'd shoved everything in my backpack and bolted, getting to the hospital in record time.

Mom had picked up some sort of infection, and because of her delicate immune system, they had insisted on keeping her in the hospital to administer antibiotics intravenously. She'd been pretty delirious for the first couple of days, awake for only short periods, and, even then, barely aware of her surroundings. By Monday, she'd been able to stay awake for an hour or so at a time, chatting with Aunt Cathy or me before falling back asleep. Yesterday had been much the same, but today, she'd managed to stay awake for several hours, eventually insisting I take a break and get out of there for a bit. Aunt Cathy had arrived, and the two had ganged up on me, shooing me out the door. I'd run home to shower and change and had stopped by The Daily Grind, hoping to get a glimpse of my favorite barista.

I hadn't meant to ask Finn out. It had just slipped out. I wasn't even sure what it was about him that I couldn't shake. There was no denying he was attractive. Those piercing blue eyes paired with his dark hair and pouty lips definitely did something for me, but it ran deeper than that. There was something about the way he carried himself, and in the way he looked at me, that made me want to know more. Combining that with the lines of poetry I'd found a couple of weeks ago, he seemed...lost.

Fuck. I should probably let it go. He'd made it clear he wasn't interested. Called me a rich pretty boy. But I thought there was more to it than that. I wanted to respect his boundaries—he certainly had a right to turn me down—but I'd also caught the way he acted sort of jittery, like maybe he was nervous or something, and I wondered if his prickly exterior was just a front.

Christ. I swiped my free hand over my face, rubbing my gritty eyes. Or maybe he just really didn't like me, and I needed to get over it.

"I can hear you thinking." I looked up to find Mom's green eyes, so like mine, assessing me. She squeezed my hand. "What's put that frown on your face, sweet boy?"

I smiled at the term of endearment, then sighed. "There's this guy," I started.

"Mm-hmm." She drew the word out in that way mothers do, like she was settling in for some good gossip.

"Do you remember when we got George?" George was

our dog who'd been with us from the time I was ten until I was about sixteen. He was a hound mix of some sort who'd been abandoned and taken to the shelter we'd rescued him from not long after Dad died. Mom had thought taking care of a dog might be good for me, that it might help with the grieving process.

"Of course," she said, her tone indicating she wasn't sure where I was going with this change of topic.

"Well, remember when we went to the shelter to pick him out? He was cowering in the back of his crate, but as soon as we got near him, he became aggressive. His fur stood up on his back and he growled at us. Even snapped a couple of times. I wanted him, but you were afraid he wouldn't be safe."

"I'd almost forgotten he was like that when we first met him. He was always such a sweet boy." She smiled fondly at the memory. My heart ached at the loss of him, even all these years later. I'd never even asked for another dog because none would ever be as good as George had been.

"That's the thing though. He wasn't *always* sweet. I spent that whole summer watching training videos and working with him until he eventually learned to trust me."

"That's right," she said, smiling. "He actually trusted you before he trusted me. You were so gentle and patient with him."

"I just knew he needed to be loved. Even at the shelter, when he was growling and barking at us, something in his eyes made me think he was more afraid than anything else."

"Is that why you begged for him? I always wondered why it was him you wanted so badly." She pushed a loose strand of hair back off her face. "Honestly, I was pretty set against him. I didn't know how I could handle him without your father being there to help. But you looked at me with those big green eyes of yours, and after everything you'd lost, I couldn't say no."

"Yeah. I just…I felt so alone after Dad died, and I was sad and scared and so…angry, and I looked at George, and I thought all his snapping and growling—well, that was how I sometimes felt on the inside, so maybe he was feeling the same. Maybe he was just scared and lonely like me."

"Oh, sweet boy," she said, tears forming.

"It's okay, Mom. It was a long time ago and it's not really the point, or at least it's not the entire point." I took her hand in mine, trying to reassure her I really was fine. "The point is, when I look at Finn—he's the guy I'm interested in—he has that same look in his eye. He's grumpy and prickly and snarky, but I think it's just a front. I think, inside, he's scared."

Her face softened as she realized what I was getting at. "You always have had the gift of looking past the surface-level stuff that most people show the world." She paused for a moment to sip her water. I helped her take a drink before placing the water on the tray table next to her. "So, did something happen today?" she continued. "Something in particular that made you upset with this boy?"

"I asked him out, and he turned me down." I didn't know if I had it in me to repeat the whole story, so I gave her the basics. "He works at the coffee shop by campus, and I've flirted a little, but he's never been real responsive. Something about him was different today. He seemed…I don't know…nervous?" I yanked the hair tie out of my bun, mostly for something to do with my hands, and with quick, jerky movements, put my hair back up. "I don't know. Maybe I just read him wrong."

"Or maybe you read him exactly right, and he's just not ready."

"Yeah, maybe. I don't know. How am I going to know when he *is* ready? Kind of feels like the right thing to do at this point is to just respect his wishes and back off."

"Definitely makes sense to do that. But perhaps he just needs a friend. You don't have to ask him out again, and maybe skip the flirty stuff, but you could try just being friendly. Let him get more comfortable with you."

Unsure how to respond, I lifted one shoulder in a half-hearted shrug. We sat quietly for a moment while I pondered her words. I honestly didn't know what the right answer was. I wanted to respect his wishes, but my gut said there was something there, some spark that was just waiting to be ignited.

Sensing that maybe it was best to table the topic of Finn for now, she patted my hand and mustered a bright smile. "Why don't you tell me about the rest of your day. Are you keeping up with your classes?"

We spoke about my day and speculated about how soon she would be released from the hospital. We talked about Aunt Cathy's kids—my cousins—and what was new with them. We avoided the topic of the upcoming Thanksgiving holiday. I didn't think either of us wanted to contemplate the possibility of her spending it in the hospital. After about forty-five minutes, her eyes started to droop, and it was clear she needed to rest.

I stayed for hours just watching her sleep, savoring the feel of her small hand in mine. When I could no longer keep my own eyes open, I decided it might be best to head home and try to catch a few hours of sleep before stopping by in the morning before my first class.

I stood from my seat, pulled the blankets up, making sure not to catch on her IV line, gently kissed her forehead, and left.

As I started my car and waited for it to warm up, I let the tears fall. The impossible reality that I might lose her washed over me, but in the midst of my despair, I felt grateful.

Grateful that I'd had that last hour with her. To discuss the ordinary, the mundane, the day-to-day moments that made up a life. Grateful that I'd held her hand, kissed her forehead, and been washed in the sound of her voice one more time.

Grateful that I'd felt her love.

IT WAS WIDELY EXPECTED that children of a certain status should be well-rounded individuals, participating in a variety of activities that would both reflect well on their status and look good on school applications.

I suspected these activities were yet another thing a parent could point to in order to lord it over their peers at their country clubs, society dinners, and PTA luncheons.

"Look at *my* son. He scored the winning touchdown!"

"*My* daughter placed first in her category *and* first in her age group at her dance competition."

"*My* son was selected as Best Young Artist at his piano competition."

Never mind that the only contribution these parents made to these accomplishments was to foot the bill. Disregard the fact that these kids spent more time with their nannies than their parents or that they couldn't remember the last time they received a proper hug. Those *small* details were irrelevant in the political games played by those in affluent circles.

The amount of pressure some of my peers had nearly

folded under trying to live up to these ridiculous expectations of success was staggering, all in the hopes of gaining their parents' attention. All so the parents could bask in their own made-up definitions of glory.

My parents, not ones to be left out of such societal games, had enrolled me in piano at the age of seven. I don't recall asking to take piano lessons, but I do remember being trotted out to perform for my parents' peers at dinner parties.

Oddly, despite my general disdain for people and my introverted nature—often confused with shyness—I didn't mind performing. Early on, I learned that when I lost myself in the music, the people in the audience simply disappeared.

In between those dinner parties and piano recitals, I practiced like mad. When I longed for my parents' attention, I filled the void with music. When I wanted to bring order to chaos, I chose Bach. To soothe, I chose Debussy. Gershwin, Chopin, and Rachmaninoff became my companions. My parents never understood my passion for music—I don't think they understood passion of any kind—but they couldn't take this away from me. Once given, there were no takebacks.

In high school, I stumbled into jazz. Everyone at my private school knew I played piano—we all came from the same country clubs and had been forced to socialize together for years—so I'd been approached by the jazz band instructor to join his group. Sports reigned supreme at our school, so the band was mediocre at best, but I didn't care. Once I'd discovered the genre, I couldn't get enough of it. I devoured the recordings of Thelonious Monk, Duke Ellington, and Chick Corea.

And when my parents asked me to leave the day after

my eighteenth birthday, I couldn't take the grand piano, but I took my electric keyboard and every scrap of sheet music. In the same week, I secured a gig at Ivory, a piano bar in the Crossroads District. They'd been reluctant to hire me, considering I wasn't even old enough to drink in their bar, but I'd convinced them to let me audition, and they'd reluctantly given me a chance to play on Tuesday nights. Over the last three years, I'd shown myself worthy and regularly played there two to three nights a week. It wasn't enough income to pay my bills, but between my shifts at The Daily Grind and my gigs at Ivory, I made do.

It served the dual purpose of supplementing my income and indulging one of the few joys in my life. Tonight, I'd walked into Ivory, the weight of my conversation with Carmen a heavy burden, but after a few hours immersed in music, I'd felt lighter. I hadn't come to any new conclusions about the Jamie situation, but it had been a good distraction.

Now, heading home a little after midnight, I heard a thump, and my car jerked to the right. The low tire pressure light lit up my dashboard. "Shit," I muttered as I carefully pulled over to the shoulder of the road. It had been lightly snowing, but as I stepped out of the car to take a look, the snow began falling harder, fat flakes swirling in the glare of my headlights.

"Fuck my life," I yelled, looking up into the night sky. It had been a really weird fucking day, and I just wanted to go home and crash since I had to be back at The Daily Grind in about six hours.

I rose from my crouch and turned at the sound of a car approaching. Shielding my eyes from the glare of the headlights, I strained to see who might be driving, and as the black Honda Accord Hybrid rolled to a stop next to me on the deserted street, I was surprised to discover the object of my thoughts from only moments ago.

"What the fuck are you doing here?" I asked in surprise after he'd rolled down his window.

He ignored my question, asking one of his own instead. "Flat tire?"

I looked at the very obvious flat and then back at him, raising my eyebrow as if to say, "*Duh!*"

He let out an exasperated sigh, tucking a strand of hair that had fallen loose from his bun behind his ear. "Look, do you want my help or not?" He sounded tired. Defeated. And maybe a little irritated. In all our interactions, I'd never heard that tone from him, and I realized I was being kind of a dick. I'd rejected him earlier today, yet here he was, offering me help in the middle of the night, and I was being a sarcastic asshole.

"Yeah, sorry. Um, can you give me a ride?" At his nod, I crossed to the other side of my Jeep, killing the ignition, and then got into his car. The snow had begun falling in earnest, and I nearly sighed in relief as the warmth of his car enveloped me. My tired eyes wanted to droop immediately. After plugging my address into his GPS, he eased back onto the road, heading toward my apartment.

I watched him surreptitiously as we drove. He wore the same jeans as earlier, though I couldn't see if it was the same sweater underneath his coat. Had he been home yet today? His blond hair was swept into a man bun as usual, but some strands had come loose, falling around his face. It was hard to make out in the darkened car, but I thought I could see dark circles under his eyes and a growth of stubble on his chin. He had a weighted air about him, as if he was carrying the entire world on his shoulders.

Whenever I'd seen him in the past couple of weeks, he'd

been the picture of perfection. Hair perfectly tied up, freshly shaved, fairly preppy attire, wide-open smiles, and eyes that danced with good humor. It had always put my back up, reminding me of the kids I'd grown up with who walked around without a care in the world, everything handed to them, with no regard for how their words and actions affected anyone else. Seeing this side of Jamie made me wonder if there was more to him than I'd originally assumed. It made me uncomfortable in an entirely different way. It made me worry about him, and I didn't want to.

"Are you okay?" I blurted out, immediately wishing I could retract my words. He glanced my direction, eyes drawn up in surprise at my outburst, before returning his gaze to the road. "Never mind. It's none of my business."

"It's okay." He blew out a breath. "It's just been a shitty week."

"I'm sorry." My words seemed trite and inconsequential, but he didn't elaborate, and I didn't know what else to say. I supposed most people would ask questions in this situation, inviting the other person to talk about it, but I wasn't most people. I wasn't comfortable talking about feelings, and I lacked practice with this sort of conversation.

We continued to ride in weighty silence before the guilt got the best of me. The guy'd had a shitty week and had still been friendly when he came in today. And when he'd asked me out, I'd been kind of an asshole. I huffed a breath. "I'm sorry I was a dick to you at the shop this afternoon."

"So you'll go out with me then?" he quickly replied.

I looked up at him, catching his shit-eating grin, and rolled my eyes. "That's still a no. But I am sorry I was such a dick about it." I paused before forcing the next part out. "You seem like a nice guy, and I'm sorry you've had a shitty week. Sorry if I made it worse."

"Nah. Don't worry about it. In the grand scheme of things, I had bigger things to worry about."

Oh. *Why did that sting?*

The silence stretched on again, filling every inch of the space around us. Jamie broke it first this time.

"Can I ask you a question?"

I glanced over at him but couldn't get a read on him. "Um, yeah. I guess."

"Why is it a no?"

I rolled my eyes. "Really, dude? Can't take the rejection?"

He chuckled. "Nah. I can take it, but I mean, what is it about me that is so offensive to you? Is it really because you think I'm just some entitled, rich asshole? You've thrown up walls from the moment I walked into that shop, even though I know you check me out when you think I'm not looking."

"Pfft. I do not."

"Seriously, what is it?"

We rolled to a stop at the curb in front of my building, and he put the car in Park. We turned to each other, and I looked—really looked—at him. I wanted to pull his hair tie free and run my fingers through the strands of his dirty-blond hair. What would it be like to tangle my fingers in those strands as I fucked his face?

The truth was, I wanted him. On some level, I'd wanted him from the moment I'd met him.

And that was why I put up walls.

"Listen, I don't do relationships. With anyone."

"Why?"

"It doesn't matter why. I just don't. It's not personal."

He considered for a moment, then reached out and brushed his hand along my cheek, sliding all the way to the back of my neck and giving a gentle squeeze before releasing me and returning his hand to his lap. It was oddly intimate and left me both unsettled and simultaneously wanting more. More of his touch. More of his warmth. More of him.

"Okay," he said.

My eyebrows creased in confusion. "Okay? That's it?"

"Someone hurt you. Maybe more than one someone. I hate that you feel you need to protect yourself from me, but I won't push."

My heart squeezed and my breath stuttered. I'd revealed nothing, yet he'd unlocked some piece of me without my permission. It wasn't quite what he was thinking, but he was still too damn close to the truth.

My palms were sweaty as I reached for the door handle.

"Look, I don't know what it is that you think you've figured out, but I do appreciate the ride, so thanks for that." I hastily got out of the car, feeling all sorts of panicky, but as I turned to shut the car door, he called my name. I leaned down to peer into the car.

"Yeah?"

"See you tomorrow," he said with a wide grin.

Our eyes locked, green versus blue, and then I shook my head, closed his door, and headed inside.

I DIDN'T SEE Jamie the next day or the one after that.

On Thursday, I had to call in to work to deal with my car. Eleven hundred dollars later, I had four brand-new tires and was approaching the maximum limit on my credit card. As it was, Carmen had loaned me half, which I absolutely hated, but I hadn't really had a choice.

Friday, I'd been scheduled to work in the morning, but

I'd picked up the afternoon shift as well, hoping to start setting aside money to go toward what I knew would be a crippling credit card bill later in the month. Against my will, I'd found myself looking at the door every time the bell jangled, but Jamie hadn't come in. I'd arrived home in such a foul mood that Carmen had packed her stuff and declared she was heading to her parents early for the holiday. They were leaving for California on Sunday, but I guessed she figured she'd rather stay a few days at her childhood home beforehand than put up with my broody ass all weekend. I couldn't really blame her.

Saturday, I rage-cleaned my apartment, tidying up the mess of clothes, doing laundry, and scrubbing nearly every surface. The only bright spot that day had been my gig at Ivory that evening. With the impending holiday, the bar had been packed, and I'd made double my normal tips.

This morning, I was sitting on my couch, notebook and pen out, attempting to write but mostly staring into space. I was due into The Daily Grind around noon, but that time was still several hours away, so I'd thought perhaps some writing would help me cleanse this endless anger out of my system.

I couldn't seem to make sense of where it was coming from. The circumstances of my life had been shitty for so long that I'd long accepted it for what it was. I had no use for anger, as it didn't change anything. Most days, I existed in a space of indifferent acceptance. This anger was useless and unwelcome. I didn't know what was driving it, and I didn't know how to get rid of it.

CICI

Are you sure you don't want to come to
Cali with me?

You know I can't afford that

CICI

And you know my parents will pay
your way

...

CICI

I know you won't accept it, but I hate that
you're spending Thanksgiving alone

It's no different than the last couple of
years, CiCi. I'm fine

CICI

You're not fine

What? Why do you say that?

CICI

Seriously? You've been a raging dick for
days. Even more than usual

Thanks

CICI

You know I love you, but you need to pull
your head out of your ass

Wow. Thanks for the chat. It's been real
helpful

CICI

I just want you to be happy

I know. Love you too

CICI

<3

I tossed the phone down on the table, then sat back and
scrubbed my hands over my face. I had to get out of here.

Fifteen minutes later, I was in my Jeep, pulling into the parking lot at Loose Park. I got out of the car, pulled my beanie down over my ears, started the music on my iPhone, and took off at a jog.

I'd never been much of an athlete, but I'd always been a bit of a runner, even running cross country in high school, though that was mostly to appease my parents. It had been several weeks since I'd gone for a run, and I found the rhythmic pulse of my feet pounding the pavement soothed the rage I'd been holding on to all weekend. It was still there underneath the surface, but it was a manageable glow of ember rather than a fiery inferno.

As I entered my second mile, I turned my mind over to examine the past week's events, flitting from one to another in no particular order, assessing each as if it held the secret to the anger burning me from the inside out. In nearly every instance, Jamie appeared in some way or the other. His relentless presence, followed by his worrying absence, and then his assistance Wednesday night, only followed by absence once again. How could one person elicit such a visceral reaction? How had I allowed his scant presence in my life to matter enough to elicit any sort of reaction at all?

I was midway through my second loop when a runner up ahead caught my eye. Dressed in a blue hoodie and black joggers that hugged his ass, my stomach clenched in recognition at the sight of Jamie on the path ahead of me. I stayed a safe distance behind him, though keeping pace, allowing myself a moment to admire the grace and athleticism of his movement.

How would that translate in the bedroom? Was he a top or bottom? I was vers, though I had a feeling being topped by him would be an experience that might break me.

I pulled to a stop, my aching cock making it difficult to

run, and stepped off the running path to adjust myself under the cover of a stand of trees. I continued to watch him covertly as he faded into the distance, feeling relieved that I hadn't been seen. After days of not seeing him, yet thinking about him nonstop, I'd suddenly hoped he wouldn't notice me.

It was at that moment I realized all the anger and rage was something else entirely.

It was fear.

CHAPTER 8

I WAS eighteen when I realized I was gay.

I was in my senior year of high school, and while I'd enjoyed dating girls and spending time with them, I'd never really pursued anything sexually. I'd kissed the girls I'd dated, of course. I'd even done some clumsy groping. I hadn't exactly hated any of it, and I even thought it could be nice having that intimacy with someone, but I had never felt the urge to take it any further. I knew guys who'd had sex, but I also knew plenty who hadn't, and I figured most guys exaggerated their experience, anyway. I wasn't particularly bothered by my lack of sex drive. I just figured it would happen when I found the right person.

On a Thursday in November, I found myself hanging out with my best friend, Asher. This was fairly common for the two of us—we'd come a long way since that almost-fight in first grade and were fairly inseparable. Most days could find one of us hanging out at the other's house when we weren't hanging out with our other friends or at whichever sports practice we were participating in that season.

On this particular Thursday, we had just come off our swim season and weren't playing any other sports until we started winter conditioning in January in preparation for the track season. Hanging out on the couch playing video games, I could tell something was on Asher's mind, but I figured he would bring it up when he was ready.

Eventually, he put his controller down and turned his body toward me, though he wouldn't quite look at me. Following his lead, I set my controller down and turned to face him, waiting until he was ready to tell me whatever was on his mind.

Seeming to steel himself, he took a deep breath and said, "I'm gay."

My entire world tilted on its axis and then, just as quickly, righted itself again. I suddenly suspected a question had been answered for me that I hadn't even realized I should have been asking. But this moment wasn't about me.

"Okay," I said, waiting for him to continue.

His eyes flashed to mine. "Okay? That's all you have to say?"

I shrugged. "I mean, yeah. What else should I say?"

"Aren't you surprised? Or mad? Or, I don't know..." He looked down at his lap before whispering, "Disgusted?"

I put my hand on his shoulder and squeezed. "Dude, I don't care who you love or who you're attracted to. I can't say I saw it coming, but it doesn't change anything."

His glossy eyes met mine. "I was so scared you'd hate me."

"Man, I'm kind of offended you'd think that of me. I mean, I get this is hard, I guess, but it's me. When have I ever given you a reason to think I was homophobic?"

"I'm sorry. You're right. It's just...I don't want to lose

you." A tear fell, followed by another, and I did the only thing I could think of in the moment. I pulled him toward me, wrapping my arms around him as he fell apart.

"You could never lose me," I said at length.

He pulled back, swiping at his eyes. "I know."

I raised my eyebrows.

"I do know. I just…once I figured out how I felt, who I am, my brain went to every worst-case scenario, and I panicked."

Asher had always been an overthinker. I suspected it was partly due to the trauma he had endured in his earliest years before he was adopted, but it was also how he was wired. He thought long and hard before making a decision, and he worried endlessly about every angle of a situation. I was sure he had been stewing on this for quite some time.

Feeling like the situation warranted some honesty on my part as well, I took a breath and confessed my own realization. "I think I may have some suspicions about myself as well."

"What?" His eyebrows raised in confusion.

"Um. I think I might be gay too."

"What do you mean you think you're gay?"

I shrugged, but my heart rate sped up as I started to think through the implications and what this would mean for me. "I guess I hadn't really contemplated the idea of being gay before, but as soon as you mentioned it, it sort of just clicked."

"What? I mentioned being gay and you decided you were too?" He sounded incredulous, almost offended, even. "You've always dated girls. Have you ever felt attraction for another guy?"

I thought a moment before responding, "I've noticed attractive guys before, but mostly in the way you'd notice anything beautiful. It just never dawned on me that it could be anything more than that. What about you? How did you know?"

His cheeks heated, and he wouldn't meet my gaze as he responded. "I, um, I've had a couple of unfortunate hard-ons at swim meets this season."

"No shit?!"

"Shut up!"

"I never noticed. How'd you hide it?"

He swallowed audibly. "I, uh, well, the first time it happened, I was standing up watching one of the other races, so I just sat down really quickly and sort of hunched over so you couldn't see it. The next time, we were on the pool deck walking to our bench, so I just moved my duffel to carry in front of me. After that, I just started carrying a towel with me as often as I could and bunched it up in front of me."

I barked out a laugh. "I wondered why you suddenly started carrying a towel with you everywhere. I thought it was like a good luck thing."

"This was definitely not good luck."

I chuckled at his sardonic tone. "So, have you acted on it? Have you, like, I don't know, made out with a guy?"

His cheeks heated again. "No. I've watched some gay porn, but I've been too scared to put myself out there. Besides, if straight is the default, how do you know if someone is gay without outing yourself in the process? It's scary as fuck."

A thought popped into my head, and without giving it much consideration, I blurted, "Do you want to kiss me?"

His eyes snapped to mine, the flush draining out of his face. "What?"

"You seem pretty certain, but you haven't tested it, and I

hadn't even suspected anything until ten minutes ago. Maybe we should test it out on each other to be sure."

"Are you crazy?"

"Thanks, man," I said, my tone dry.

He rolled his eyes. "I just mean, don't you think this could fuck things up between us?"

"I don't think so. I'd rather try it with you, someone I trust, than with a random stranger. If I'm going to upend my entire life, I'd like to know for sure, first."

He thought about it a moment. I could practically see the wheels spinning, and I found myself hoping his answer would be yes. Now that I had this suspicion about myself, I just had to know for sure. Resolved, he sat up straight and angled his body toward mine, one leg crossed in front of him and the other planted on the floor as he sat sideways on the couch. "Okay. Let's do it."

I reached out my arm, brushing my hand against his cheek before grasping the back of his neck to pull him toward me. I could feel the rise of my pulse rate as our faces moved closer. My eyes flicked toward his lips and his breath caught before I closed the distance, crushing his lips to mine.

I had intended to ease into it, starting with a brush of the lips and progressing from there, but at the last second, I'd surged in, going for broke. Thankfully, Asher didn't seem to mind, meeting my lips with just as much gusto.

We explored each other, teeth clashing and tongues tangling as we swallowed each other's moans. Wanting to feel more of him, I got both hands around his shoulders and tugged, bringing him down on top of me as I sank back against the arm of the couch. He came willingly, settling on top of me with a groan as our cocks aligned next to each other like pieces of a puzzle fitting together.

My hands roamed his body, finding their way under his shirt and trailing along the muscles of his swimmer's physique. He whimpered as I tore my mouth away from his and began trailing kisses down his jaw. Dimly, I registered how different the feel of his scruff was against my skin, how hard his body felt pressed against mine. I liked it. I liked it a lot.

As I nipped his ear, licked down his neck, and sucked at the base of his throat, he rutted into me. My hips responded automatically, chasing the friction, frantically seeking release.

Nothing had ever felt like this. Never had my blood been lit on fire, nor had I been so desperate to come. I reveled in it.

There would be no turning back.

Lightning fast, my orgasm slammed into me with the force of a hurricane. I groaned as it ripped through me. My body stiffened as my cock pulsed endlessly in spurt after spurt, my cum soaking through my shorts.

Above me, Asher stiffened as well, his mouth open in a silent scream as he came. I held him through it, stroking his back and noting for the first time how beautiful he was. How had I never noticed that before?

Eventually, he dropped his forehead to mine, our panting breaths mingling as we tried to return our heart rates back to normal.

"I think I can safely say," I said between stuttering breaths, "that I'm gay."

Asher smiled, his eyes locking on mine. "Yep." He leaned in and brushed his lips across mine before sitting up. Suddenly aware of the mess I'd made in my pants, I looked down at the stain spreading across the front of my joggers. Glancing over at Asher's lap, I noted he had a similar situation. My eyes darted to his and held for a moment before we burst into laughter.

THE DAY after I gave Finn a ride home, I walked into The Daily Grind and he wasn't there. I wasn't sure whether I was relieved or disappointed. The conversation we'd had the night before had left me with more questions than answers. Who had hurt him? What had happened that made it so difficult for him to let anyone in?

He'd tried to play it off like I hadn't figured it out, but I suspected his front was because I'd gotten a little too close to the truth for comfort. He'd panicked and fled. The self-preservation instincts were strong with that one.

I didn't begrudge him that. I'd never truly had my heart broken, but I'd experienced grief, and I understood what it was like to want to wrap yourself in protective layers so you never experienced those awful, ugly feelings again.

Unfortunately, or fortunately, depending on your perspective, I wasn't wired that way. I wore my heart on my sleeve, and even when I tried to hold back, tried to protect myself from hurt or disappointment, my big feelings always rose to the surface, bursting forth for better or worse. I'd learned that, for me, it was better to be upfront with those feelings, good or bad, and deal with the consequences head-on.

But just as I understood that about myself, I understood that it didn't work for everyone. With Finn, I would have to be patient. It was going to take time to peel back all those layers until I found the very center of who he truly was.

I also understood that the biggest rewards came from the things you had to work for. Something told me Finn was going to be worth it.

I didn't make it back into the shop again until Tuesday. Classes were out for the Thanksgiving holiday, so I didn't even have a reason to be in the neighborhood. But despite my best efforts to give him space, I found myself in my car and on my way almost before I realized what I was doing.

I stood out of the way just inside the door, leaning casually against the wall, and simply watched him work. The shop was fairly busy, so he hadn't noticed my presence, allowing me the freedom to observe him in motion. There was a grace to the way he moved from counter to machine to customer and back again as if he was performing the steps to some intricate choreography created specifically for him. The barista next to him moved frantically amid the morning rush, clearly overwhelmed with the number of orders coming in, but Finn was the picture of calm. His movements were quick and efficient, competent, as he moved from one task to the next without skipping a beat.

I stepped into the line, continuing to observe him, patiently waiting my turn. At the counter, I ordered my usual and then, on impulse, added two pastries for Mom and Aunt Cathy.

As he called my name for my order, I noticed the barest of a hitch in his flow. Had I not been watching his movements, I wouldn't have noticed it.

I stepped up to the counter and caught a flash of...something...in his eyes. It was gone before I could identify it.

"Haven't seen you in here for a while," he said as he handed me my coffee.

"You watching for me?" I hadn't meant to be flirty, but Finn brought it out in me. He shrugged but didn't answer the question, instead asking one of his own. "You having a better week?"

I was so used to Finn brushing me off that his question took me aback. "What?"

"You said last week was shitty. Is this one better?"

A broad smile stretched my face. Our interactions usually involved a little flirtiness from me and a sarcastic smirk from him. Never had they involved anything personal. Was it possible I was wearing him down? Peeling back that first layer? "Yeah. Much better. My mom came home from the hospital yesterday."

His face grew serious. "Oh shit. Is she okay?"

I waved him off. "She has cancer, so no, she's not really okay. But she *is* better, and that's all I can ask for. I'm excited to spend Thanksgiving with her."

He looked down as one of the other baristas placed a couple of pastries in brown paper sleeves on the counter next to where Finn's hand rested. He picked them up and handed them over to me, his fingers brushing mine in the exchange. "Wow, um, that sounds really tough." His voice was quiet, hesitant like he wasn't sure how to respond. Most people didn't. Cancer made people uncomfortable. It didn't discriminate—everyone was susceptible—and mention of it was a reminder that it could hit them or someone they knew next. In my experience, it was absolutely heartbreaking to watch someone who meant the very world to you suffer so dramatically, but it also made me laser-focused on the things that truly mattered. I didn't have time or patience for the bullshit that most people seemed to get worked up about. I savored every moment I got to have with Mom and tried to find as much joy in my own life as I could.

Perhaps that was why I continued to pursue Finn. One might have argued that life was too short to waste chasing someone who didn't want you. But I would argue that this wasn't about the chase, not really. This was about seeking a connection with someone who you knew absolutely deep in your core would fundamentally change you for the better.

Logically, I didn't know Finn well enough to truly know this type of connection could be made, but I'd stopped questioning the logic of anything having to do with Finn almost from the moment I'd walked into The Daily Grind that first time. I'd simply accepted that the path to him was a path I was destined to take. There was only one direction: forward.

"Yeah, it's been a rough couple of months, but she's an absolute badass warrior, so we'll be extra grateful on Thanksgiving to still have her with us." I smiled, thinking about how a week ago, we weren't sure she'd be out of the hospital in time. It was a relief to have her home.

"How do you do it?" he asked.

"How do I do what?"

"How are you so goddamned cheerful about everything?"

I chuckled. "I don't know any other way to be. Mom's cancer is pretty serious. She may not make it." I swallowed past the lump in my throat. "But if I'm only meant to have a few more months with her, I'd rather not waste them walking around being a dick to everyone. It won't change the outcome. I'd rather fill our time with laughter."

He shook his head. "I just—"

"Hey, Finn! You gonna stand around talking to your boyfriend all day, or are you going to help us out here?" one of the baristas called from down the counter. I had been so intently focused on him that I'd forgotten they were in the middle of a rush. I looked around, noting that the line was even longer than it had been when I'd come in.

"I better go. You have plans for Thanksgiving?"

"You asking me out again?"

I chuckled. "Nah. But if you need a place to hang, you're welcome with us."

"That's all right, man. I'm good."

"All right. Happy Thanksgiving, Finn."

"Yeah, uh, you too." He nodded and turned to get back to work.

I got to the car, placing my coffee in the cupholder and the pastries on the passenger seat, my stomach heavy. I suspected his turn down of my Thanksgiving offer wasn't because he already had plans but because he thought he didn't need them. Without stopping to consider my actions any further, I opened the glovebox and riffled around until I found a piece of paper and a pen that would actually write. I jotted down a note and ran back inside.

I caught Finn's attention, and he approached with a question in his eyes.

"I know you're busy. Just take this. You can read it later when you have time."

"What is it?"

"Just take it."

Without waiting for further response, I shoved it in his hands and walked out.

WHEN I WAS SIXTEEN, Carmen walked in on me making out with a boy. It was my first kiss. I'd known I was gay for as long as I could remember, almost before I even had a name for what it meant to be attracted to other boys. The hard lines and sleek planes of the male body just did it for me. I tended to prefer those with an athletic build, but really, if he had a dick, there was a decent chance I'd at least be mildly interested. But between the fact that I didn't particularly like talking to most people and the distinctly straight makeup of our elite preparatory academy, opportunities for hooking up were few and far between.

Joey, the only out person at our school, wore his sexuality like a goddamned badge of honor. He wore mascara and carried lip-gloss and a compact in a little purse, and while he wore the traditional male uniform of slacks, navy sweater vest, and striped tie, he often paired it with chunky platform shoes similar to the style worn by the girls at our school.

A little too tall and broad to be considered a twink, he carried the stereotypical attitude of one. He seemed to get a kick out of making people uncomfortable with his flirtiness and overt sexuality. I found him both obnoxious and fascinating. Even as he annoyed the shit out of me, I was envious of his ability to put himself out there and say *fuck it* to anyone who dared to insist he be anything other than himself.

Joey remained the only out student at our school because I had no desire to draw attention to myself in that way. For as long as I could remember, I had done my best to go unnoticed at school. I wasn't shy, per se, but I had no desire to fill my days with meaningless conversations with my peers, who, for the most part, seemed to be motivated solely by trying to gain the attention of others. I was well aware that most others thought I was an odd loner, but that was fine with me. As long as they left me alone, I didn't care. The only thing I did to put myself out there was to play in the jazz band, but even that was solitary in its own way. I could communicate musically, but once rehearsal was over, I was out.

So, no one was more surprised than me to find myself lip-locked with Jason Donovan, senior starting center for the basketball team, in an empty classroom on a Friday in November. As far as I knew, he had a girlfriend, but that didn't stop me. I didn't know why he'd chosen me or how he'd figured out I'd be into it, but he'd grabbed my hand and pulled me into the classroom. Before I knew it, his tongue was down my throat and we were kissing with all the desperation that comes with teenage hormones.

I loved it. The way he tasted as our tongues tangled together. The feel of his fingers tugging my hair as he pulled me closer. I didn't stop to think about his motivations or the ramifications of what any of this meant. I was just along for the ride.

So when the door opened and Carmen came in to return a textbook she'd borrowed, I hadn't heard her. But Jason had. One minute I'd been lost in sensation, marveling at the feel of him pressed against me, and the next, my ass hit the edge of a desk as I was roughly shoved away from him.

"If you fucking tell anybody, I'll kick both your asses," he said as he hastily ran a hand through his hair and bolted out the door without a backward glance.

I stood there in the center of the room, my erection deflating, wondering what the hell had just happened. This had to have been the weirdest ten minutes of my life by far.

A face came into focus as Carmen approached me. I knew her in the way I vaguely knew everyone at our school. Enrollment here was relatively low, allowing the school to maintain its elite status, so we all knew each other, regardless of what grade we were in. Carmen was a feisty, curvy Latina girl in my grade, making her stand out in a sea of otherwise thin blonde society girls. I knew her parents managed some sort of nonprofit, but I didn't know much else about her.

I wasn't sure what I expected to see in her eyes, but compassion was all I saw reflected there. She offered a smile, asking, "Are you okay?"

Cautiously, I took her hand, rising. "I'm fine."

"I won't say anything. Not because that douche threatened me, but because it's not cool to out someone."

"Uh, cool. Thanks." Not sure what else to say, I turned to leave, but her hand on my shoulder stopped me. I turned to look at her, my eyebrow raised in question.

"So are you? Gay, I mean? Or bi?"

I turned more fully to face her, crossing my arms over

my chest, adopting a defensive stance. "That's really none of your business."

"I know. But listen…I'm a lesbian. And my parents are organizing this big gala this weekend and keep pressuring me to bring a date, but they don't know I prefer pussy over dick. You could be my date, and it would take some of the heat off me…"

"Seriously? Rubbing elbows and making small talk with a bunch of society douchebags? That sounds like my worst nightmare. If I say no, are you going to tell everyone about…?"

Her face fell, her disappointment with my noncompliance evident in her expression. "No. I wouldn't do that. It was just an idea."

I huffed a breath, shocked that I was about to agree to this ridiculous plan, but I knew it would take some of the pressure off me too, even if it did sound like my worst nightmare. My parents were never going to be okay with my sexuality. They'd never said anything homophobic, but they didn't have to. And they'd be thrilled I was attending some society to-do. The last couple they'd tried to get me to go to, I'd flat-out refused. God, I hoped I wouldn't regret this.

"What time should I pick you up?"

FUCKING JAMIE. I'd been perfectly fine spending Thanksgiving alone. Both The Daily Grind and Ivory were closed for the holiday, so I planned to spend time sleeping in, catching up on chores, practicing my piano, and maybe doing a little writing. All in all, a pleasant way to spend a day. I didn't mind the solitude. In fact, I generally preferred it.

Part one of my plan was a success, which was nice, considering I'd played a gig at Ivory the night before and hadn't gotten home until after midnight. I rose from bed around ten, started some laundry, and settled at my tiny kitchen table to write while I enjoyed my coffee. An hour later, I'd only written two paragraphs and had checked the clock roughly twenty-seven times.

I got up from the table, moving to the kitchen to warm up my coffee and switch the laundry from the washer to the dryer. I showered, hoping that would help me focus, but with the absence of Carmen's things in my bathroom, all it did was remind me that I was, once again, alone.

I liked being alone though. No one to bother me. No

one to nag at me to make the bed or pick up my clothes off the floor. No one chattering nonstop. No one to fight with over what we'd eat for dinner. No one to disappoint.

Pulling on gray sweats and not bothering with a shirt, I moved to the kitchen, grabbed an apple, and sat back down, determined to get some words on the page.

Twenty minutes later, I was still staring at a blank page.

Fuck it.

I moved back down the hall, again checking the clock, before picking up the little piece of paper Jamie had shoved in my hands at the shop on Tuesday.

Finn-
I know you said you were all right, but the offer still stands.
Dinner is at 1:00 on Thursday.
1076 W 56th Parkway
-Jamie
816-555-9375

I LET my head fall back, eyes closed, as I contemplated the madness I was considering. Because surely that's what this was...utter insanity. Was I really contemplating showing up at the house of a guy I barely knew, who had low-key been stalking me for weeks, to crash a holiday meal with a family I knew nothing about?

I let out a sigh. I had about forty-five minutes to change and get there.

Shit. Apparently, I was doing this.

THIRTY MINUTES LATER, I was on the road to Jamie's, descending into an epic downward spiral. My right foot was occupied with driving while my left knee was bouncing up and down at a frantic tempo. I almost turned around three times but managed to talk myself out of it.

God, I was losing it. This wasn't like me. I didn't do nerves. Years of playing piano in front of an audience and disappointing my parents over and over again had drummed that out of me.

I pulled up my contacts and dialed Carmen.

"Finn?" she answered, worry in her tone.

"Yeah, it's me."

"Is everything okay? You never call me."

"Yes, I do."

"Nope. You always text. Never call."

"Okay, fine. I never call. But I'm calling you now."

"Right. So what's wrong?"

I already regretted calling her. This conversation was ridiculous.

"Nothing's wrong. I'm fine. I just wanted to wish you a Happy Thanksgiving."

"Okay, now I *know* something's wrong. What's going on?"

I sighed. Might as well rip off the Band-Aid. Now that I'd called her and given her reason to be suspicious, she wasn't going to let it go.

"I'm, um, on my way to Jamie's."

"Seriously? Oh my God, that's awesome!" I winced as her excited squeals filled the interior of my car, her voice coming through the speakers. "How did this come about? Tell me everything."

I rolled my eyes but told her about Jamie coming into the shop on Tuesday and giving me the invite. "I don't know, CiCi. It feels weird barging in on their dinner like this. Maybe I should turn back."

"Don't you dare!" she exclaimed. "He invited you, didn't he? He wouldn't have done that if he didn't want you there."

"I don't know. It could be a pity invite. He's a nice guy. Totally the type to collect random strays and invite them to dinner."

"Oh my God, stop it! You are not a pity invite. The guy has been after you for weeks. He's totally into you. Stop overthinking it and just enjoy yourself."

Turning onto 56th Parkway, I glanced at the GPS to ensure I had the house number correct. Three houses down the block, I found the house and pulled up on the curb.

"Well, I was right about one thing. He's fucking rich. I'm about two blocks from Loose Park." The historic neighborhood built in the 1910s and 20s consisted of million-dollar homes, many of which were listed on the national historic register. We had gone to school with kids in this area, though my parents lived a little farther away across the state line. I marveled that Jamie and I hadn't crossed paths before now. I rested my head on the steering wheel.

"Okay, so? Why does that matter so much to you?"

"Do you not remember the people we grew up with? My parents? Their friends?"

"Your parents are narcissistic assholes. And yeah, we went to school with some entitled dicks, but not all rich people are like that." Her voice softened, and I thought I could sense some hurt in her tone. "My parents aren't like that."

"Your parents are the best, CiCi, but in my experience, they're the exception, not the norm."

She let out a sigh. "Look, just do me a favor and give him a chance."

"Why? For as much as I've tried to tell him no, you've pushed me toward him. You've never even met him. Why are you pushing this?"

"Because you wouldn't have called if there wasn't some part of you that wanted to see where this goes. Because while you're so busy pushing everyone away, there's a boy who cares enough to see past your bullshit. Because you deserve it, Finn. You deserve to be happy."

There was an ache in my chest at her words. I felt hollowed out and raw and, dammit, near tears. What if she was wrong? What if I was fundamentally unlovable?

"I'm scared," I whispered, head still resting on the steering wheel.

"I know, baby."

She didn't say anything more. Just stayed on the line, letting me breathe while I willed the ache in my chest to subside.

"I love you, Carmen. I don't know where I'd be without you."

I heard a sniffle on the line. "I love you too, you big idiot. Now go in there before you turn me into a puddle of goo and fuck up my makeup."

I chuckled at her sass, knowing it was her way of trying to lighten the mood. "All right, I'm going. Thanks, CiCi."

"You got this, sweets. Text me later."

I STOOD in our formal dining room, surveying the place settings and taking a moment to collect my thoughts. I had been moving almost nonstop since Aunt Cathy arrived around ten a.m. She'd immediately gotten to work in the kitchen, employing me as her sous chef and dishwasher as she prepared the Thanksgiving meal for our family. Mom had insisted on helping and had peeled potatoes and carrots while sitting on a stool in the kitchen, chatting as we worked. Around noon, my Uncle Bill arrived with my cousins Cody and Ashley in tow. Uncle Bill and Cody had commandeered the TV, turning it to football, while Ashley had coaxed Mom into sitting with her on the couch under the guise of asking her advice on what to wear to the winter formal at her school. At fourteen, Ashley was mature for her age and had recognized that Mom needed to take a break. I was grateful for all of them.

At some point, Mom had fallen asleep, and Ashley pulled a blanket over her, sitting next to her and scrolling social media on her phone. Overcome by the sight of my mom looking so pale and vulnerable on the large, overstuffed couch, I'd needed to take a minute to pull myself together. I'd headed to the dining room under the pretense of setting the table, and with that task accomplished, I found myself staring at the table, lost in memories of past Thanksgivings.

I remembered that last year my dad was still with us, and our house had been nearly bursting with both sides of our family in attendance. Warmth and laughter had been plentiful. I thought of the years Asher had joined us, first as my friend and then as my boyfriend. Some years Aunt Cathy's family had joined us, and others, they'd been with Uncle Bill's side. But no matter how big or small the gathering, our house had always been filled with love.

What would next Thanksgiving look like? Would Mom still be with us? Or would I be the last remaining person in my family, an extra place setting added at Aunt Cathy's table or tagging along at a friend's gathering?

God, what a melancholy thought. It wasn't like me to let this type of thought occupy space in my mind, but I supposed I was only human. I let out a shaky breath, my head turning sharply at the sound of the doorbell ringing through the house.

"I got it!" I hollered back toward the kitchen as I hurried to open the door.

"Finn! You're here!" My grin stretched wide across my face, chasing away the sad thoughts from moments ago.

"Um, yeah. I hope it's still okay?" He was adorably shy, standing on my front step dressed in dark jeans with his jacket open to a sweater the color of fresh blueberries.

"Yeah, of course! Come in!" I held the door open wide and gestured for him to enter. He stepped past me into the entryway and shrugged off his jacket. At The Daily Grind, he was usually dressed in well-worn jeans and a T-shirt, so I took a moment to admire the way his sweater molded to his shoulders and his slim-fit jeans hugged his ass. I didn't think there was anything he wouldn't look hot in, but I sure as shit enjoyed this look on him.

I hung his jacket in the closet behind the door and led him back toward the kitchen, where Aunt Cathy was pulling rolls from the oven. "Oh good, Jamie. Can you pull that basket down from the cabinet for the rolls? I can't reach it." I crossed to the cabinet she indicated, pulled the basket down, and handed it to her. "Thanks, honey. Oh, who's this?" she asked, finally catching sight of Finn, looking awkward, standing just inside the doorway.

"This is my friend, Finn." I gestured back to her. "This is my Aunt Cathy."

"Hello," Finn said with a little wave.

Looking past her into the living area, I could see all heads turned toward us, eyeing Finn with open curiosity. I hadn't mentioned I'd invited him because I hadn't actually thought he'd show up, so I was sure they were confused about this mysterious visitor.

I grabbed his hand, delighted he didn't immediately pull it back, and led him into the living room to make introductions. Mom had woken from her catnap at the commotion and was eyeing me with a little smirk. "Hey, everyone, this is Finn. He's a...friend."

Mom looked pointedly at our hands still clasped together but didn't comment. I made the introductions and was saved from further explanation by Aunt Cathy's announcement that dinner was ready.

We made our way into the dining room, each of us taking a serving dish from the kitchen while Ashley added a place setting to the table next to mine. After saying grace, we dug in, passing dishes around the table, loading our plates with turkey, potatoes, gravy, green beans, and rolls. Conversation flowed around us, my family making efforts to include Finn without being overly pushy. I soaked it all in, savoring the feeling of being surrounded by those I cared about most.

After dinner, we all worked as a team to clear the dishes, insisting that Aunt Cathy relax on the couch with Mom after working so hard to make dinner. With six of us working in the kitchen, it didn't take too long before we were finished. Cody and Ashley headed down to the basement to play pool while Uncle Bill dozed on the couch in front of a football game on TV.

I hung the dishtowel I was holding on the oven handle and turned to Finn, holding out my hand for him to take. He eyed it for a moment before returning my gaze, those piercing blue eyes unreadable as he ever so cautiously reached out and laid his palm against mine.

I wrapped his hand in mine and pulled him closer. I wanted to hug him, to pull him all the way into me and wrap him up in my arms, but I didn't think he was ready for that. Instead, I turned, tugging him down the hall toward my bedroom.

Mom had always been one for recording every moment and milestone with photos, and many of these lined the hallway in mismatched frames. While many of my friends' houses growing up had been decorated by professionals, ours had been filled with the things that had caught Mom's eye. The result was a mix of style and decor, all reflecting my mother's vibrant warmth. I loved that the frames didn't match and there was a mix of artwork and photographs and posters adorning our walls. It was comfortable.

Finn took it all in, eyes wide as he studied the pictures as we passed. There were pictures of me in my soccer uniform in second grade with popsicle juice staining my face and jersey. A family photo in front of the Christmas tree when I was nine. That had been our last Christmas with Dad. There was one of me looking terrified while holding an infant Cody and another a couple of years later of me holding Ashley, looking a little more confident. There was Asher and me at prom and another with the swim team the year our relay won State. Milestones, big and small, were captured, moments that made up the fabric of my life.

I started pulling Finn into my room, but his feet were rooted to the spot, his eyes locked on the picture of Asher and me dressed up for prom. We had chosen matching tuxes but with different colored bow ties that complemented each other. It was cheesy as hell, but we hadn't cared. We'd just wanted to have a little fun with it. In the picture, we stood side by side, hands clasped together, dopey grins plastered across our faces as we looked at each other.

"Who's this?" Finn asked.

"That's Asher. He's my best friend."

"Best friend? Looks like more than that here."

"Yeah, we dated for most of our senior year in high school, but we've been friends longer than that. Since first grade, I think."

He pulled his hand free of mine, putting both hands in his pockets as he stared at the picture, a little crease forming between his eyes. "So you dated in high school but were friends before that, and you still...what? What is he to you now?"

"He's still my best friend." I put my hands in my pockets, mirroring his pose. "We broke up when we went off to college. He went to Mizzou and I went to KU, and neither of us wanted to do the long-distance thing—"

"Wait. You go to KU? I guess I assumed you went to UMKC..." His eyebrows drew up in confusion.

"I do now. I transferred at the beginning of the semester so I could move home to help take care of Mom."

He was quiet for a moment. Most people didn't know what to say when I mentioned Mom's cancer. Eventually, he turned back to the photo, returning us to the original line of questioning. "So you said this Asher guy is still your best friend?"

I chuckled at the way he'd said "This Asher guy." I thought maybe he was a little jealous, and I kind of liked it. "Yeah, it was hard to be apart from him when we first left for school, but we worked at staying friends, and both of us have dated other people since. He's engaged, actually. Just happened over the weekend." I paused to gauge his reaction, but I couldn't tell what he was thinking. He continued to stare at the picture, his face unreadable. As much as I liked the thought of Finn being jealous, I worried this would be an issue between us. "Is this going to be a problem? My friendship with Asher is important to me."

Finally, he turned to look at me. "What am I doing here, Jamie?"

"What do you mean?"

"Am I just some guy to replace your old flame? He gets engaged, and you're feeling a little lonely, so you ask the sad barista to Thanksgiving to fill the void?"

"Is that really what you think?"

He shrugged. "I mean, why else would you invite someone you barely know to your family's Thanksgiving? People don't just invite random strangers to family meals."

"One, I want you here. Just you, for no other reason than that I like you. I told you weeks ago that I want to know you. I still do, now maybe more than ever. There's no other motive here. I'm not into playing games.

"Two, Asher has been a huge part of my life for almost as long as I can remember. He was there when my dad died, he was my teammate in both swimming and track, and yeah, he was my first love. But we broke up over three years ago, and neither one of us has regrets about that. I'm not holding out some hope we'll get back together, nor am I resentful that he's found happiness." I reached up and placed my hand gently on the side of his face, turning him to look at me so he could see the sincerity in my eyes. "You're the one I want, only you, okay?"

I held my breath while I waited for his response. I didn't want to argue over Asher, but he was important to me, and I hoped Finn could understand that. I wanted him to see that they could both fit into my life, just in different ways. His eyes searched mine as if assessing the veracity of my claim, and I refused to look away, returning his gaze with the hope that he could see the truth of my words.

Finally, he tore his eyes away from mine, pulling away from my touch, his voice small as he responded, "I'm not very good at this. I told you I don't do relationships." He scratched at the back of his neck. "The thing is, I never have, so I don't really know how. I don't know how to trust anyone's motives. How do I know you won't hurt me, Jamie?"

My shoulders sagged and I let my breath out in a whoosh as the tension left my body. I suddenly understood that he hadn't meant any of this as an accusation but as a way to try to make sense of my actions. It was a defense mechanism to protect himself. At its simplest, he was scared, just like George had been all those years ago.

I reached out, tipping his chin up, forcing him to look at

me. "You don't. And I can't guarantee that I won't. Because sometimes people hurt each other. But I can promise you that I'll do my best not to. And you'll always have honesty from me. I meant it when I said I don't play games."

"But why me? No one has ever pursued me even half as relentlessly as you have. It's weird, and I don't understand it. I'm not anything special. My life isn't anything extraordinary. I'm a simple guy living a simple existence. You could have anyone. Why me?"

God, he twisted my feelings into knots. I hated that he thought so little of his own worth. It made me even more determined to break through all those layers and show him how much he had to offer the world.

"I said honesty, right? I don't know what sparked that initial attraction besides the fact you're obviously hot. You know that, right?" His cheeks flushed and the corner of his lips turned up in a small smile. "And maybe I'm stubborn and like a challenge, but I don't know...there was something in the way you poured your soul out on paper that afternoon I came in when you were writing. And in the way you turned me down flat and called me out for being a rich pretty boy. It made me want to know why that bothered you. The more you push me, the more I want to understand why."

He shook his head but still held that little smile as if he couldn't understand me but was willing to humor me nonetheless. I hoped that was the case.

"I'm hard to know. My best friend Carmen knows me better than anyone, and she'd tell you I'm a pain in the ass. But..." He took a deep breath as if in resolution. "But I think I don't want to be alone anymore. I'm scared, and I'll probably be a dick to you more often than not, but since you seem so damn determined to 'know me,' as you put it, then I guess I'm willing to give it a try."

I put my hand on his shoulder and squeezed. "I'm not proposing marriage, you know...I just want a couple of dates. We can keep it as simple as you need it to be. One step at a time."

"Yeah, um, I think that would help."

I smiled broadly. "Can we start with a hug? I'd really fucking like to hug you."

He returned my smile, though it was a little softer than mine. "Yeah, I think I'd like that."

I pulled him into me, wrapping my arms around him, enveloping him in my warmth. I wasn't a huge guy, but I was a little taller and a little broader than him, and he fit perfectly, molded against me. He seemed unsure where to place his head, so I tucked it against my shoulder, leaning mine against his. His arms came around me, and at length, I felt him begin to relax. I don't know how long we stood like that, heart beating against heart, breathing in the scent of him, but I do know it was the best hug I'd had in a long, long time.

CHAPTER 13

FINN

THE WEEK FOLLOWING Thanksgiving flew by in a blur. With the holiday season fully upon us, I was working almost nonstop. I'd seen Jamie briefly a few mornings when he'd come into The Daily Grind, but each time, we'd been slammed and I'd only managed a few words as I'd handed him his coffee order. He'd come in to work between classes a couple of afternoons, but I knew he was on end-of-semester deadlines, so I hadn't wanted to bother him. I knew he could have found a place to work on campus, but he chose the coffee shop because I was there. I hated how much I loved that.

Still, it seemed every time I started to doubt the wisdom in pursuing any kind of relationship, no matter how casual, during such a busy time, Jamie'd send me a text just to let me know he was thinking of me. Sometimes it was a meme, sometimes a GIF, sometimes just a line or two of text. Nearly every time one of those messages came through, I'd roll my eyes, even as my pulse stuttered in response. I'd found myself frowning at my phone on more than one occasion because several hours had passed and I hadn't heard from him.

What the hell was wrong with me? Since when did I care how often a guy, or anyone really, texted me? I started leaving my phone behind the register rather than carrying it in my pocket just to prove I didn't need constant interaction. I was already starting to become addicted to those little messages. What would happen when I was actually able to spend time with him? What would happen when he inevitably decided I was too much work to continue to pursue? Would I survive the withdrawal? Or would I spiral out like a junkie badly in need of their next fix?

Better to avoid the addiction altogether.

And then...I'd eventually cave and check my phone to find that he'd sent three more messages, and I'd be right back to where I started. I was starting to suspect I'd never be able to quit him.

While my days were spent at The Daily Grind, my evenings were spent at Ivory. One of the other pianists had gotten sick, and they'd asked me to pick up a couple of extra nights in addition to the two I already had booked. One of those had led to three more bookings for private parties later in the month. I was thrilled at the money coming in. At this point, my tires would be paid off by the end of the month and I might even be able to set some back in savings rolling into the new year.

By Saturday night, I was fucking exhausted. I hadn't managed more than five hours of sleep a night for the last week and wasn't sure how much longer I could maintain at this pace. Thankfully, Ivory was closed on Sundays, so while I was scheduled for an afternoon shift at the shop tomorrow, at least I'd be able to sleep in and still have most of my evening free since my shift at the shop was relatively short.

I was sipping a Manhattan off to the side of the crowded bar between sets when I caught sight of Jamie across the room. As he removed his wool peacoat, I took stock of him. He wore a fitted charcoal sweater over a button-down that he'd paired with black slacks. His dirty-blond hair was swept up in his usual man bun, and he'd grown out a bit of scruff in the last week. As I watched, he unbuttoned the cuffs of his sleeves and pushed the sweater and button-down to his elbows, revealing his toned forearms. He tucked a loose strand of hair behind his ear as he sat, his back to me. Two guys who appeared to be about our age took seats next to and across from him, but his attention was elsewhere as he scanned the room. I assumed he was looking for me, and that knowledge came with a little flutter of nerves that I wasn't used to experiencing.

I never got nervous when I performed, but I suddenly felt anxious at the thought of performing for *him*. The lead bartender caught my eye, nodding to the stage, and I knew my time was up. It was probably for the best that I didn't have a chance to overthink it any further. I finished off my drink and headed toward the stage.

I didn't want to look at him as I took my seat, but I couldn't help myself, and when we locked eyes, he gave me a wink. I rolled my eyes, instantly more comfortable, and dove into the set, starting with "Last Christmas." He barked out a laugh, the sound carrying over the din of glasses clinking and chatter, and I was glad he got the joke.

As one Christmas tune gave way to another, my gaze kept wandering back to Jamie and his friends. God, he was beautiful. When he threw his head back and laughed, eyes sparkling with mirth, I was captivated. Fortunately, my fingers played with a mind of their own because I couldn't take my eyes off him.

Lust coiled hot in my belly. Now that I'd given myself permission to consider pursuing something with him, I wanted him. Desperately. It had been a long time since I'd fucked anyone, let alone someone I actually felt a connection with. I was terrified, even as I knew I wouldn't be able to stop myself if the opportunity presented itself.

I finished my set with a jazzy rendition of "Sleigh Ride" before announcing I'd be back in ten. I nodded to the bartender as I made my way over to Jamie's table, bracing myself for the inevitable small talk I knew I'd have to make with his friends. God, I hated that, but I knew I should make an effort. It wasn't like I didn't know how. It was just exhausting after doing it all day at The Daily Grind. Jamie was a raging extrovert, so I supposed this was something I'd have to get used to.

Dating someone was a pain in the ass.

Jamie rose from his chair as I approached, brushing a soft kiss against my cheek and gesturing toward the open seat to his left. Courtney, one of the regular servers, slid a Manhattan in front of me before slipping away to check on another table.

Jamie made the introductions. Sitting to his right was Asher, who looked so different from the photo I'd seen at Jamie's house that I hadn't recognized him. He was tall, but where he'd been rather lanky in his pictures, he'd definitely filled out since. He wore black-framed glasses and his short dark hair was neatly styled. He was objectively attractive, in a nerdy professor sort of way, with his navy sweater worn over a button-down and tie. Any jealousy I'd felt died as I saw the way he looked at his fiancé. Their hands clasped on top of the table, Joshua returned the same adoring look before bringing his gaze to me, openly curious.

Shortly after introductions were made, Asher stepped away to the restroom while Joshua signaled Courtney to bring their check. I took the opportunity to lean into Jamie, saying, "I didn't expect to see you here tonight."

"Is it okay that I'm here? I missed you."

"Yeah, um, I'm just not used to having anyone come to hear me play. Carmen has come once or twice, but that's pretty much it."

He seemed genuinely shocked by that. "Really? You're amazing."

I was pretty sure I blushed at the compliment, but I ignored the heat in my cheeks. "I'm not exactly loaded with friends. Who would come to hear me?"

Something passed over his face. Was that pity? For fuck's sake. I didn't need his pity. I rolled my eyes. "Relax. I don't need or want a ton of friends. It's not a big deal." I tossed back half of my Manhattan, searching for a way to change the direction of the conversation. "So what's the deal with Asher and Joshua? I thought you said you were helping your uncle with his Christmas lights and then working on a big paper you have due?"

"I did help with the lights, yeah, but Asher and Joshua came into town and wanted to take me out to dinner, so I suggested we come here after." He leaned in a little closer. "I wanted to show you off."

"You told them about me? I thought we were taking it slow. We haven't even been on a date yet." A knot of panic formed in my gut. It was bad enough I'd already met his whole family before we'd actually been on a date, let alone meeting the best friend/ex-boyfriend. That implied a seriousness I wasn't yet ready to contemplate.

"He's my best friend. I tell him—"

"Hey, guys." We both turned to see Asher and Joshua standing behind their chairs, tugging their coats on. "We're going to head out. It was good to meet you, Finn."

Jamie hopped out of his chair, reaching over to shake Joshua's hand, then leaned in to hug Asher and whisper something in his ear. Logically, I knew there wasn't anything between them, but they had a history, and my gut churned at the intimacy of the moment. Their presence here, all three of them, left me feeling confused and agitated. I slammed back the rest of my drink and pushed my chair back to stand.

Wordlessly, I turned to head back to the stage, leaving the three of them behind me. I knew I was being rude, but I didn't care. I didn't want to continue our conversation and my break was up anyway. I felt a hand on my elbow, but I shrugged it off and kept walking. I took the two steps up to the stage and settled in at the piano. Without looking at Jamie, who I knew was still standing there, I dove right in with "O, Holy Night."

By the end of my set, Jamie and most of the other patrons had cleared out. I didn't know if I was relieved or angry that he'd left. Did I want him to fight for me, or did I want to avoid a fight altogether? I was too damn tired to figure any of it out.

Twenty minutes later, I walked into my apartment, stripped down to my boxers, crawled into bed next to Carmen, and crashed.

I slept until eleven and woke with a start. Looking around, I tried to figure out what had woken me. The bed was empty next to me, and I strained to listen for any clues as to whether Carmen was home.

A buzzing on the nightstand next to me alerted me to an incoming message. Swiping open my phone, I noted that I had three missed messages. I figured that must have been what woke me.

JAMIE

I'm sorry I upset you last night

I wasn't trying to be pushy

Can we please talk?

I flopped back in bed, debating how or even if I wanted to respond. Scrubbing my hands over my face, I heard Carmen's footsteps as she approached the bed. She nudged my hip, and I moved over, making space for her to climb in next to me.

"Hey, sleepyhead," she said softly, running her hand through my hair. "I wondered how late you were going to sleep."

"I'm fucking exhausted, CiCi."

"I know. You're running yourself ragged."

I sighed. It was on the tip of my tongue to remind her that we didn't all get an allowance like she did, but that was a shitty thing to say, even for a dick like me, so I held my tongue.

My phone buzzed again. Carmen turned to reach for it. "Leave it," I said, my tone brooking no argument.

She ignored me, grabbing it anyway and punching in my code. So much for boundaries. She read it and then shoved it in my face so I could read it too.

JAMIE

At least tell me you made it home safely

I frowned.

"Are you going to respond?"

"I don't know. I'm still half-asleep."

She was quiet a moment, but then, "What happened last night?"

"I don't really want to get into it."

"Too bad. Tell me."

With a frustrated sigh, I threw the covers off me and climbed out of the other side of the bed. "Why can't you just drop it?"

"Because I care about you and you're too fucking stubborn for your own good."

"What makes you think this is about me being stubborn?" I tossed the question over my shoulder as I walked into the bathroom and shut the door without waiting for her response. I took a piss and washed my hands, but then I just stood there, staring at myself in the mirror, letting the events of the previous evening roll through my mind.

Dammit. I overreacted last night. It had been really sweet of Jamie to come see me play last night. And so what if he'd mentioned me to his best friend? Hadn't I done the same with Carmen? Then I'd seen the exchange between Jamie and Asher, and despite knowing there was nothing more than friendship there, it had made something clench inside me. So, I'd panicked and been rude, and like a selfish asshole, I'd bailed without even giving him an explanation.

Fuck.

Disgusted with myself, I walked out of the bathroom to see Carmen still lying in the same spot, holding out my phone to me. "Text him. At least let the poor guy know you got home okay."

I took the phone, opened my messages, and typed a response.

I'm fine

I should probably have said more, should have apologized, but I didn't even know how to begin. I wasn't used to anyone caring about my words or actions, and I certainly hadn't worried about how I made someone else feel in a very long time. I watched as those three little dots appeared and disappeared several times, but when it finally seemed like no message would come through, I laid my phone face down on the nightstand and climbed back into bed.

I felt Carmen wrap her arm around me but made no move to turn toward her. Still, I didn't shrug her off either.

We lay there for a while like that, listening to each other breathe. I needed to get up and shower before work, but for all my insistence on pushing everyone away and my determination that I was fine by myself, it felt good to be held. To be wrapped in her warmth. To be cared for. To *matter*.

"I met someone," she said, her voice quiet. There was a hesitation as if she was afraid of my reaction. I rolled over to face her, eyebrow lifted in question. "Her name is Isa. We met on the beach over Thanksgiving. She's a ballet dancer from Denver. She's..." The expression on her face was a mix of wonder and apprehension. "Finn, she's everything."

Her wide eyes were full of so much damn hope. I felt my heart lurch in my chest. Carmen's dating history was absolute garbage. She was so quick to fall in love, and she inevitably ended up falling for a horrible excuse for a human. She loved the thrill of the fall so much that she allowed herself to be blind to the other person's faults.

Still, this time, the look in her eye was different. She looked so damn hopeful, but I could see a little bit of fear there too, and it may have seemed odd, but I actually thought that after all she'd been through, a little fear was healthy. It meant she might be a little more cautious rather than throwing herself at someone who didn't deserve her.

God, I hoped Isa was worthy of her. I wasn't sure I could pick up the pieces of Carmen's love life again.

"Wow, CiCi. That's really great. I'm happy for you!" At least, I *wanted* to be happy for her. I wasn't sure what to think, honestly.

She narrowed her eyes but didn't say anything.

"What's that look for?" I asked.

"I don't know. Aren't you going to tell me it's too fast and lecture me about how I just got out of a relationship and how hard long-distance relationships are?"

"Would it do me any good?" I threw back, heavy on the sarcasm. "Sounds like you've already covered all of that for me."

"Dick." She shoved my shoulder playfully. "I've over-thought the shit out of this, about all the things I just said and all the ways it could go sideways. But my gut says this is different."

"How? How is it different?" She shot me a look, fire in her eyes, but I cut her off before she could snap at me. "Calm down. I'm not judging. I'm genuinely curious. What about this feels different to you? Different from all the other girls who've promised you the moon only to turn around and treat you like shit?"

She flinched at my words but didn't try to deny their accuracy. "I don't know. I guess the best way I can say it is that I've honestly never felt like I could truly be myself with someone so quickly. Usually, when I'm starting to date someone, I feel like I have to be on my best behavior, with my makeup flawless and my hair perfect. I'm always thinking about the perfect thing for us to do, the perfect topic of conversation, the perfect response to every question. Then, about the time I start to actually get real with someone, they fuck me over somehow or other. But Isa sees past my bullshit and won't accept anything less than real. She pushes me to be myself but somehow puts me at ease at the same time. It's scary as fuck to have someone really see the heart of who you are, but it also feels so damn good, like it's a relief that I can relax and be myself, and she still wants me around."

I honestly couldn't imagine what that was like. Aside from Carmen, I couldn't think of a single person in my life that I'd allowed to get close enough to actually see the real me. Was I willing to let Jamie in that far? With the way I'd fucked up last night, I wasn't sure I would get the opportunity to find out.

"Well then, I hope it works out. Seriously. I want you to be happy."

"Thanks. Me too." She was quiet for a moment like she was pondering what she was going to say. "I want that for you too, you know."

"What?"

"I want you to be happy. I want you to find someone you're willing to let your guard down for."

"I don't know, Carmen." I sat up in bed, placing my feet on the floor and turning my back to her. "I don't know if that's in the cards for me."

"So, what? You're just giving up on Jamie?"

"I fucked it up. I told you I wasn't built for this shit." I ran my hands through my hair, scrubbing my curls a couple of times before swiping my hand down my face. "I don't know how to do this."

"Bullshit."

"What?" I asked, turning back to look at her.

"I said bullshit. You keep saying you don't know how to be in a relationship, but you've been friends with me for years."

I rolled my eyes. "A friendship isn't the same as a relationship." I stood from the bed and turned to face her, the corner of my mouth turned up in a smirk. "Besides, I don't know if it counts since you pretty much browbeat me into it."

I was trying to go for light. I was tired of this conversation. Tired of feeling like a failure. Tired of dealing with all these *feelings*. Things had been so much easier before.

Before Jamie.

Carmen didn't take my bait. "It's okay to be scared. But don't run away. Don't cheat yourself of the possibility."

"I have to go to work," I said, deliberately choosing not to respond, instead making my way around the bed toward the closet.

"Finn..." she called out.

I came back out of the closet with a pair of jeans and a long-sleeved T-shirt. "Leave it, Carmen. I know you mean well, but not everyone is built like you. You dream of love and marriage and family, and I...I just can't see that for myself. Just let me be."

I was almost to the bathroom door when she wrapped her arms around me from behind, stopping me in my tracks. I sighed. "Come on. I need to shower so I can get to work."

"I know. But you know you deserve those things, right? You deserve love and happiness."

"Yeah, sure. Of course." We both knew I didn't mean any of that, but what was I supposed to say?

She came around to stand in front of me, grasping both of my hands, her big brown eyes earnest as she said, "I mean it. You're an amazing person, Finn. And I know I already said it before, but I want you to be happy. I want us both to be happy."

"I'm not amazing. I'm a grumpy asshole barista who plays piano on the side. I'm just an average guy trying to get by like everyone else."

"That's the thing though. Life shouldn't be about 'getting by.' There is joy and happiness and *love* out there, Finn, and I want you to know that you deserve those things. I want you to let yourself have them."

Her words were like tiny paper cuts on my heart. So small you could barely see them, but they hurt like a bitch. She was trying to make me feel better or inspire me or some shit, but they only made me feel worse. She was wrong. Those things weren't for me.

I squeezed her hands before releasing them and stepping back. "I know you believe those things, CiCi."

"Don't push me away, Finn," she said, sadness weighing down her words.

"I'm not pushing you away. I just have to go." I leaned down and kissed her forehead, and then I fled.

THE DAILY GRIND had been slammed with customers most of the afternoon, with students studying for finals and folks trying to get ahead on their Christmas shopping. I'd been grateful for the distraction as it hadn't given me time to contemplate the events of last night and my conversation with Carmen before I'd left.

But now, as I headed home, exhausted from the day, my thoughts couldn't help but wander over the last twenty-four hours and everything that had been said. I wasn't sure what I thought about whether I deserved love and happiness, but Carmen had definitely been right about one thing.

I was scared.

And goddammit, I was tired of feeling that way. Tired of living in fear. Tired of not really living at all.

I turned into the parking lot of my apartment and pulled into a slot in front of my building but didn't turn off the ignition. Instead, I sat with my Jeep idling, staring at the darkened window of my third-floor apartment. Carmen had texted earlier, letting me know she was going over to her parents' for dinner, and I suddenly found myself, maybe for the first time ever, not wanting to be alone.

Was this what the rest of my life would look like? Whether it was Isa or someone else, Carmen was going to find love. She would move in with someone else someday, maybe get married, maybe have that family of her dreams, and where would I be? Still a grumpy barista coming home to a shitty apartment alone.

Fuck it.

I pulled out of the spot and headed toward Jamie.

I WAS WATCHING an episode of *Ted Lasso* with Mom when the doorbell rang. "Were you expecting someone?" I asked.

"Nope," she said with a tiny shrug.

I paused the show and got up to answer the door. I was floored to find Finn standing on my doorstep. His hair was disheveled like he'd been running his hands through it, and he wasn't wearing a jacket, despite the chilly temperature.

He looked fine as fuck in his skinny jeans and hoodie, but I crossed my arms and leaned against the doorway, preventing his entry. It took a lot to push me over the line, but I was frustrated. And exhausted. Tired of studying and worrying about Mom and playing what felt like an endless game with him. I'd told him I would be patient, and I wanted to be, but his silence today had *hurt*. How could I understand anything if he refused to talk to me?

I arched one brow but said nothing.

"I'm sorry," he said simply, eyes not quite meeting mine.

"What are you sorry for, exactly?" I hadn't expected the

apology, though I hadn't really expected him to show up here either.

He raked his hands through his hair in frustration, visibly agitated. "I just...it was a lot coming at me at once. You at Ivory. Asher and Joshua. We haven't even been on a date, and you showed up with your best friend and his fiancé—people I don't even know—like it was just no big deal, and I panicked."

"You said it was okay that I was there..." I still didn't understand. I'd asked him, and he'd said it was okay.

"It was, and then it wasn't." He let out another sigh, really a sound of frustration more than anything else, and swiped his hands through his hair again, this time rubbing all the way down the back of his neck before dropping them roughly back to his side. "I'm not like you, Jamie. I don't people very well. I *was* glad to see you." His face heated as he said it, softening some of my rough edges. "But I guess I just hadn't really given any thought to you telling other people about me, and I certainly wasn't prepared to meet your best friend. I didn't know what to do with that. It made me feel like things were moving faster than I was ready for."

I was starting to get it. I'd texted Asher a bit about Finn over the last month. He was my best friend, and we told each other everything. So when he'd come into town and the three of us had gone to dinner, the idea of taking them to Ivory had popped into my mind, and I'd jumped on it. I'd promised to take things slow, and then I hurtled past a couple of steps without thinking.

I hung my head as it all came crashing down on me. I'd promised not to push, and then I'd done just that. I looked back up at him and nudged the door open wider. "Would you like to come in?" I asked.

He looked hesitant like he wasn't sure whether that was

such a good idea, but when a gust of wind kicked up, causing him to shiver, he nodded and stepped past me into the entryway. I led him into the kitchen, where I pulled down two rocks glasses and poured a healthy shot of bourbon in each. Handing one glass to him, I gestured for him to take the stool at the island while I leaned against the counter opposite.

"I think maybe I'm the one who owes you an apology. I promised we could take it slow, and then I didn't follow through with that. In my excitement, I honestly didn't see it as rushing things, but looking back on it from your perspective, I can totally see how it felt that way to you. I'm sorry it made you feel like you were being pushed. And I hate that I'm the one who made you feel that way." I wanted to touch him, even just to take his hand, but I didn't know if it would be welcome, so I kept my position across from him. "I don't ever want to hurt you, Finn."

"You didn't hurt me. I just felt...cornered, maybe? I don't know if I'm saying this right." He took a healthy swig of the amber liquid before placing his glass on the counter in front of him. Then he pushed it back and forth from hand to hand in either a stalling tactic or a gesture of nerves. I wasn't sure which. Finally, he tossed the rest of it back, setting the glass firmly on the counter, and looked up at me, face resolved.

"Look, I'm not comfortable getting into all the personal shit just yet. I don't know if I ever will be. But let's just say that my parents really fucked me up. I never had much of a relationship with them, and what little we did have, blew up in my face after graduation." He looked at me, appearing to gauge my response, and I nodded, encouraging him to continue. "I've also never really been much good with people. I don't know if it's a learned behavior from my parents, a survival thing, or just the way I'm wired, but I don't let people in, and I don't trust anyone. It's not personal, or at least, I don't mean it to be." His eyes dropped to the counter in front of us, and I almost missed it when he said, "I don't want to hurt you either."

All the tension, frustration, and confusion I'd felt melted out of my body. I reached out, gently placing my hand under Finn's chin, urging him to look at me. There was a vulnerability in his eyes that I'd never seen before, and for a second, it took my breath away. "Thank you for trusting me with that," I said, sincerely appreciating the glimpse of what lay behind those carefully constructed walls of his, even as much as it broke me to hear it. "I've said from the beginning that I want to know you, and I mean that. I want to know the things that scare you and the things that hurt you. I want to know all the good as well as all the ugly."

The space between us shrank until there were just inches between our lips. I wasn't sure whether I'd leaned into him or he'd leaned into me, but it was as if some invisible force was pulling us together and we were both helpless to stop it. "The thing about me is that I feel everything deeply. I wear my heart on my sleeve. When I go in with someone, I go all in. I don't really know how to do it any other way." I watched his face carefully, praying I wouldn't see panic there. He gulped but didn't pull away, so I continued. "I know that's probably too intense for you, and I'm terrified that by telling you this, I'm going to scare you away, but I'm scared too because, Finn, you have the ability to wreck me, and I..." I looked down for a second, swallowing past the lump in my throat. *Shit.* "I know I said I just wanted a few dates and we could take things slow, and I really will do my best not to push you, but the reality is, I'm already invested. I'm drawn to you in ways I can't explain." I brushed my thumb over his lips wanting desperately to taste them. "It doesn't make a damn bit of sense, but I can't shake this feeling that you're meant to be mine. So if this is too much, let me know now while I still have the ability to walk away."

By the time I'd finished my speech, we were both breathing heavily, the air thick between us. I'd probably fucked this all up, laying it on the line like this. He was probably going to run for it, but I had to fucking know. I had to know before I was crushed.

He pulled away from me, my hand falling from his chin where I'd been holding him. I felt the rejection like a punch to the chest. My chin dropped and I released the breath I'd been holding.

Okay then. Now you know. Now you can move on from this insanity you've been living for the last month.

I felt him come up behind me, but I was afraid to turn around, afraid of what I'd see when I looked into his eyes. I kept telling him I wouldn't push, but I'd been unable to keep the words inside me any longer. His vulnerability had unlocked something inside me, and I'd suddenly needed him to know how I felt. Needed him to know what he did to me. That I was scared too.

"Is that what you call 'not pushing?'" he asked with... was that humor? I cautiously turned around, leaning against the counter, but didn't respond to his question, waiting to see what he'd do or say next. "Maybe I need to be pushed." He stepped forward, one foot sliding between mine so we stood hip to hip, our groins just a breath away from each other. "Maybe I've spent too much of my life playing it safe, hiding in the shadows, avoiding conflict." His hands came up to rest on the nape of my neck, their heat scorching my skin. I forgot to breathe as he leaned in closer, his lips nearly brushing against mine. "Maybe I need you to show me what it's like to take a risk. Push me, Jamie."

Like a switch, I closed the distance between our lips, slamming my mouth down on his, my hands landing on his hips, holding him there against me. Some part of my brain registered I was holding him hard enough I might leave bruises, but I made no move to soften my grip. In fact, I *hoped* I was leaving a mark on him so that days from now, he wouldn't be able to deny this moment. He wouldn't be able to run from it.

Tongues tangled and twisted, tasting, seeking, fighting for dominance. He nipped my lip, and I groaned, backing him into the opposite counter. He bit my lip again, this time tugging it between his teeth before releasing it and diving back in again.

That pinch of pain set fire to my blood, lust shooting straight to my cock like a bolt of lightning. Liquid fire coursed through my veins, igniting everything inside me into an inferno of need. How could one kiss spark such a blaze? I was in danger of burning from the inside out.

A blast of cold air swept over us, having a similar effect as being doused with a bucket of ice water. We burst apart, lips puffy and bruised, chests heaving, eyes locked as we tried to gain control of our rapidly beating hearts.

"Oh, hello, Finn! So good to see you again." I spared Aunt Cathy a cursory glance before returning my gaze to Finn. I searched his face, trying to get any sense of what he was thinking after that kiss, but his intense stare was inscrutable.

Oblivious to the sexual tension permeating the air, Aunt Cathy bustled about the kitchen, putting containers in the fridge and the freezer before carrying three grocery bags into the pantry.

"We weren't expecting you tonight," I called out, my eyes never leaving Finn's. My hands slid from his waist to wrap his hands in mine. I was thrilled when he didn't pull away. I finally tore my gaze away to look down at his hand resting in mine, marveling at how beautifully they fit together.

"I just had a few things I wanted to drop off since I won't be able to come over tomorrow. I don't want you and your mom to go hungry." Aunt Cathy emerged from the pantry, empty bags tucked under her arms.

"You didn't have to do that! I do know how to cook a few things around here."

"Aw, it's cute that you think that's true." I shook my head as she winked at me. "I'm just going to say hi to your mom before I leave." She crossed the kitchen to head down the hall, but I stopped her.

"Wait!" I called out, her words finally registering in my lust-addled brain. "Did I know you weren't going to be here tomorrow?"

"Yeah, honey. Remember we talked about it on Thursday? I have jury duty. I'm going to try to get out of it, but I at least have to show up for the initial selection process." Shit. I had totally forgotten about that. The stress I felt must have shown on my face because she asked, "What's wrong? I thought you said you had it covered."

I groaned, releasing Finn's hand to tuck a loose strand of hair behind my ear. "It's finals week. On a normal Monday, I'd be able to skip class and borrow notes from someone, but I have two finals tomorrow, and there's no way I can miss."

"Well, is there any way to reschedule? Maybe explain the circumstances?'

"I mean, I can try, but I doubt they'll let me. The university is pretty strict when it comes to maintaining the integrity of finals. They rarely let anyone reschedule."

"What's the issue?" Finn asked, and I turned to look at him. "Mom is pretty weak right now, especially after that infection before Thanksgiving," I said. "We try to work it so one of us is here with her at all times in case she needs anything."

"What time are your finals?" he asked.

"One's at eleven-thirty and the other is at two, I think."

"Okay, I open at the café tomorrow, but I'm off at ten-thirty. I can come over and hang out for the rest of the day until you get home from your finals."

"Um, wow. That would be amazing!" I was astounded at the generosity of his offer. He'd only met my mom the one time at Thanksgiving. "Are you sure?"

"It's not a big deal. I can be here around eleven if that works for you?"

"Yeah, that's perfect." I placed my hand on his face, rubbing my thumb over his cheekbone. "Thank you. Seriously, this is...just thank you."

Aunt Cathy cleared her throat and said, "Sounds like you boys have this handled. I'll just go say hi to your mom."

Struck by Finn's kindness, I leaned forward and kissed him. This kiss was sweeter than before. A gentle press of lips before I pulled back. "Please let me know if there is anything I can do in return."

"No need to thank me. Hanging out with your mom isn't a hardship, Jamie." He pulled away. "But I should get going. I have some things to get done around my apartment, and I need to be up early tomorrow."

As I walked him to the door, I tried to work through the myriad of emotions I'd experienced in the last half hour. It'd been a damn rollercoaster of feelings, and though I wasn't ready for him to leave, I also knew I would be better off if I gave myself some space to process everything. And even though I was terrified that as soon as reality set in, Finn would make a run for it, I knew he needed the processing time too. I wanted him to be sure this was what he really wanted. He'd made some bold declarations tonight, and it would kill me if he came to the conclusion that this was all too much. I didn't want him to regret making a decision with his dick. If he truly wanted this, wanted us, then I wanted him to make that decision with a clear head.

At the door, we turned to face each other, staring awkwardly while waiting for the other to speak first. Finally, he broke the silence. "I really am sorry, Jamie. I'm sorry I freaked out." He released his breath in a whoosh before continuing, "You asked me to let you go if I couldn't handle it, and I'll be honest, your intensity scares the shit out of me. It's fucking terrifying." He ran his fingers through his hair before reaching for my hoodie and yanking me closer. "But I'm drawn to you too, and I'm not ready to walk away."

He pulled me into him, lips meeting mine in another searing kiss, but this time, before I could get my bearings, he was already pulling away. "I'll see you tomorrow at eleven," he said before pulling the door open and walking out without looking back.

WHEN I WAS SEVENTEEN, I came down with the flu. I'd woken up that day feeling a little off, but my mother had insisted I go to school because she had "things to do" and didn't have time to deal with a sick kid, even though I was old enough to take care of myself.

I made it through third period before I puked.

In the middle of AP World History.

And again in the hall on the way to the nurse.

I knew my mom would be upset that she had to drop what she was doing to pick me up, and though I'd driven myself to school that day, I was in no condition to drive home. I kind of thought she deserved to have her day interrupted. Had she let me stay home, she could have done whatever she needed to do and left me home to sleep in my own bed. It wasn't like she'd actually taken care of me when I was sick in years.

Ninety minutes later, she arrived, having been in the middle of a massage where she couldn't be interrupted. Even if it was the school calling regarding her sick child.

She entered the nurse's office, her face reflecting the

appropriate amount of motherly concern as she fluttered about, feeling my forehead and remarking on how clammy I felt. She picked up my backpack, helped me up, and eyed me with concern as we made our way through the main office and out to the car.

It was all an act, of course. The moment we stepped up to her compact BMW, she dropped the facade, tossing my backpack in the back and leaving me to fend for myself. With a sigh, she put the car in gear, not saying a word on the ten-minute drive home. She pulled into the garage, got out, and headed into the house without bothering to look back at me.

I climbed out of the car, grabbing my backpack out of the backseat, and made my way to my bedroom, pausing once to sit on the stairs when a wave of light-headedness washed over me. I dropped my backpack near the door before stumbling over to my bed, where I stripped down to my boxers and climbed in.

I had no idea what time it was when I woke next, but with the sun setting so early now that it was December, the room was fully dark.

My sheets were damp, my skin clammy, and my body was wracked with chills. I turned to switch on my bedside lamp, and my head immediately started pounding as my stomach rolled with nausea. I hastily threw off my covers, knowing another vomiting episode was imminent, and made a run for my bathroom across the hall.

Thankfully, I made it to the toilet this time, but since I hadn't eaten anything since breakfast, I mostly retched stomach acid and bile. The whole episode left me feeling shaky and weak, so I curled up on the bathmat and fell back asleep.

"Finn! What the hell are you doing on the bathroom floor?"

I squinted, my face scrunching up in a frown against the blazing overhead light my mother had switched on. My head was still pounding, and I felt hot all over.

"I threw up again and I guess I fell asleep," I responded feebly.

"Get up off the floor and get back in bed. Honestly, I can't imagine why you wouldn't have just gotten back in bed after you got sick."

She turned and walked from the room without bothering to help me up. I managed to pull myself to a standing position but took a moment to brush my teeth and pop a couple of Tylenol before moving to the hall, where she stood waiting with her arms crossed, her forehead creased in impatience.

"Can you move a little faster, please? Your father and I should have left five minutes ago."

I gave her a cursory glance, noting her attire. Dressed in a long satin skirt, paired with a deep-red cashmere sweater, and wearing heavy makeup, it was clear she was heading to a holiday event.

I didn't bother to acknowledge her as I passed by, climbed back into my bed, pulled the covers up, and closed my eyes.

"Your father and I are heading out to the symphony. Now, he is working a very important deal with one of his clients, so there's a possibility we will be coming back for a nightcap after the performance. I was hoping you'd be up for a little piano performance, but I suppose, under the circumstances, we'll pass on that."

"Heaven forbid your sick child mess with your plans, Mother."

I didn't bother to open my eyes to gauge her reaction, but I could imagine the flat line of her mouth as she glared in disapproval. "Your smart mouth really isn't appreciated, Finneas. Just make sure you stay in your room. We don't need you vomiting all over our guests."

Without waiting for a response, she walked out my door.

I lay there for a while, but despite my exhaustion, I was achy all over and couldn't get comfortable enough to fall asleep. I found my phone next to my bed and picked it up to message Carmen.

> I feel like death

CICI

> Sorry sweets. I heard what happened

> I'm sure everyone did

CICI

> No worries. In seventh period, Shelly Smithfield and Jenny Lawrence got busted for vaping in the second-floor bathroom and were suspended for 3 days. Code of conduct calls for expulsion, but word is their daddies made a huge donation and got it down to a suspension. It's bullshit, of course, but at least that bit of gossip took the heat off you

> Lucky me

CICI

> Lol

> Seriously, tho. You gonna be ok?

> Yeah. My parents are pieces of shit, but I'll live

CICI

??

I sighed.

> Don't worry about it. Just the usual shit. Having a son is such a huge inconvenience for them

CICI

Boo

Want me to come over?

> Nah. No need to get you sick too

She didn't respond after that, so I spent some time scrolling TikTok, but before too long, my eyes got heavy, so I set my phone aside and fell asleep again.

Sometime later, I woke to the feeling of being jostled as someone climbed into bed with me. I immediately recognized Carmen's perfume and relaxed, though I wasn't sure how I felt about being only in my underwear. We were both gay, but still...I'd never been nearly naked in bed with anyone. Too tired to give it any more thought, I scooched over to make some room.

"What are you doing here, CiCi? I told you I didn't want you to get sick," I mumbled.

"Shh. No one should have to be alone when they're sick. Go back to sleep." My chills were back, so even though part of me wanted to kick her out, I couldn't resist snuggling into her warmth.

"How did you know I was alone?" I asked.

"You said your parents were assholes, so I guessed."

A massive shiver rolled through me as I responded, "I

think my exact words were that my parents are pieces of shit.”

“Hang on,” she said as she climbed back out of bed. I pulled the covers around me as I continued to shiver in the bed. She returned with a glass of water and a couple more Tylenol. “Here, take these,” she said, handing me the pills and water. I swallowed them before handing the water back to her to place on my side table.

She climbed back into the bed with me, again pulling the covers over us and draping her arm over me.

“You’re crazy, you know that?”

“Eh, you love me anyway.”

We lay there for a moment, my chills slowly subsiding as I absorbed some of her warmth.

“Thanks, CiCi,” I whispered.

“You’re welcome, sweets.”

CHAPTER 16

I WASN'T sure what had possessed me to volunteer to hang out with Jamie's mom. Carmen gave me a smug smile when I told her, which I ignored. All I knew was that when I saw the panic on Jamie's face, I hadn't even thought before offering. Jamie had always struck me as kind of go-with-the-flow, yet yesterday I'd first seen him frustrated, then stressed, and all I knew was that I wanted nothing more than to see him back to his usual chill, happy self. I hated that I'd been responsible for the frustration, but at least there was something I could do about the panic.

I arrived at the Felton residence promptly at eleven a.m. Walking up the steps to the door, I was struck by an intense bout of nerves. My stomach fluttered with butterflies and my hands were sweaty, despite the cold December air. I'd come over here last night intending to apologize, to make things right after I'd shut him out Saturday night. What I hadn't expected was for *him* to apologize to *me*. And I certainly hadn't expected his impassioned declaration about his feelings toward me. It had unnerved me, but surprisingly, rather than making me want to flee, it'd made me want to stay. I'd wanted to know what it felt like to be cared for so intensely, and for the first time in my life, I'd wanted to take a risk. But now, in the bright light of day, I wondered if Jamie would still feel the same way. Or would he regret everything?

Just as I was about to knock, Jamie opened the door with a huge smile. He was so damn beautiful. I was relieved to see that smile again, and my nerves melted away.

"Hey, you!" He leaned forward, pressing a quick kiss to my cheek before moving aside so I could step through the door. "Mom is asleep at the moment. She was up for a bit this morning, but ever since her infection, she tires even easier than before." He took my coat and hung it on the hook by the door before leading me to the kitchen. "There's some soup in the fridge that Aunt Cathy brought over, so that would probably be good to heat up for lunch. Her appetite can be kind of iffy, but she should at least try to eat something so she can take her pills." He gestured to those sitting out on the counter. After going over the instructions for her meds, he picked up his backpack and headed toward the door.

He turned to me as he pulled on his coat and said, "Thanks again for coming over today. I can't tell you how much it means to me."

"It's not a big deal."

"Nevertheless..." He leaned in, pressing his lips to mine and holding them there for a moment before pulling back. "I'd really like to continue where this is going, but I've got to get going. Stay for dinner with us tonight?"

"Yeah, I can do that."

He gave me another one of his bright smiles. "Great! See you tonight!"

I shut the door behind him and made my way into the

living room, carrying my messenger bag with me. Sitting on the couch, I pulled out my AirPods and selected a playlist, making sure to keep the volume low enough that I could hear Mrs. Felton if she needed me. I then pulled out my notebook and began to write.

For the next hour, I lost myself in the act of putting words on the page. The last week had been absolute insanity, so I'd barely had time to put pen to paper. Today, as I wrote word after word and line after line, it felt good to finally pour my thoughts and feelings out on the page.

It seemed to me that most people preferred to talk out their thoughts and experiences with their friends, bouncing off ideas, seeking input and perspective, but I'd never been comfortable opening myself up that way. Writing words allowed me to make sense of my life. It'd been this way for as long as I could remember. Playing piano allowed me to express my emotions while writing allowed me to express my thoughts.

Around noon, I got up from my spot on the couch, stretching, my neck stiff from sitting hunched over the low table. I tip-toed down the hall, peering into Mrs. Felton's room, where she still appeared to be fast asleep.

Knowing she needed to take her pills, I returned to the kitchen, where I heated up some soup. Placing a bowl, some crackers, and her pills on a tray, I made my way back to her room.

As I entered, her eyes fluttered open, her lips slowly curving in a smile. "Finn! I'm so glad you're spending time with me today!"

Uncomfortable with her enthusiastic declaration, I simply nodded as I crossed over to her. She struggled to pull herself into a sitting position, so I quickly set the tray aside on the bedside table so I could assist her. She waved me away, saying, "I'm fine, kiddo. If you could just help me stand, I can make it to the bathroom, and then let's take this food back out to the kitchen. I'd rather not eat like an invalid."

"Are you sure?" The look she returned reminded me that up until this year, she'd been a teacher. There would be no arguing with her. "All right," I mumbled as I took her cool hand in mine and helped her stand. I watched her make her way across the room to the bathroom, her leggings and T-shirt baggy on her thin frame. I made sure she looked steady on her feet before taking the tray back out to the kitchen, then returned to her room to guide her to the table. I knew she didn't want my help, but Jamie would kill me if I let her fall.

We successfully made it to the kitchen, where she sat at one end of the table and invited me to sit next to her. I sat awkwardly while she scooped up some of the chicken noodle soup, blowing on the spoon to cool it a bit before taking a bite. "Where is yours?"

"Oh, I'm fine."

"Don't be ridiculous. I'm sure my sister made enough for a family of twenty. Go heat yourself up a bowl."

"Yes, ma'am," I said and got up to pull the large container of soup back out of the fridge. As I retrieved a bowl from the cabinet and began to ladle a portion for myself, she said, "Jamie says you work at a coffee shop by the university. Are you in school then?"

"No, ma'am. I'm not in school." I always got a mixture of responses when I told people I wasn't in school. They ranged from judgment to pity mixed with the occasional patronizing "You'll figure it out." Most people didn't ask why. They were generally too busy making assumptions regarding my motivations and telling me what I *should* be doing without knowing anything about my background or life story. The thing was, I had *wanted* to go to school. But that option had been taken from me.

When she didn't respond, I chanced a glance at her. I sensed no judgment or pity, just open curiosity. Surprising myself, I felt compelled to elaborate. "I came out to my parents the day after graduation. They kicked me out of their house and cut me off from the trust fund that was supposed to pay my way."

The microwave chimed, and I took my soup over to the table to sit next to her. My pulse was racing. I hated talking about my personal life, but somehow these Feltons had a way of pulling it out of me. I didn't look at her. She hadn't been judgmental so far, but I was afraid I'd see pity. "Did you apply for loans?"

"All the deadlines had passed, and my parents are in a pretty high tax bracket, so I really couldn't qualify for anything anyway." I blew gently on my soup spoon before taking a bite. "Besides, I was more concerned with where I was going to live and how I would support myself at that point."

"How'd you survive?"

"My friend, Carmen. Her parents took me in over the summer until I could save enough for a small apartment. I've been working at The Daily Grind and playing gigs at Ivory ever since."

"Jamie says you play piano?"

"Yeah. It was maybe the one thing my parents did for me that I can be grateful for. I mean, they got me piano lessons so I could be more well-rounded, which made them look better to their society friends. I don't think they counted on it being something I would be so good at. And, as it turns out, not only has it helped me make money, it's been one of the few things that was solely mine. They could kick me out, but they couldn't take that away."

We were quiet as we continued to eat our soup. Dropping stories of your sad childhood was a real conversation killer. I couldn't believe I'd just poured all that out to her. I hadn't even told Jamie about a lot of it. Finishing my soup, I set my spoon down, but before I could reach for my water glass, I felt her hand on my arm.

"Our job as parents is to love our kiddos, no matter who they grow up to become. Apparently, your parents didn't get that memo." She squeezed my arm. "I'm proud of you."

"Proud?"

"Of your strength. Your resiliency. You've survived in spite of them."

I shook my head. "I just did what I had to do."

"Maybe. But I've taught a lot of affluent children over the years. They have every advantage in the world, earn top grades, get accepted to elite schools, yet most wouldn't have the first clue how to make it out there in the real world."

She wasn't wrong, and while I was incredibly uncomfortable with her praise, a part of me was hungry for more. I couldn't remember the last time someone had told me they were proud of me. "Um, thank you," I said, rising to collect our bowls and move them to the sink. As I finished loading the dishwasher, she asked, "Would you play for me?"

"The piano?"

"Yes. I have such happy memories of Jamie's father playing Christmas carols at this time of year. It's been years since anyone's played for me."

Unable to deny anything she asked of me, I escorted her to the living room, making sure she was comfortable with a blanket across her lap. The piano was surprisingly in tune despite having sat virtually unused for years. I took requests for about thirty minutes until I noticed her eyes had closed. I pulled the blanket over her shoulders, then quietly retrieved my notebook and sat on the other end of the couch where I would be nearby if she needed anything.

As I watched her sleep, my notebook closed in my lap, I thought of the vast differences between Mrs. Felton and my mother. They couldn't be any more dissimilar. Jamie and I had grown up in wealthy households, but as far as I could tell, that was the only similarity.

This house had a warmth I hadn't experienced in my own home. It was tidy but lived in. Blankets were loosely folded and tossed over the backs of chairs and couches. Pictures and knick-knacks were mixed among books, some clearly well-worn, crowding shelves. Mismatched candles sat on the mantle at various heights, their black wicks showing evidence that they'd been lit at some point.

My home had been all sleek lines and dark leather. Pictures were chosen carefully and used sparingly in favor of dramatic artwork. Books were leather-bound and shelved in the study. I was sure none of them had ever actually been cracked open. Candles were never, ever burned.

What would my life have been like had I grown up in a home such as this? Comfy furniture. Cozy blankets. Hugs. Laughter. Love. Parents who not only accepted their gay son but who cherished and encouraged him to be whoever he wanted to be. People who did whatever they could to support their child rather than use their child as an accessory to somehow elevate their own status.

My heart hurt for the little boy I'd been, for the childhood I'd never even known could be possible. And my heart raged on behalf of the man I'd become. The man who pushed everyone away because it hurt too damn much to let anyone in. It was easier, just so much fucking easier, to shut out all that warmth. To exist in a state of numbness where there was no expectation of joy or happiness. If you didn't expect it, you couldn't miss its absence.

I was starting to get a glimpse of all that I had missed. Sure, I'd seen it with Carmen's family, but this was different somehow. I didn't know if it was because Carmen was a daughter and I was a son, and seeing Jamie accepted and loved as a son made it feel more real, but it honestly didn't really matter. In this moment, what mattered was that I was finally starting to see all I'd lost and all I'd closed myself off to. It fucking pissed me off.

My fingers itched to play. I wanted to pound out some Beethoven or Rachmaninoff until I couldn't think or feel anything anymore. But I didn't want to disturb Mrs. Felton, so I opened my book and began to write.

I WALKED in the door around four o'clock to a quiet house. I'd come in through the garage, and when I didn't see my mom or Finn in the kitchen, I made my way down the hall toward my mom's room. Her bed was unmade but empty, so I retraced my steps, turning off into the living room, where I found them both asleep on either end of the oversized sectional.

Finn's notebook was open in his lap, his pen dangling loosely in one hand as if he'd stopped in the middle of writing. His head was leaned against the back of the couch, slightly tilted to one side.

I studied him as he slept, his face relaxed in sleep. My eyes drank in every detail, from the dark hair resting on his forehead to his strong jaw and full lips. I itched to brush that lock of hair from his face and press my lips to his, but I didn't want to wake him. I knew he'd worked himself ragged last week and was probably still trying to catch up on sleep.

Still, as always, I was inexplicably drawn to him and found myself carefully sinking onto the couch next to him.

In his sleep, he released the pen, which rolled off the notebook and onto the carpet, and laid his head on my shoulder. I managed to get my arm around him, pulling a blanket over us and savoring the feel of him tucked into my side.

I sat like that for a long time, my eyes closed, not in sleep, but in contentment. I thought about the path we'd taken to arrive at this point. All the times he'd pushed me away. What was it about him that kept me coming back for more? I'd never pursued someone so relentlessly, yet he was like a drug I couldn't quit. I was always desperate for that next hit.

The events of last night played through my mind like a highlight reel. Glimmers and flashes of our conversation, of the way he'd kissed me, the way we'd kissed each other. Fire and passion and need coursing through my veins. The way he'd felt in my arms. The sound of his panting breaths as our tongues fought for dominance. Heat pooled low in my groin, and though Finn and my mom were asleep, I was thankful I'd grabbed the blanket because it was doing a bang-up job of hiding my erection.

A rustling on the other end of the sectional caught my attention, and I opened my eyes to see my mom slowly rising to stand. I started to inch forward, willing my erection down while trying to figure out the best way to extricate myself from Finn's hold without waking him, but she waved me off. "I'm fine," she whispered. "I suspect he needs the rest."

"I think so too," I whispered back. "Are you sure?"

"I'm just going to watch some TV in the sitting room. I'll be fine."

"I don't want you to fall."

"Stop it. I can still walk. Just love on him for a little while. He needs it."

A battle was waged inside me, but ultimately, holding on to Finn won. Still, I stared after her with a watchful eye to make sure she appeared steady on her feet. When I heard the faint sounds of the TV coming down the hall, and it seemed she'd successfully made it without falling, I turned my attention back to Finn.

Giving in to the temptation of touching him, I pressed a kiss to his temple before laying my head back and closing my eyes.

I BLINKED AWAKE, looking around in confusion. It took me a moment to realize I had fallen asleep while holding Finn. His head had drooped so he lay more on my chest than my shoulder, hunched over in what must have been an uncomfortable position. I was sure his neck would be achy.

Gently, I nudged him, trying to wake him. His eyes opened slowly, and he sat up, looking at me cautiously, obviously confused about how he'd gotten into such a position. "When did you get home? What time is it?" he asked as he slowly rolled his head from side to side, stretching his neck.

I raised my smartwatch, wincing as I realized how long we'd been napping. "It's close to seven. I got home around four, but you were out cold, so I thought maybe I'd join you."

He rubbed his eyes. "You should have woken me."

"Did you have someplace to be?" I asked. "You said you could stay for dinner, so I figured it'd be okay to let you sleep."

"No, I just...I don't know. I feel bad that I slept all over you."

I grinned. "No need to feel bad. Gave me an excuse to hold you."

He looked at me out of the corner of his eye, one side of his mouth tilted up in a smirk. "You don't need an excuse. All you have to do is ask."

I raised my eyebrows in surprise. This little bit of flirty banter was new. "Yeah?"

"Yeah. But first, I gotta pee."

I chuckled as I watched him head down the hall toward the powder room, shamelessly admiring his ass in his black joggers as he walked away. My stomach rumbled, and I reached over to pull up an app on my phone to place a pizza delivery order. Unsure what Finn liked, I ordered a basic pepperoni and some garlic knots.

I was just finishing placing the order when Finn reappeared from the hallway. "I hope you like pepperoni on your pizza..."

"I'm actually a vegetarian..."

"Bullshit. I watched you eat plenty of turkey on Thanksgiving."

"Fuck. I forgot about that." He chuckled. "Yeah, pepperoni's fine." He sat next to me on the couch but angled his body so he faced me. "Do you have studying to do? I don't want to keep you..."

"I only have one more final, and it's not until Wednesday, so I have plenty of time to study." I grabbed his hand, examining his fingers, mapping every vein, line, and fingerprint, before threading our fingers together and resting our joined hands on my thigh. "So, can I hold you now?"

The corner of his mouth curled up in another sexy smirk. I wanted to lick it.

"No," he said.

"No?"

His smirk deepened into a full-on smile that nearly stole my breath, and I found myself grinning just as wide.

With our eyes locked, he swung one leg over mine and lowered himself onto my lap. My hands settled on his hips, holding him in place. He draped his arms over my shoulders, his hands playing with the hair at the nape of my neck as he pulled me in for a kiss. "I was thinking of something a little *dirtier* than cuddling," he whispered before his lips met mine.

I opened immediately, and his tongue swept in, leisurely sliding against mine. Tasting. Teasing. Tempting. Heat flooded my veins, and I lowered my hands to grab his ass, pulling him closer. I could feel his erection pressed against mine. My dick was achingly hard as I kneaded his ass, loving the feel of him in the palms of my hands.

He rocked his hips, grinding his cock against mine, and I groaned. It was a feral sound full of hunger and need, want and desperation, as our kiss turned from a leisurely exploration of tongues and mouths to a frenzied quest for dominance.

My hips bucked up, my cock seeking more contact with his as we rutted against each other. Dimly, I recalled my thoughts from the previous evening about not rushing things and not letting my dick do the thinking, but I was too far gone, lost in the feel of him. He tore his lips away from mine, nipping at my jawline, earlobe, and neck. My hands found their way under his hoodie, and he hissed as my fingers trailed up the ridges of his spine. I loved the feel of his skin, smooth and hot under my fingers.

Our movements became more frantic as we ground against each other, chasing our release in the middle of my goddamned living room. I hadn't come in my pants since my freshman year of college when I'd drunkenly dry-humped a guy from my Western Civ class in his room at his frat house, but I wasn't about to stop now. Not when I was this close. Not when I had Finn in my lap and his movements were just as sloppy and desperate as mine.

"Want to feel you," I mumbled into his ear as I reached for his waistband, pulling the elastic of his pants and briefs down, releasing his dick. I continued holding the elastic down with my left hand as I wrapped my right around his cock, smearing precum down his length and then giving a long stroke from root to tip. He groaned as he bit into my shoulder, and I gave him another stroke. This one was a little firmer, my palm rubbing against the head.

He felt so good in my hand. I couldn't see him, but I could feel his thickness and imagined what it would feel like in my mouth. In my ass. My own dick jumped at the thought.

As I pumped him harder and faster, his little nips became bites and his moans whining pants of neediness. I hoped he was leaving teeth marks. This felt like a fever dream, and I wanted there to be evidence later.

Without warning, he buried his head in my chest, grunting as his cock swelled in my hand before shooting hot ropes of cum all over the front of my hoodie. I kissed the top of his head as he continued to pulse and mutter incoherently into my chest.

He jerked as I stroked his oversensitive head one too many times, and I chuckled and did it again just to be an ass.

"Fucker," he muttered but didn't move to get off my lap, his chin still resting on my chest as he tried to regulate his breathing.

I wanted to hold him, wrap my arms around him, his rapidly beating heart pressed against mine, but my right hand and a good portion of my hoodie were covered in jizz. He pulled his head away from my chest, sitting a little straighter in my lap, and I groaned as his ass brushed against my neglected dick.

"Ah, poor baby still needs to come, doesn't he?" Finn smirked at me. I pushed my hips against him in response, then carefully tucked his dick away and wiped my hand on a dry portion of my hoodie.

He climbed off my lap, moving to his knees on the floor while reaching for my waistband when the doorbell rang, startling us both.

"Fuuuuck. That's probably the pizza." I sighed and looked down at the mess on my shirt. "Why don't you get the door while I go clean up. I already paid in the app."

While Finn made his way to the door, I jogged down the hall to my room, carefully removing my hoodie and throwing it into the hamper. My balls were aching with the need to release, so on impulse, I grabbed the hoodie back out of the hamper and pulled out my dick. Three strokes later, I was coming all over the hoodie, my release mixing with his, my knees practically giving out on me as I shot over and over in a never-ending stream of cum.

A knock on my door scared the bejeezus out of me. "Just a sec," I called out, quickly wiping myself off and once again tossing the hoodie in the hamper. I pulled my pants back up before crossing to the door.

Finn leaned against the wall opposite my door, arms crossed languidly, one ankle crossed over the other. He gave me a look as if to say *I know what you were doing in there,* but he didn't say a word.

I closed the distance between us, pulling him away from the wall and into my arms. Just like the last time we'd hugged, he stiffened as if he wasn't sure what to do. I didn't care. I was a hugger, and he would have to get used to it. We stood like that until, eventually, his body relaxed and his arms tentatively came up around me. Thrilled that he'd caved and hugged me back, I gave him one more squeeze and then released him.

"I'm starving. Let's eat!"

WE ATE our pizza in the living room, the box resting on the coffee table between us. Jamie's mom—she insisted I call her Annie—joined us for a slice. I ate quietly, marveling at the simplicity of eating in the living room and enjoying how their conversation flowed so easily. My mother would have lost her shit had we ever dared to bring food into her pristine living room, yet Jamie's mom sat on the couch with us, eating straight out of the box, forgoing plates.

They talked about his finals—the ones he'd taken so far and the one he still had to take—and spoke about Christmas shopping and family gossip. Aunt Cathy had texted to say she'd successfully gotten out of jury duty, so she would be able to come over on Wednesday while Jamie took his last final. Cody had a basketball game coming up on Thursday and Ashley was singing at Crown Center with her high school choir on Friday. With Annie's weakened immune system, it wasn't safe for her to be out in the crowds, and she and Jamie both seemed bummed to miss it, so I offered to come over and hang with her on Friday while Jamie Face-Timed the concert to us. I had a gig on Thursday night, so I couldn't do anything about the basketball game, but I had a window of time between my shift at The Daily Grind and my gig at Ivory on Friday, so I could help during that time.

They both seemed reluctant to accept my offer, but in the end, they conceded. The truth was, I'd enjoyed spending time with Annie today. In all the time no one had been looking out for me, I'd not had anyone to look out for as well. It felt good to be able to give that to someone. Not just because I wanted to help Jamie but because I wanted to help Annie as well. I was no longer content to sit idly on the sidelines of my own life. I wanted to be an active participant. I wanted to be useful. I wanted to be needed. I wanted to care.

Had they begun to care for me as well?

After dinner, Jamie's mom retired, saying she wanted to read a bit before bed, so while Jamie settled her in her room, I cleaned up the boxes and wiped down the coffee table, making sure not to leave stray crumbs. Jamie returned just as I was finishing up and grabbed my hand, tugging me down the hall to his room.

He closed the door behind us and crossed to the bed, pulling me down with him. We lay on our sides facing each other, one of his legs thrown over mine, his hand laying loosely on my hip. He stared at me intently, his moss-green eyes laser-focused on me as if searching for something. It was such a serious look on a face usually so merry. I could feel my cheeks heat under his scrutiny.

At length, he leaned forward and pressed his lips to mine. It was a sweet kiss, with just a brush of his tongue against mine, before he pulled away to turn that intense gaze on me again.

"What?" I asked, unable to take the silence any longer.

He reached for my hand and threaded our fingers

together. He finally tore his gaze away from mine to look down at our joined hands. I followed his gaze and watched as he slid his thumb up and down over mine, savoring his touch. His eyes slid back to mine as he said, "I just...I was just wondering what changed..."

"What do you mean?" I asked though I had a feeling I knew.

He pulled our clasped hands up so they were folded against us, sandwiched between our chests. He smiled a little as he said, "You just seem...lighter tonight, flirting and making out with me—"

"Making out? Are we teenagers now?" I interrupted, choosing to ignore the rest of what he'd said. I was deflecting, and we both knew it.

"You rode me, and then I jerked you off until you came all over me. Call it whatever you want, but we basically humped each other like teenagers, so I'm going to call it making out." I chuckled as he waggled his eyebrows before continuing. "Man, don't get me wrong, I love seeing this side of you. I love seeing you smile." He reached up and brushed his thumb across my lips before taking my hand in his grasp again. "But if I'm being totally honest here, I'm scared to trust it. What made you open up with me and what if you shut down again?"

His wide green eyes were open with so much vulnerability that I nearly collapsed under the weight of it. I'd made him scared to trust me. The world hadn't given me a reason to trust feelings given so freely, and so I'd dulled just a little bit of his shine, and I hated it. He didn't deserve that, yet a part of me was relieved to know I wasn't the only one in it. I wasn't the only one fighting my way through the muck of complicated feelings.

I wasn't the only one afraid.

I knew I owed him an answer or at least some sort of explanation, but talking about my feelings was hard as fuck. Writing was better, but I had to learn to verbalize these things. I couldn't press pause on a conversation so I could quickly grab my journal and write that shit out.

"How did your parents take it when you came out?"

His forehead wrinkled at the seemingly unrelated question. "My dad died when I was ten, so I never got the chance to tell him, but my mom gave me a hug and then three days later cornered me into an embarrassing lecture about condoms and lube. Turns out, after I announced Asher and I were dating, she'd done a bunch of research and felt like I needed to have 'the talk' again, only this time the gay version." He chuckled. "Lucky me, I got to have the sex talk twice."

I tried to muster a smile, but I must not have been successful because his face fell. I couldn't bear to look at him for this next part, so I rolled over, turning away from him. He didn't let me get too far, pulling me back against him, the little spoon to his larger one. He lifted his head and pressed a gentle kiss to my temple. "I'm guessing it didn't go so well for you," he said softly.

"No, but it's not exactly what you think. My parents weren't homophobic so much as they were afraid of how *my* sexuality might make *them* look. They couldn't care less who I fucked, as long as it didn't reflect poorly on them. I never got a sex talk other than my dad tossing me a box of condoms and telling me I damn well better not get a girl pregnant. I was fifteen and had known for years I was gay, but I didn't bother correcting his assumption that I was straight." I paused, waiting to see how Jamie would respond, but when he didn't say anything, I took a breath and continued, "The day after graduation, I told my parents I was gay.

I don't know what possessed me to do it. The only people who knew at that point were my best friend, Carmen, and this kid I'd kissed once, who was very, very closeted. He was a couple of years older than me, and after he graduated, I didn't mess with anyone after that." Jamie said nothing but started pressing small kisses to my head, neck, and shoulder as I talked.

"Anyway, we were sitting at dinner in our formal dining room, just the three of us, which was unusual because they rarely bothered to dine with me, but for whatever reason, we were eating together, only it was as if I wasn't even there. They were talking around me and over me about *my* college plans as if I wasn't sitting right there next to them. They'd chosen the college. They'd chosen the major. And they hadn't bothered to ask for my opinion on any of it. I'd gone along with all of it. Written the essays and applied to the colleges they wanted. Declared a respectable major. Earned academic scholarships, even though they could pay every cent on their own. I'd gone along with all of it. It's what I'd always done. At least it was what I'd done when they bothered to pay me any attention at all.

"So in the middle of dinner, three bites into my braised beef risotto, as my parents debated the merits of me rooming with Henry Davidson, whose father was a partner in my dad's firm, or with Edward Helzberg, whose mother was a partner in my dad's rival firm, I calmly put my fork down, announced I didn't think Henry or Edward would be comfortable with a gay roommate, and declared that I would not be attending Northwestern to pursue pre-law in the fall."

Jamie stopped kissing me, instead resting his chin on my shoulder and squeezing me tightly as I continued. Now that the words had started, I couldn't even begin to stop them.

"There was a lot of yelling. Mostly at me, but some directed at each other, as if one of them held some sort of responsibility for 'making me this way.' They didn't bother to ask me to explain myself. Nothing I had ever said mattered, so why would this be any different? Eventually, I got up and walked out without a backward glance. I spent the night at Carmen's, unable to stand the thought of a night spent getting yelled at or, worse, suffering their cold indifference. When I returned the next day, they'd changed the locks and refused to let me in. My father opened the door long enough to tell me I was to get my shit together and toe the line, or they'd cut me off.

"I'd like to say I held strong to my convictions, but I did consider going back and playing by their rules. As much as I hated the world I was brought up in, I hadn't known anything else. I had no idea what else I might make of my life. I just knew I didn't want to be their puppet any longer. But it was the idea of going back in the closet that ultimately made my decision. I refused to turn back and deny that part of myself any longer. The housekeeper, who'd always been more like a mom to me than my own mother, snuck me back into the house while my parents were out later that evening so I could grab a few of my things. I made it out with a backpack full of clothes, my keyboard, some sheet music, and a couple of notebooks. Oh, and my Jeep." I shrugged as if any of that was as simple as asking whether I preferred pepperoni on my pizza. "I haven't spoken to them since."

He was silent for a while. I assumed he was processing the shit show I'd just dumped on him. It was so different from his own family that I couldn't begin to imagine what he must think about mine.

"You're amazing," he said at last, his voice low next to my ear.

I scoffed, uncomfortable with his praise. "I don't know about that. I should have stood up to them years ago rather than letting it get to that point."

"Eh. Would it really have made a difference? It might have made your high school years even worse." He tugged me so I rolled to face him once again. "You're a survivor. You did what you had to do to get through high school, and then you've continued to do what you've needed to since. You're fucking brave, Finn."

He looked at me like I was some sort of goddamned hero when, in reality, I was nothing of the kind. I was just a broody asshole barely making ends meet with the emotional capacity of a teaspoon.

Unable to bear the look in his eyes any longer, I yanked myself out of his hold and sat up on the bed, turning away from him. "I wasn't brave. I was a fucking coward my whole life, and all that one act of defiance got me was kicked out of my house without any way of supporting myself. I could have gone to college. I might have eventually convinced them to let me change my major. I could have fucked my way through half the men on campus, and they would've never known."

"And you would have died a little more each day that you had to deny who you really were."

"How is that any different from who I am now? Yeah, I'm open about my sexuality, but I'm locked in an endless cycle of trying to make ends meet. I'm not living, Jamie. I'm simply existing, bouncing from one shitty job to the next, barely making rent, barely sleeping, barely even fucking. Carmen is the only friend I have, and I'm not even sure why she puts up with me."

He sat up and put his arm around me, pulling me into his side. "You have me. You have my mom. Stick around a little longer, and you'll have Aunt Cathy and her family too."

My heart was racing, pounding the inside of my chest so hard I wondered if it was possible to bruise from the inside out.

I wanted that. I wanted family and love and acceptance so badly that it was an ache inside me. I was absolutely terrified it would all be gone with a snap, and I'd never recover. How could I want something so desperately that I'd never even known was missing until now?

And yet now that I'd had a taste, there was no turning back. I needed this. Craved it. Even as I feared what it could do to me.

I took a shaky breath and turned my head to look at him, steeling myself for the words that would come next. I felt like Wile E. Coyote barreling off a cliff only to look down and realize the ground was gone from beneath my feet. The question was, would I plummet to the bottom of the canyon, or would there be something there, *someone*, to catch me when I fell?

"You asked me what changed. It was you. You and your family. I've spent my entire life closing myself off from everyone because it was safer that way. Carmen has been the only one to penetrate that wall, mostly because she's a wrecking ball of a human who won't take no for an answer. Honestly, other than you, she's the only one who's even tried."

"I think I like Carmen already," he said, pulling a small smile out of me.

"She'd like you too, but I'm afraid if the two of you ever meet, you'll gang up on me, and I won't survive it."

"Perfect." He grinned at me shamelessly.

I shook my head before continuing, knowing I needed

to get this out. "Since you walked into my life, I've realized that in my effort to protect myself, I've missed out on so much, and I don't want to do it anymore. I don't want to sit on the sidelines while life passes me by." I swallowed past the lump in my throat, pressing on. "You said I have the ability to wreck you, but I think I could say the same to you. And I'm so damn scared, but I want that. I want someone in my life who thinks I'm worth risking that kind of heart-break. And if you're willing to risk that with me, then I'm willing to risk it with you too."

"So fucking brave," he murmured before pulling me into him in a fierce embrace, holding me tightly as if he could somehow fuse all my broken pieces back together.

Tears fell without my permission. I hadn't cried once over my parents in the last four years, not even the night I walked out of their lives, and yet this guy had managed to pull down all my walls in a matter of weeks. He'd worked brick by brick until, eventually, they'd all come crashing down, and I couldn't be sorry for it.

He pulled me back down beside him, lying with his arms wrapped around me, my head on his chest, my tears soaking his shirt. He stroked my back, ran his hands through my hair, and murmured words of comfort in my ear. I had no idea what he said, but the sound and tone of his voice soothed me, and eventually, I slept.

FOR LIKELY THE fiftieth time in the last half hour, I caught myself staring at Finn as he worked the coffee shop counter while I attempted to study for my last final. The truth was, I didn't really need to study. I knew the material and my grade was strong enough that this final wouldn't make a big impact, but I'd needed an excuse to see him again.

His confession Monday night had left me feeling raw, my heart aching for him. What kind of heartless bastards could treat their only son like that? What must the rest of his childhood have been like living in a house like that?

He'd finally cried himself to sleep, but I'd stayed awake for another hour watching him and marveling over just how strong he was. I'd never known fear like he had. I'd been nervous to tell my mom about Asher and me, but not once had it ever occurred to me that she would turn me away. I'd never had the experience of having everything I could ever want, only to find myself living paycheck to paycheck to survive.

He'd bruised my ego when he'd called me a rich pretty boy a few weeks ago, but the truth was, to some degree, he'd been right. Oh, I wasn't nearly as shallow as the term pretty boy might suggest, and I certainly had compassion for those down on their luck, but all from a safe distance. I'd never had to examine it up close. I'd never had to give it more than a passing thought before returning to my cushy life.

Finn had lived it. Was still living it.

He was amazing.

He made me want to be better. To not take the life I'd been lucky to live for granted. To appreciate the people who'd supported me, who *still* supported me. I wanted to do the same for him. To be the same for him. I wanted to show him how beautiful life could be when you were surrounded by love.

The man currently occupying all my thoughts caught my eye and gave me a small smile before returning his attention to the customer in front of him. His curls were covered in a beanie today and he wore a Henley that hugged his slender frame paired with worn jeans slung low on his hips. He reached for something on the shelf above him, and I nearly drooled at the sight of a sliver of bare skin when his shirt rode up his abs. I wanted to lick it.

"You must be the mysterious Jamie," a voice said next to me, her tone laced with humor. Startled, I turned to find a curvy Latina woman staring at me, arms crossed, eyebrow raised, red-painted lips curved up in a smirk. Her ebony hair was pulled back into a smooth high ponytail, large hoops dangling from her ears. I instantly knew who she was.

"And you must be Carmen." Her smirk widened to a broad smile, her eyes alight with humor. "Damn right," she said as she pulled out the chair opposite me. Even if I didn't know what she meant to Finn, I would have liked her immediately.

"How did you know who I was?" I asked.

"Broad frame, dirty-blond hair in a man bun, staring at my best friend like you want him to be your next meal...the signs were there."

I barked a laugh, pleased that her description signaled Finn must have been talking about me. "Busted," I said. "Did you come here looking for me, or is this a coincidence?"

She took a slow sip of her coffee as she studied me. "He might have mentioned that you were coming in this morning." She shrugged. "I was curious."

I raised a brow. "And?"

"And...I haven't completed my assessment."

"Fair enough."

"Oh no. Nothing good can come of this," Finn said as he approached my—now our—table.

I looked up at him and grinned. "Scared?"

"Of the two of you together? Fuck yes."

I laughed. "Ah, baby. You don't have anything to worry about," I said as I took his hand, his eyes softening at my use of the endearment.

He turned toward Carmen, though he didn't let go of my hand. "What are you doing here, CiCi? I thought you had a final this morning?"

"Calm down, Finn. I took it first thing this morning and then thought I'd come get a cup of coffee."

"You haven't been here in weeks and just so happen to swing by after I told you Jamie would be here this morning?"

"Mm-hmm," she said as she took another sip, her eyes wide with false innocence.

"You two are unbelievable. I have to get back to work." He leaned over and kissed my cheek. "Be good," he said as he walked away.

Turning back to Carmen, I said, "So...what do you want to know?"

She made a show of crossing her arms, leaning back in her chair, and giving me an assessing stare. "What are your intentions with my best friend?"

"My intentions?" I laughed. "Why do I feel like I'm being interrogated by his ninety-year-old grandma?"

She dropped the pretense of being my interrogator, her face taking on a genuinely worried look as she leaned forward, speaking quietly. "Listen, you seem like a nice guy, but Finn is...he's fragile."

"Fragile?" I scoffed. "I think he might be the strongest person I've ever met."

"He is, in so many ways. But emotionally, he's...well, he's never let himself care about anyone. He's never risked himself that way."

"He has you," I argued.

Her face softened. "I love that boy so much, but that's a different kind of love. There's a difference between the kind of love you have for a best friend and romantic love. It's a much bigger risk...one he's never taken."

"I do know that. He's shared a little about how his parents treated him, and I have a feeling there's a lot more to the story, but I promise, I want nothing more than to show him how amazing a relationship *can* be. And that he's worthy of it." I took a deep breath and put it all out there. "I'm half in love with him already, and we're only getting started. I have just as much to lose."

"Maybe. But if it all falls apart, you still have people in your life to help you pick up the pieces. He just has me."

"Jesus." I scrubbed my hand over my face. "No pressure."

She reached across and placed her hand over mine,

offering me a smile. "Don't get me wrong. I'm pulling for you. I want him to see just how beautiful love is, and I think you might be the one to show him. Just...be careful with him."

I placed my hand over hers. "I'm glad he has a friend like you. Now," I said as I picked up my coffee and leaned back in my chair, "got any embarrassing stories about him?"

I WALKED into my house around three o'clock on Friday to the scent of sugar in the air and the sound of Michael Bublé singing "Holly Jolly Christmas" coming through the Bluetooth speakers we had installed throughout the house a few years back. I stripped off my coat and scarf, hanging them on the hook in the mudroom, before stepping into the doorway to the brightly lit kitchen. I paused, leaning against the doorframe, and took it all in.

Mixing bowls were piled in the sink, several types of cookies were lined up on a cooling rack, and there was a bag of flour sitting open on the counter, along with a half-used carton of eggs.

And at the end of the island, farthest away from me, were my mom and Finn. She was sitting on a stool, scooping dough and rolling it into balls before dropping each one into a bowl. Finn swirled each ball around the bowl and then dropped them on a parchment-lined cookie sheet next to him. My eyes stung at seeing them working together, smiling and laughing.

As I watched, Finn placed the last ball on the cookie sheet while my mom set aside the cookie scoop and stuck her pointer finger in the bowl, scraping off some cookie dough from the side and popping it in her mouth. My grin spread impossibly wide as my mom's eyes closed in pure bliss as she sucked the raw dough off her finger.

"Isn't it unsafe to eat raw cookie dough?" Finn asked her.

"Worth it," she said as she stuck her finger back in the bowl, her eyes twinkling.

"Looks like you two have been busy!" I said as I stepped forward into the kitchen. Both of them turned to look at me, twin smiles lighting up their faces. I didn't think I'd ever seen Finn smile so wide, and the sight made something flutter in my chest. I leaned in and kissed Mom on her cheek before placing another on Finn's lips. I kept it chaste out of respect for my mom, but even that small contact set my blood humming in my veins.

A timer sounded, and Finn moved past me to pull one pan out before placing another in the oven and setting the timer again. I stepped over to the sink, pushing up the sleeves of my hoodie as I started the sink to do a round of dishes.

"You don't have to do that," Finn said. "I can clean it all up."

"That's not how it works in this house. When one person cooks, it's up to the other to clean it up." I looked over at Mom, giving her a wink. "Mom would kick my ass if I didn't help."

"Damn right," she said, stealing a treat off the nearest cooling rack. Since I had taken over at the sink, Finn slid around to the other side of the island, sitting beside Mom and grabbing a sugar cookie.

"Did you get a chance to talk to Ashley after her performance?" Mom asked. "The choir sounded great!"

"Yeah, she said to tell you she'd be over later tonight to hang out."

"Pfft. What high school girl wants to hang out with their aunt at home on a Friday night?" I inwardly cringed, knowing how much she hated feeling like she was being babysat, but the fact was, Ashley had offered. She really was a great kid, and she loved her aunt.

"She offered, Mom. Said she's going to bring over popcorn and hot chocolate and wants to watch Hallmark Christmas movies in her PJs."

Finn came up next to me and began drying the dishes I'd already washed. "What time is your gig tonight?" I asked him.

"Not until eight. Why?"

"I thought we might go out to dinner beforehand to celebrate."

"Celebrate? What are we celebrating?" He looked so adorable, his eyebrows drawn up in confusion.

"I got my placement today. I'm student teaching at Swope," I said with a huge grin.

"Oh, Jamie! That's great news!" Mom said, clasping her hands together in excitement.

"Yep. I'll be teaching seventh-grade language arts with Mr. Davis."

"Oh, he's so great. The kids love him!"

The timer went off, and Finn swapped out another sheet of cookies, setting the timer again before turning back toward me. "Congratulations," he said softly before placing a quick kiss on my cheek.

He started to turn away from me, but I pulled him back, placing his arms around my waist before putting my own around him. "So, what do you say? Celebrate with me?"

"Um, yeah." He looked down at his hoodie. "Can we run by my apartment so I can change?"

"Of course. I'd love to see your space."

"Okay then. Let's do it!"

WE DROVE through the streets of Midtown, Jamie's black Honda following my Jeep to my place so I could change my clothes. It had dawned on me that this would be our first official date, and I had never really been on one. I'd taken Carmen to events over the years, and I'd participated in the occasional hookup, but I'd never been on an actual date.

I was nervous as fuck.

We pulled into the parking lot of the complex, and I waited for Jamie to join me so we could walk up to my apartment together.

I unlocked the door, proud when my hand only shook a little, and walked into the empty apartment, flipping on the switch as we entered. Carmen was gone for the weekend. With her finals complete, she'd flown to Denver to see Isa perform with her ballet company in the Nutcracker, so we had the place to ourselves.

"So, um, can I get you something to drink?" I asked, fidgeting with the strings on my hoodie. I was suddenly very aware of how small my apartment was and how that must look to him.

Jamie didn't answer my question, instead crossing over to me and pulling me into his arms. He wasn't much taller than me, so my head rested perfectly on his shoulder, and I breathed in the scent of him. He smelled like the forest after it rains, and it calmed my racing heart.

"Don't be nervous, baby. It's just dinner," he said, stroking his hand down my back.

"I'm not nervous," I lied.

He chuckled, pulling away and pressing a kiss to my forehead. "Show me around your place."

"There's not much to see. We're obviously standing in the living room. The kitchen's right there." I pointed to the tiny kitchen adjacent to the living space. "And back there is my bedroom."

He waggled his eyebrows, saying, "My favorite room."

I rolled my eyes but felt more of the tension melt, just as I was sure he'd intended.

"Come on," I gestured for him to follow me back to the bedroom, glad I'd spent some time folding and putting away laundry yesterday. We entered the space, and I moved to the closet to pull out my black slacks and button-down, my standard gig attire.

I turned to find Jamie sitting in the chair next to the bed, watching me.

"I'll just be a second," I said, crossing to the bathroom.

"Where are you going?" he asked, eyebrows raised, mouth curved in a sarcastic little smirk.

"I'm just going to change in here," I said, hooking my thumb over my shoulder and gesturing to the bathroom behind me.

"Shy, Finn?"

"Um, no...maybe." I let out a frustrated sigh. "Cut me

some slack, Jamie. I've never dated before. I don't know how to…do…this."

He stood and crossed over to me, his features softening as he placed his hands on either side of my hips. "I'm sorry. I was just flipping you shit. The only wrong way to do this is to do something you're uncomfortable with." He kissed my forehead and stepped away. "Why don't I just go back out and wait in the living room?"

"No," I said, reaching for his arm. "Stay."

I made my way back to the bed, setting my things down as I pulled my hoodie over my head, exchanging it for the button-down. "So tell me about this student-teaching gig. What's the deal with Swope?"

His eyes watched my hands as I worked my way down the buttons, and he swallowed, his eyes darting back up to mine before responding. "Swope Middle School is the school I attended, as well as where my mom taught. I could student teach anywhere, really, but Swope feels like home, you know?" I reached for my pants, turning my back to him as I dropped my sweats and pulled my slacks up. "I'm hoping student teaching there will lead to a permanent position in the fall," he continued. "A couple of teachers in the English department are retiring, so there will be some openings."

Facing him again, I buttoned my slacks and then reached for my belt, threading it through the loops at my waist. "That's cool," I said. "I figured you went to private school."

"Nah. My mom is a big believer in the public school system, so that's where I went. Swope Middle and then Ward High." I sat on the edge of the bed closest to him to put on my socks and shoes. "Where'd you go to school?" he asked.

"KC Prep Academy. I think we played you guys in basketball."

"Yeah, most sports, actually. I competed against you guys in swim and track."

I ducked my head. "I used to run cross country, mostly to appease my parents, but other than that, I'm not really a sports sort of guy."

He leaned forward, placing his fingers under my chin, forcing me to look up at him. "You know I don't care about that shit, right?"

"It just feels like we have nothing in common. We both grew up rich, but our experiences in that world couldn't have been more different. I don't do sports, and you don't do music. You're a semester away from graduating from college, and I'm a barista and a freelance musician. How's this supposed to work, Jamie?"

"Listen. We don't have to share all the same interests to be compatible. You also enjoy writing, and I'm going to be an English teacher. I may not know anything about music, but that doesn't mean I don't enjoy listening to you play. And the only one who has a problem with the barista thing is you. I don't care how you make your living." He scooted closer as he spoke, one of his knees sliding between mine. "Besides," he said, sliding his hand to the nape of my neck, "we have this..."

He pressed his lips to mine, tracing the seam of my mouth with his tongue, urging me to open for him. I met his tongue with mine, his flavor seeping into my soul as we fused our mouths together. Heat pooled pleasantly in my core as our tongues tangled and twisted, exploring each other.

He nipped at my bottom lip once, twice, and a third

time, pulling it into his mouth before releasing me and plunging back in again.

Want and need raced through me, urgency fueling the fire in my blood as I pulled him down on top of me. Lying on the bed, my feet still planted on the floor, he straddled my hips, his hard cock rubbing against mine through our clothes, sending jolts of pleasure radiating through my body.

I may not have known how to do relationships, but this...this I could do.

Abruptly, he tore his lips from mine, and I whimpered, chasing his retreating mouth, not ready to give up the taste of him.

"Shh, baby. I've got you," he said as he pushed my knees apart to kneel on the floor between them. He reached for my belt buckle, the one I'd just put on moments ago, and made quick work of undoing it and my fly before yanking my pants and briefs down to my ankles in one fell swoop.

I leaned up on my elbows, contemplating how quickly we'd gone from talking about where we'd attended school to Jamie kneeling on the floor before me, nose buried in my groin, and then I stopped contemplating anything at all when he took me in his mouth, all the way to the back of his throat in one swift motion.

"Fuck," I grunted as he pulled back and then slammed down once again. He swirled his tongue around my crown, licking at the underside, swiping precum from my slit.

"You taste so good. So fucking good," he said, his voice raw with lust, before drawing me all the way back in again. I buried my hands in his hair, just as I'd fantasized about, pulling the silky strands free of their bond and yanking him impossibly farther onto me. He moaned as I tugged at his hair, bringing his hand up to massage my balls as he hollowed out his cheeks, sucking me harder than I'd thought possible.

My hips bucked wildly as he moved faster, his head bobbing up and down relentlessly, the friction almost unbearable. Just when I thought I couldn't take anymore, I felt my balls draw up and the telltale tingle in my spine, indicating my imminent climax.

"Jamie! Jamie, I'm going to come," I said as I tried to pull him off me, but he doubled down his efforts, and with a couple of wicked strokes of his tongue, I was coming in pulse after pulse down his throat. Moments later, as I began to come down off my high, I felt his arm against my leg, moving in rhythm, and I realized he must be getting himself off. I'd been so lost in the best blowjob of my life that I hadn't even noticed he'd undone his pants.

Hastily, I pulled my shirt up to my shoulders and yanked him up just as he found his own release, thick ropes of cum landing hot on my belly. He was stunning, standing above me, his long hair loose around his face, lost in the ecstasy of his orgasm, marking me with his load. I vowed that next time, I would be the one getting him off. I wanted to be the one responsible for that look on his face.

His knees nearly gave out as his dick shot one more time before he collapsed on the bed beside me.

We lay there, breathing heavily, side by side. Jamie turned his head toward me, and I mirrored his position.

"That was fucking amazing," I said, still trying to gain control over my breathing.

"*You're* amazing."

He got up, walking awkwardly to the bathroom, holding on to his pants with his clean hand, trying to keep them from falling down. I chuckled at the ridiculousness of it, amused at how he could give me the blowjob of a lifetime yet move so awkwardly in the clean-up phase. I had to admit, it was nice to see Mr. Perfect might not be so perfect after all.

I heard the water running before he returned, his pants pulled back up to rights, a washcloth in his hands. He cleaned me tenderly, making sure to remove all evidence of his release before helping me put my clothes back on.

I grasped the hand he held out to me, and he pulled me to standing. He retrieved his hair tie, efficiently pulling his hair back into its messy bun. He was sexy as fuck, but I couldn't wait to pull that hair down and mess him up again.

He turned back toward me, his eyes locked on mine, wide and open. "Do you like me, Finn? Do you like spending time with me?"

Confused by the abrupt question, I answered simply. "Yes."

"Did you like what we just did? Do you want to keep doing it?"

"Well, yeah...don't you?"

"Of course I do." He pulled me in for a kiss. I wasn't sure how he could simultaneously make it hot and tender, but that's exactly what he did. "Then let that be enough. Stop overthinking this. Stop worrying about compatibility. Just...enjoy it."

Finally, it dawned on me that he was referring to the conversation we'd been having before he'd kissed me. And he was right. If I was going to be all in, I had to stop questioning everything. I had to stop questioning him.

"All right. I will."

"Yeah?" He smiled wide, his eyes alight with happiness.

"Yeah."

I'D EXPECTED we'd go to a nice steakhouse, so Jamie surprised me when he took me to a little out-of-the-way Mexican restaurant on Southwest Boulevard. He told me the only true way to celebrate anything was with tacos and margaritas. Knowing I still had to play a gig, I limited myself to one Modelo but thoroughly enjoyed watching Jamie get a little sloppy after a couple of margaritas.

He approached food the same way he approached everything, with exuberant delight. And in between bites of tacos, rice, and beans, and sips of his margarita, he regaled me with tales of his childhood. How he broke his arm when he was twelve in a sledding accident, of summers spent learning to ski at their lake house in the Ozarks, and winning the 100m freestyle race at State his senior year. He teared up when he told me about his childhood dog, George, a hound rescue who'd died when he was sixteen, and laughed until he cried when he told me about the time he locked himself out of his car while it was running and how when he called Asher to come to the rescue, Asher had run out of gas on his way to help. They'd both had to call his mom, who'd laughed her ass off before arriving with a spare key for Jamie and a gas can for Asher.

He'd had an all-American childhood, while mine had been...something else. Something less. He'd lived his life in color while mine had been endured in shades of gray. I told him how I'd fallen in love with the piano and played in the school jazz band. I shared about the poetry competition I'd quietly entered my freshman year and how I'd placed third, but I hadn't told anyone. I told him about my parent's absence in my life and how I'd always done my best to go unnoticed because that was easier than making waves. I'd long ago stopped yearning for their love and had simply wished for them to leave me alone. I told him about how I'd met Carmen that fateful day in an abandoned classroom and how she forced me to attend prom with her and still drug me to charity events with her when she didn't have a date.

I hadn't wanted to bring the mood down, but I'd wanted—needed—to be honest with him. I hadn't felt like we could move forward if Jamie didn't understand where I'd come from. I didn't want to spend the rest of my life drowning in regret over the way I'd handled my upbringing, but I didn't think I could move forward without confronting the reality of it either.

Through all of it, Jamie listened as if the meaning of life was held somewhere within the story of my childhood. He listened without pity and without offering any sort of platitudes. He just...listened. And when we were finished and it was time to go, he pulled me to him in a hug, offering comfort without words.

We'd originally planned to take two cars to dinner so Jamie could head home while I headed to Ivory, but I was glad we'd ultimately decided to take one since Jamie was not in any condition to drive. Ashley had texted that she was spending the night at the Felton's, so Jamie was free to spend the rest of his evening with me.

Throughout my gig, Jamie sat at the bar, sipping water while I played, listening attentively. He didn't fiddle with his phone or make small talk with his bar mates. His attention was on me as if he and I were the only ones in the room.

We were quiet on the way home, lost in our own thoughts. The day had been one I was sure I wouldn't soon forget. Making cookies with Annie and spending time with Jamie all filled me with a warmth I wanted to wrap myself in like a blanket.

We made our way up to my apartment just after one in the morning and prepared for bed. I was less shy about stripping in front of him this time, climbing under the covers in just my briefs. He climbed in behind me, pulling me close, my back to his chest, just like we'd slept on Monday, only this time with a lot less clothing. His heat permeated my skin, and my dick gave a halfhearted twitch, but I wasn't sure I had the energy to do anything about it. I'd been up at five for my shift at the The Daily Grind and had been going nearly nonstop since. Paired with the emotional energy I'd expended today, I was a virtual zombie.

"Thank you," I mumbled.

"For what?" Jamie asked, the whisper of his breath tickling my neck.

"For today. For everything. For just...being you." My words were a jumbled mess in my punch-drunk state. I hoped he could understand them.

He pressed a kiss to the spot right behind my ear, and I thought he whispered, "You're worth it. You're worth everything." But I might have heard that in my dreams.

WHEN I WAS TEN, my father passed away. He had a massive stroke and collapsed in his office at work. He had been relatively young and healthy, so it came as a shock to us all. I missed school for two weeks. Our house seemed to be constantly full of people. Aunt Cathy and her family were there nearly every day, though Ashley and Cody were just two and four, so it was a little harder for her to help out since she was constantly chasing my cousins. My paternal grandparents, who were still living at the time, came to stay with us for a month.

And it seemed no matter where I turned, no matter which room I walked into, someone was crying. My mom carried a box of tissues with her everywhere she went. I didn't know how someone could cry so many tears, but I knew my mom and dad had loved each other very much, so I supposed she was bound to cry a lot.

I, on the other hand, couldn't cry. I thought perhaps something was broken inside of me. I was old enough to understand that death was permanent, that my dad wouldn't be coming back. And I felt sad about it...really,

really sad. But I still couldn't cry. I wanted to ask Asher about it, but his bio dad had hit him when he was really little, so I thought he would probably feel differently about it.

The funeral came and went. Our house was full of crying people and more food than we could ever eat. The number of visitors waned, I went back to school, and eventually, my grandparents went back to their home in Arizona.

It was on the first Saturday after everyone had left, that the dam finally burst.

Like a moth to a flame, the scent of coffee and bacon drew me into the kitchen. But when I climbed on the stool to see what my dad was cooking for breakfast, I realized it wasn't my dad cooking. It wouldn't be my dad ever again.

Mom made most of the meals in our home, but breakfast had always been Dad's domain. He said Mom deserved to sleep in and have someone else cook her a meal for a change, so nearly every Saturday, and sometimes on Sunday, he made breakfast. Omelets. Pancakes. Waffles. Biscuits and gravy. If it was a breakfast food, he made it.

Sometimes he let me help, and those were my favorite times. It didn't matter if I made a mess of the batter or accidentally flipped a pancake onto the stove. Dad always patiently helped me clean it up or showed me the right way to do it the next time. And when it was all finished, we'd arrange everything on a tray and take it to Mom. He always let me take the credit, even though he'd done most of the work.

But on this Saturday, it was my mom doing the cooking. And I didn't know why, but it made me angry. This was our thing, mine and my dad's. It wasn't hers. She didn't know that the secret ingredient in the pancakes was the extra splash of vanilla or that the key to a good sausage gravy was heavy whipping cream rather than that low-fat stuff.

I watched while she stirred the batter, immediately noticing it was too thick.

"You're doing it wrong!" I shouted at her. "It's all wrong!"

She turned and looked at me, eyes wide with concern. I wasn't prone to outbursts. This was completely unlike me. I felt unhinged and out of control, but I didn't know how to stop it.

She set the batter aside and turned the burner down on the bacon before approaching me, her hands held out in front of her as if approaching a wild animal. "Honey, it's okay. Everything's okay."

"No, it's not!" I shouted again. "The batter's all wrong! You're messing it all up!"

I jumped off the stool and tore up the stairs to my bedroom, where I slammed the door, throwing myself on my bed, hot tears streaming down my face. I cried and cried, big, ugly, hiccuping sobs. Two weeks of tears had been bottled up inside me, and it seemed I was going to let them all out at once.

I didn't hear the door open, but I felt my mom's hand on my back. I tried to shrug it off, but she wouldn't be deterred. She just kept rubbing soothing circles as the tears continued to fall.

"I wasn't trying to take your dad's place," she finally said.

"I know," I mumbled with a sniffle.

Guilt washed over me. I'd never yelled at my mom before. Dad would be so disappointed in me. A few more tears fell at the thought.

"I'm sorry I yelled," I said at last.

"Oh, sweet boy. It's okay." She smoothed some of the hair off my forehead.

"It's not. I shouldn't have talked to you like that. I don't know why I did."

"Grief is a funny thing. It makes you say things and do things you might not normally do."

I turned to look at her. "I hate it. I hate feeling this way. It feels like I'm going to be sad and angry forever."

"I know, honey. I feel that way too. And I think we'll probably feel that way for a long time. But hopefully, as the days pass, that weight will get lighter, and we'll be able to carry it easier."

"I miss him, Mom." I squeezed my eyes shut against the new round of tears threatening to fall.

"I know, baby. I miss him too."

She held me for a long time after that, as both of our tears fell.

I WAS neither a morning person nor a night owl, falling somewhere in between. Still, when I awoke Saturday morning, the time on my phone read ten-fourteen. The warmth of Finn's body next to mine made me smile. Unused to sleeping with someone else next to me, I'd awoken several times throughout the night, and each time, some part of him had been touching some part of me. Almost as if he was afraid to break the connection.

This morning, he looked so peaceful, his usually serious face relaxed in sleep, a curl hanging loose over his forehead. I wanted to brush away that curl and kiss his forehead, but I also knew he needed to rest, and I didn't want to wake him. Finn was one of the hardest-working people I'd ever met, and at the rate he was going, he was going to wind up ill.

I lay there for a while, just watching him, but eventually, my bladder forced me out of bed. Having taken care of that business, I pulled on my jeans and made my way into the kitchen, taking my phone with me so I could text Ashley.

> Good Morning! How's Mom doing?

When she didn't respond right away, I put the phone back in my pocket and started opening cabinets, looking for the coffee. After starting the pot to brew, I opened the fridge, scanning the contents to see if I could whip up some breakfast. It would be nice to be able to spoil my guy.

Expecting the nearly empty fridge of a typical bachelor, I was pleasantly surprised to find it fairly well-stocked. Pulling out bacon, eggs, some veggies, and cheese, I located the tools I'd need to whip up an omelet.

I paused for a moment when I felt my phone vibrate in my pocket.

ASHLEY

She's doing great, actually! I think yesterday's baking adventures with Finn wore her out, so she headed to bed early, but she woke up this morning with more energy than I've seen in a while

> That's great! What do you have going on today? What time do you need me home?

ASHLEY

Actually…my mom is coming over in a little bit, and we're all going to do a little Christmas shopping

I frowned at that. Mom really shouldn't be out shopping in big crowds. Before I could respond, another text came through.

ASHLEY

Don't worry. We're just going to go a couple of places, and she's going to wear her mask

> She said it didn't feel like Christmas if she didn't go into an actual store. We couldn't refuse her

> Please don't be mad

I sighed. I supposed I couldn't keep her in a bubble forever, even though that's exactly what I wanted to do.

> I'm not mad. Just don't let her overdo it and make her use hand sanitizer.

ASHLEY

> Of course! We should be back by 3 if you want to head home around then.

> Sounds good! Have fun!

Bacon was popping and sizzling on the stove when I felt arms envelop me from behind. Finn placed light kisses on my back, starting at one shoulder blade and moving across to the other. A shiver of delight rippled through me at the feel of his lips pressed against my skin. I didn't think I'd ever get tired of the way it felt when he initiated contact. It was so often me pursuing him that I treasured the moments when he came to me.

"Mmmmm," I said as I turned around, wrapping him in my arms. He hadn't bothered with a shirt, and the feel of him in my arms, pressed skin to skin, had my cock filling and desire humming through my veins.

We stood there like that for a moment, just savoring the feel of each other, before I had to release him to pull the bacon off the pan. I removed it to a paper towel-lined plate, turned the burner off, and pulled him back into me.

"Mmm. You feel good," I said, inhaling his scent. He placed a trail of kisses on my neck, starting at the curve of my shoulder and moving up to that spot just below my ear. Another shiver ran through me, and goosebumps broke out on my flesh even though the body pressed to mine was still warm from sleep.

"That feels good too," I murmured as he nibbled my earlobe. My dick was impossibly hard now. I was sure he could feel it against his leg. I *hoped* he could feel it, feel what he was doing to me.

I ran my hands along his back, loving the feel of the lean muscle tapering down to a narrow waist. I continued my path down, down, down, slipping beneath the waistband of his sweats, discovering he hadn't bothered with underwear. My hands followed the perfect curve of his ass, and I grabbed a handful and pulled him into me. I groaned at the feel of his erection against my thigh, glad I was having as much effect on him as he was on me.

His lips trailed from my ear across my lightly stubbled jaw, nipping and licking as he went until he arrived at my mouth. There, he paused, pulling away just enough to look me in the eyes for the first time this morning. His pupils were blown wide, the look of pure lust on his face sending a jolt straight to my cock.

"I want you," he said, his voice gravelly with need.

"Thank God," I returned before bringing my lips to his, claiming him in a kiss so hot that I feared we'd set the whole place ablaze.

Without breaking the kiss, I walked him back, bouncing off the counter as I tried to angle him toward the hallway. Impatient, he yanked me around, reversing our positions so he was the one pushing me. When we got to his bed, he shoved me on it, following me down to straddle me.

"If you're going to leave me with bruises, I'd rather they

come from your mouth, not from running into every wall in my apartment."

"That can be arranged," I said before sitting up and pulling one nipple into my mouth and sucking. Hard.

He let out a hiss, throwing his head back, his hips rocking against mine in response. I let out a hiss of my own as our cocks brushed against each other.

I ripped my mouth away from him, suddenly desperate to eliminate the barriers between us. "I want to feel you," I said as he rocked against me.

Without hesitation, Finn scrambled off my lap and yanked his pants down, kicking them off to the side. He was beautiful, standing naked before me, his body long and lean, his dick jutting proudly from a nestle of dark curls.

I wanted to touch him.

I wanted to lick him.

I wanted to ride him.

"You okay there?" he asked, jolting my gaze from his dick back up to the smirk resting on his lips.

I wasn't a bit embarrassed at getting caught looking. Finn was a goddammed work of art. "I'm more than okay. C'mere," I beckoned.

"Aren't you forgetting something?" he asked, nodding at my lower half.

"Shit. I guess I was a little distracted." I grinned as I shifted to take my pants off, but he put a hand out to stop me.

"Let me," he said, all traces of humor gone now as he lowered to his knees in front of me.

What a sight he made, kneeling naked before me. He licked his lips as he reached forward, gripping my waistband and tugging down. I lifted my hips as he inched my pants and boxers down my legs, finally pulling one foot out and then the other.

I leaned back on my elbows, watching his face as he blatantly eye-fucked me.

"Are *you* okay?" I asked, teasing him as our roles had become reversed.

Eyes snapping to mine, he smiled and said, "I'm fucking fantastic."

Now that we were both undressed, I repeated my command. "C'mere."

Finn climbed back onto my lap, our dicks leaking all over each other as they made contact for the first time without any barriers between us.

"Fuuuuck," I ground out as he rocked against me, rolling his hips leisurely, ensuring every millimeter of my erection rubbed against every bit of his. I looked down, thrilling at the sight of our dicks rubbing against each other. It was hot as fuck. "Look at you. You're so fucking perfect."

His forehead rested against mine, his breath coming out in little pants, as we both stared at the sight of our cocks rubbing against each other. Reaching between us, Finn ran his thumb through the bead of precum gathering on the head of my dick and smeared it down my length as he took both of us in his hand and gave a leisurely stroke from base to tip.

We both groaned in pleasure as his hand worked us in long, steady strokes. The feel of his cock sliding against mine, both of us wrapped in his fist, was heaven, but I needed more. Impatient, I reached up with one hand, pulled his face down to mine, and took his mouth in a brutal kiss. I wrapped my leg around his waist and flipped us so I was on top. I pressed myself into him, wanting as much skin-to-skin contact as possible.

We rutted against each other, our hips moving faster and faster in rhythm as we both frantically sought release. I ran my lips down his neck, licking and sucking my way to his collarbone. Finn knotted his fingers in my hair, holding me to him as I sucked a bruise into his shoulder, marking him.

"Fuck, Jamie. I'm so damn close," he said, his voice breathless as he drove his hips up into mine, meeting me thrust for thrust.

"Me too. So good."

Letting go of my hair, his hands moved down to my ass, where he grabbed both cheeks, pulling me into him and holding me there as he arched his head back and let go with a shout. The sound he made was something primal and triggered my own release as our cocks pulsed against each other, our cum mingling between us, coating our bellies in a hot, sticky mess.

Panting and unsteady, I rolled over to lie beside him before my arms gave out.

"Next time, I want to be inside you when you come. I want to watch your face as I take you apart, piece by piece," he said, his voice raspy.

I turned to look at him, my eyes wide. *Fuck*. I hadn't given a lot of thought as to whether I wanted to top or bottom our first time, but suddenly, I found myself really damn happy to bottom. Still, I couldn't resist flipping him some shit.

"Oh yeah? How do you know I won't be the one taking you?"

"Because your dick twitched just now when I mentioned it, even though we both came not more than a minute ago. You liked that idea. You liked it a lot."

My lips curled up slowly, smiling wide like the

Cheshire cat. "Yeah. I really did."

He smiled back at me, just as wide.

———

WE CLEANED UP, and I finished cooking breakfast. We ate at the coffee table, sitting on the floor of his living room, our backs propped up against the couch, bare shoulders touching.

"This is a damn good omelet. Can you cook other things as well, or do you specialize in breakfast?"

"I can cook a few other things, but mostly just breakfast." I took another bite of eggs before continuing, "My dad and I used to cook together on the weekends before he died. It's one of my favorite memories of him."

"Oh, I'm sorry. I didn't mean to bring up something painful."

"No, it's okay. I don't mind talking about him. Makes it feel like he's still here, you know?"

He was quiet for a moment before asking, "How old were you when he passed?"

"Ten. He had a massive stroke while he was at work. No one saw it coming."

"Jesus, Jamie. That must have been..."

"Awful," I finished for him. I munched on a piece of bacon, contemplating how best to describe my feelings for the man who had shaped me, who still had an impact on the man I was today. "Dad was...he was my idol. He didn't have this big, larger-than-life personality—I get my extroverted side from Mom—but everyone loved him. There was a kindness about him...a warmth. When you spoke with him, you always got the sense that he really listened and was genuinely interested in what you had to say. Even as a kid, I felt that way. Most adults sort of listen to kids with half an ear and have a tendency to downplay their thoughts and feelings, but Dad always made me feel like what I had to say was real and valid and important. He did that with everyone."

I swallowed past the lump in my throat. He'd been gone from my life longer than he'd been in it, yet it still sometimes felt like it had only been moments since I'd last heard his voice or felt his embrace.

I set my now-empty plate down on the table and turned to look at Finn, wanting him to understand. "I'm never going to have that quiet, calm nature that he had, I'm just not wired that way, but I try to remember that feeling when you really feel like someone hears what you're saying, that they truly see you, and I try to do that with others as well."

Setting his plate down next to mine, Finn reached up to tuck a stray strand of hair behind my ear, his hand lingering on the side of my face as he said, "You do that with me, Jamie. No one has ever seen me the way you do. No one has ever even tried except maybe Carmen." The intensity in his eyes as he looked into mine had my heart beating faster. "Do you know how special that is? My parents never heard a damn thing I had to say, but in a matter of weeks, you've managed to unlock pieces of me even *I* didn't know existed."

I reached up and clasped his hand that was still resting on the side of my face. "Your parents were selfish assholes who should've never been allowed to have children. You deserved so much more than to be paraded about when it suited them and ignored when it didn't. But it's their loss, Finn. Their huge, gigantic loss because the person I see has so much more to offer than they'll ever know. He has depth and humor and kindness. He has an achingly beautiful soul.

He has..." I had been dangerously close to finishing that sentence with 'my heart,' but I hesitated, unsure how that would be received.

"What? He has...what?"

"You have my heart, Finn." I held my breath, unsure how he would respond. Not quite an outright declaration of love—it was still pretty damn heavy a sentiment so early in this relationship—but I'd never been one to hold back. I didn't think I had it in me to do so. And loving Finn, if that's what this was, wasn't something I could stop. My heart was barreling over the cliff at a breakneck pace, and I was helpless to stop it, nor did I want to. Still, I knew he was out of his depth with all this, and I prayed I hadn't scared him away with my statement.

"Damn, Jamie. What are you doing to me?" He pressed his lips to mine, and I sighed into him, releasing the breath I'd been holding, thankful he wasn't running away. I moved my hand to cup the back of his neck, holding him to me as our tongues twined in sensual exploration. This kiss wasn't a horny prelude to sex. This was tenderness and vulnerability, and passion. It was *thank you* and *I'm falling for you* and *I'm still here* and *I think I might love you*. It was a million little things and just one big thing all at once.

At length, Finn pulled back, those beautiful eyes focused intently on mine. "I wish I'd met him. Your dad, I mean," he said.

"Me too." I squeezed the back of his neck where my hand still rested. "He would have liked you."

He shrugged that off like he didn't really believe it. "I'd thank him. I'd thank him for teaching you to be the kind of man who'd take a chance on a person like me. Who saw me even when I did my best to be invisible to everyone."

"I'd thank him for that too."

I STARED up at the sprawling mansion in front of me as a wave of nausea rolled through me. The massive Tudor-style home sat back from the road atop a small hill, allowing it to exert its understated yet clear dominance over the other mansions that dared to line the street in its presence. Located in Mission Hills, the third most affluent municipality in the country and just on the other side of the state line from Kansas City, Missouri, houses in this Kansas neighborhood regularly sold in the millions, and the house I was staring at likely had sold at the top end.

Built in the 1930s, this house had been home to a railroad magnate, professional baseball player, aspiring presidential candidate, and currently, a partner in the highest-rated law firm in the Midwest with offices in Kansas City, Chicago, and Dallas.

The other partner of the aforementioned law firm was my father.

I banged my head on the steering wheel twice before pulling out my phone. My thumb hovered over my contacts list as I realized that the one person I'd always reached out to, my ride or die, was not the person I was reaching for today. I pressed the button and waited.

The sound of Jamie's rich baritone filling up the space inside my car as he answered with a "Hello," rolled through me like a warm summer breeze. I closed my eyes, breathing in and out as I tried to settle my frantic thoughts. "Baby? What's wrong?" he asked, and I realized I hadn't responded to his initial greeting.

"I'm, uh, I guess I'm having a bit of a freak-out."

"Why? What happened? Aren't you at your gig?" His voice was laced with concern. In my mind, I could see the worry etched into the lines on his forehead.

Exhaling, I did my best to explain. "Yeah, I'm at the gig. I'm sitting outside the house."

"Okay..." he prompted, clearly waiting for me to clarify the problem.

"The house...it's the home of my father's partner. In his law firm. I'm ninety-nine percent sure my parents will be in there." Another wave of nausea rolled through me at the thought of seeing them again. It had been three and a half years since the day Dad had given me the ultimatum and I decided I wasn't going back in the closet. In all that time, they hadn't reached out, and I hadn't looked back. I thought I'd had zero fucks to give where they were concerned, but apparently, my body's reaction to the very real possibility of seeing them again signaled that maybe there was at least one fuck rattling around in there somewhere. Or maybe Jamie had melted my ice-cold heart, and now I was feeling things I'd thought I'd long buried. Either way, it felt like my insides were trying to rearrange themselves.

"It was an executive assistant who booked me for the gig, and the host's name is Richardson. I didn't know it was *that* Richardson. They offered me twice as much as I usually take for this sort of thing since it's Christmas Eve, so I didn't ask a lot of questions. But I should have known. My parents have been coming to this party on Christmas Eve for years. It's tradition. How did I not put it all together?" My hands were shaking and my voice had pitched up as I word-vomited in a panic.

"Breathe, baby. Are you sure it's the same Richardson as your dad's partner?"

"Oh yeah. I may not have initially recognized the address, but I was forced to come to enough events here over the years. There's no doubt it's his place."

"Damn. Okay. So what are your options?"

"Options?" I asked. I didn't have any options. I was trapped in my own personal hell with no way out.

"Yeah, options. Can you bail? Call and tell them you got sick?"

God, that was tempting. And at the rate I was going, not far from the truth. I felt like I was going to vomit any minute now. But I was a professional, and I might not have a lot going for me in my life, but I had integrity. I wouldn't bail on a gig, even if it meant facing my parents. "No, I can't do that. I don't need word getting around that I'm not professional. And shit, the money on this gig is ridiculous."

"Okay. So you're going in there then... Want me to come with you?"

"What?" I was stunned. The thought of having him there, just so I wouldn't be alone, nearly broke me, but that was crazy. "I can't just waltz in there with my boyfriend when I'm playing a private party."

"First of all, I like the sound of 'boyfriend.' We're circling back to that later. And second, I went to my fair share of these things growing up when my father was still alive. I know how to rub elbows with the rich, and I know how to blend into the background. No one will even notice me."

That was absolutely not true. There was never a room Jamie inhabited in which he wasn't noticed. If not for his gorgeous smile that lit up a room or his stacked body that made women and men alike take notice, he simply had a personality that naturally drew people to him. Still, his offer was amazing. I knew he had plans with his family tonight to drive around looking at Christmas lights while sipping hot chocolate in their PJs. They'd done it since he was a kid, and even though he was grown now, they'd continued the tradition because it made his mom and Aunt Cathy happy. He'd invited me to come with them, but I'd had this gig, and now he was offering to drop everything just to be there for me. My eyes burned and the Christmas lights on the massive home in front of me blurred as my vision clouded with unshed tears.

"I can't ask you to do that, Jamie. You should be with your family. This is one of the few holiday traditions your mom is still able to do this year. She deserves to have that with you."

"You're my family too, you know. Mom will understand."

God, he always knew the right things to say. Family. I'd never let myself wish for one, but this man had me yearning for it. "You're amazing, you know that?" I took a shaky breath. "You go with your mom. I'll be okay."

"Are you sure?" I could hear the worry there, so I infused my voice with as much false bravado as possible. "Yeah. I'll be okay. Just hearing your voice has helped." I glanced at the clock. "Um, I should probably go though. I'm supposed to be set up and ready to play in ten minutes."

"All right. Call me when you're done?"

"It'll be late..."

"That's all right. I'll be up."

"Yeah, okay. Thank you."

"No need to thank me, baby. That's what *boyfriends* do."

With that, he finally pried a smile out of me. "Not letting that go, are you?"

"Damn right, I'm not." I could hear the smile in his voice and maybe a bit of pride too. "Go. You got this, okay?"

"Yeah, okay. Talk to you later."

I hung up the phone, took a deep breath, and pulled into the driveway.

It wasn't lost on me just how much my life had changed in just a few years. Tonight, I'd come in the back through the service entrance rather than through the grand front entrance we'd used in my youth. I had a bottle of water sitting discreetly underneath the piano bench I was sitting on rather than a glass of bourbon in hand, not that I would have been openly drinking alcohol all those years ago, but I might have snuck a shot of vodka into my Sprite. And rather than eating canapés and avoiding conversation with pretty much everyone, I was currently playing light Christmas melodies at the grand piano in the center of a very ornate entryway.

This house, I knew, held not one but two grand pianos, and while I'd hoped they might station me at the one situated out of the way in the corner of the formal living room, they'd decided it would be more festive if I sat at the one in the middle of the grand entrance so the music could both welcome guests as they entered as well as filter throughout the house. The lid was propped on the tallest peg, allowing sound to reverberate around the massive two-story space. Two elaborately decorated, twelve-foot Christmas trees were positioned in the curve of the twin staircases that led to the second floor and what I knew to be the private quarters for the occupants of the house. I once hid in one of the bedrooms when my father's secretary had imbibed too much wine and gotten handsy with me. I'd been sixteen, and I was fairly sure she'd been my father's mistress at some point and had decided she wanted to see if there was any family resemblance between father and son.

I moved from "O, Holy Night" into a lively rendition of "Rockin' Around the Christmas Tree" as my eyes continued their scan of the space's occupants. I'd recognized quite a few guests as employees of my father's firm and had even spotted a couple of my former classmates standing with their parents, sipping cocktails, likely trying to finagle an internship at one of the hottest law firms in town. Connections were everything in this world, and no one was above using anyone they could to get ahead.

A few curious eyes had lingered on me, but they'd either been unable to place how they knew me or, more likely, had decided to ignore my existence altogether. I had no idea what my parents had told people after I'd been cut off, but it was clear that I was now no better than "the help," my existence not worthy of acknowledgment, which was fine with me. I was here for a hefty paycheck. The rest of them could fuck off.

A couple of hours into the party, I was fairly sure most of the guests had arrived, but I'd yet to see my parents, which surprised me. But then again, I had no idea what was going on in their lives. Perhaps my dad had left his firm. Perhaps they'd had a falling out and were no longer welcome. Richardson had always seemed like a decent sort, as much as any high-powered attorney ever had, and maybe he'd caught my father sleeping with his secretary one too many times and they'd parted ways.

As I moved on from one holiday favorite to the next, I imagined all the scenarios in which my father might have fucked up enough to have caused a parting of ways. I didn't even know if they'd separated. My father simply could have been sick or otherwise engaged tonight. There could have been any number of reasons to explain his and my mother's absence, but the idea of him on the outs with his partner, that he'd fucked up enough to have caused some sort of rift between them, was enough to send my imagination into overdrive.

As it happened, I wasn't lucky enough to avoid the people who'd raised me but hadn't cared for me. Deep into the evening, just fifteen minutes before midnight, I'd finally begun to let my guard down. Surely this close to the end of the evening, I was safe. In just a bit, I'd collect my payout, then call Jamie, relieved that my worry had been for nothing, and promise to see him in the morning for Christmas.

A slender brunette with high cheekbones and immovable eyebrows, thanks to Botox, crossed in front of the piano carrying a glass of wine and a judgmental smirk as she conversed with the woman next to her. Her hair was smoothed back into a sleek knot at the nape of her neck. She wore a fitted black gown she'd no doubt had to starve herself to fit into, and I could see the emeralds my father had given her for her fortieth birthday winking at her ears. She glanced my way and did a double take, her eyes going wide with recognition as she caught sight of me in the middle of performing "Baby, It's Cold Outside." Her feet came to a complete stop, and the woman she'd been chatting with turned back to see what had stopped her, having continued walking, oblivious to the distress my mother was so obviously experiencing.

My stomach again began to tie itself in knots, but my face gave away nothing as I continued playing without skipping a beat. I held her gaze, daring her to look away as she quickly schooled her features before turning back to her friend. She murmured something to her before walking away into the other room.

I finished the song and let out a breath, checking the time on my iPad to calculate how quickly I could escape before word got back to my father that I was there. I played two more songs and, at eleven fifty-eight, determined it was close enough. I closed my iPad and picked up my bottle of water, turning on the bench to exit through the kitchen, where I knew my check would be waiting before I slipped through the service entrance.

Three steps from freedom, I was stopped cold in front of the man who'd both given me life and denied my very existence. He wore a dark-gray suit accented with a red tie that would look festive on anyone this time of year. Though, on him, he merely resembled the gatekeeper to hell.

I'd gotten my curls from him, yet he never wore his hair long enough to let those curls show. He wouldn't dare allow his hair to be anything other than perfectly neat, so he kept it trimmed short. The last couple of years had added a bit of salt to his pepper, but it only served to make him appear more dignified.

I knew better.

For all his appearance of class, he was nothing more than a cold-hearted, opportunistic snake. He pulled people into his inner circle in the way one might gather first aid supplies in case of emergency. If he thought there might be something to gain in acquainting himself with you, he culti-vated that relationship, becoming your most valued friend. And when the depth of your usefulness had been wrung out, he discarded you like an apple core in a compost pile.

It didn't matter if that person was his only son.

He glared at me as if my presence was offensive to him, as if the fact I still existed on the earth was too great a burden for him to suffer.

"Father," I said as I moved to pass him by.

He shifted, completely blocking my exit. "What the *hell* are *you* doing here?" he gritted out, jaw tight, teeth clenched.

"Merry Christmas to you too," I responded with a smile, infusing it with every bit of disgust I could muster. "I believe that's no longer your business."

I stepped forward again, attempting to pass him. We were standing in the doorway between the hallway and the kitchen, and while there weren't any guests mingling in this part of the house, I still didn't think Dad would want to risk catching anyone's attention with this little chat he was trying to have.

"I'm assuming since you never came crawling back to my house, you've decided to live your gay fuckboy lifestyle?"

The assumption that I was a fuckboy was laughable. I'd been too busy trying to keep myself alive and off the streets to have time to be any sort of fuckboy. The assertion that being gay was anyone's choice was just ignorant.

"Fuckboy? Jesus Christ, Dad. You really never knew a damn thing about me, did you?" I sneered at him, letting my disgust show. "Awfully bold of you to accuse me of being a fuckboy, considering you've probably slept with at least half of the women at this party."

"Now listen here, you ungrateful little shit. I don't know what you think you know about me, but you don't know a damn thing." He gave me a once-over, looking me up and down from head to toe, no doubt finding me lacking. "I can't believe I raised someone like you."

"Someone like me?"

"I gave you everything you could ever want. Sent you to the best schools. Paid for years of those damn piano lessons. Paid off admission counselors at Northwestern to get you into a good law school. And what did you do? You threw it all in my face so you could what? Be some pussy who fucks men?"

Adrenaline surged through me. "For fuck's sake, Dad. It's not a choice. It's who I am. And frankly, I don't give a shit whether you approve or not. I never wanted to go to law school, never wanted to be a partner in your practice, and I sure as shit didn't need you to pay off admissions counselors." I was seething with rage at this new revelation. "All I ever wanted from you was for you to pay attention to me. Listen to me. Support me. Love me. But you're not capable of any of that, are you? You're not capable of loving anyone but yourself." I shook my head, absolutely disgusted that any part of this person's blood coursed through my veins. I wanted nothing to do with him ever again. "You made it clear how you felt a long time ago. Now let me pass."

He crossed his arms, his stance wide, continuing to block my path.

"Why are you here? What do you want from me?" he demanded.

"Jesus, Dad. You are such a conceited, arrogant asshole. Why do you assume my presence here has anything to do with *you*? I've lived on my own for years now, without you and without Mom. You know what I want from you? Not a goddamned thing."

Deciding I'd had enough of this entire evening, I shoved past him, bumping his shoulder with mine as I passed. I expected some sort of rebuttal or snarky comment as I walked away, and when it didn't come, I couldn't resist turning to look back at him one last time.

He stood in the doorway, staring at me, eyes wide in shock as if he couldn't believe someone had stood up to him. Shaking my head, I made my way through to the kitchen, picked up my check, and walked out.

WHEN MIDNIGHT CAME and went and I hadn't heard from Finn, I started to worry. When it passed one a.m., I added frustration to the mix. By two, I'd entered into a state of agitated panic. Had something happened? Was he okay? Had he been hit by a drunk driver? Had he gotten into a fight with his father and been arrested for assault? He had said he'd call. I thought we'd gotten past the stage where he closed himself off from everyone, or at least where he no longer closed himself off from me. Was he avoiding me? Was he shutting me out?

Why hadn't he called?

Frustrated, I tossed my phone on my bed as I paced my bedroom. I ran my hands through my hair for what seemed like the hundredth time, the strands long since pulled free of their bond.

I'd had a really lovely evening crammed into Aunt Cathy's minivan with my mom and my cousins, sipping hot cocoa and looking at the lights. My mom and my aunt shared stories of Christmases from their childhood, and we all laughed at the retelling of the time Uncle Bill dressed up as Santa one Christmas Eve, only to show up at our house to find my dad had also dressed up as Santa. There had been a lot of confusion from the kids and quick thinking from the adults to explain that one without giving away any of the magic.

It had been so nice to laugh with my family and have an evening that felt normal for maybe the first time since my mom's diagnosis, but underlying it all was a layer of worry over what might be going down at Finn's gig. Usually so stoic, it had pleased me that he'd reached out to me, but I hated the reason that had necessitated it.

Having been raised in a household surrounded by love and constant support, it baffled me that anyone could treat their child the way Finn had been treated growing up. Children deserved nothing less than unconditional love. To be mostly ignored his entire life, only to then be tossed out simply because of his sexual identity, was a damn travesty. They didn't deserve a moment of his thoughts, and I vowed to love him enough to make up for it.

My phone buzzed with an incoming message, and I lunged for it.

FINN

Hi

Baby. Are you okay?

FINN

Yeah

No

Three dots flashed over and over across my screen for a full minute before the next text finally came through.

I rushed for the front door before his reply had even come through. Just as I reached the door, my phone buzzed with his response.

I yanked the door open, and there he was. Standing on my front porch, his breath coming out in little puffs in the cold December air. He looked...lost.

"Baby. Have you been standing out here in the cold all this time?" I asked as I yanked him inside and shut the door behind him. I pulled him into me, rubbing my hands up and down his arms, trying to warm him up.

"After the gig, I drove around for a while, and then I parked on the curb. I didn't want to go home, but I didn't want to wake you." He shrugged, his arms limp at his sides, his face pressed into my shoulder so I could barely make out his words. "I've only been standing outside for about ten minutes. I couldn't decide what to do."

"What to do about what?" I pulled back to look at him, trying to puzzle out the source of his distress. "What happened tonight?"

"My father... I don't think my parents ever really loved me." His eyes were hollow. No tears. No pain. No anguish. Just empty, as if he'd bled every feeling he'd ever had dry and there was nothing left but emptiness.

My heart cracked. Just split right in two. Maybe he was numb, but I wasn't, and I ached for him. "Oh, baby. Come on." I grabbed his hand, pulling him behind me down the hall to my room. I closed and locked the door behind us and turned to find him standing in the center of the room, staring into nothing. I stripped off his coat, tossing it on the chair in the corner, then nudged him to sit on the edge of my bed. Gently, I kneeled and removed his shoes before pushing him back to lie on my bed. He went willingly, moving as if he wasn't even aware of what he was doing.

I'd seen Finn angry and I'd seen him sad. I'd delighted in one of his rare smiles and thrilled to see his head thrown back in ecstasy. But I'd never seen him like this. As if the world had finally beaten him down and just taken every-thing he had until there was nothing left.

It scared me.

"Talk to me, Finn. Tell me what you need."

His eyes found mine, and he shrugged. Shit. Maybe he didn't know what he needed. But *I* needed to touch him. To hold him. To reassure myself that he wasn't going to float away like dust in the wind.

Wanting him to be comfortable, I stripped him down to his boxers, then did the same before climbing into bed beside him and pulling the covers over us.

We lay like that for a long time, his back to my front, my arm wrapped tight around him. I kissed the back of his neck, pressing my lips to his chilled skin, infusing as much love and warmth as I could into the touch.

His breathing had evened out, so I thought he might have fallen asleep, but finally, he spoke. "When I was thir-teen, I walked in on my father having sex on the desk in his home office. The woman he was with was not my mom. I don't know who she was, probably some woman from the country club or maybe his office. She was laid across his desk on her back, legs over his shoulders, and he was pounding her, going to town. Hadn't even bothered to remove his tie."

His voice was robotic, devoid of emotion as he spoke, as if he was simply laying out the facts in stark black and white. I leaned up, propping my head on my hand so I could try to at least get a glimpse of the side of his face. I wanted to turn him to face me, but I had a feeling he needed to get this out without looking at me. Still, I brushed his hair back and kissed his temple as he continued, hoping that those small actions would somehow break through the icy shell he'd drawn up around himself.

"I was old enough to know what was happening, and I tried to back out of the room without getting caught, but I stumbled over the leg of a side table, knocking a book onto the floor in the process. I froze, terrified of my father's reaction, but he never stopped fucking her. Just yelled at me to get out as he pumped into her over and over again. She never even looked at me."

I kissed him again, this time behind his ear.

"I worried about the incident for days. Was my father going to punish me? Threaten me? Should I tell my mom? Did she know? My relationship with my mother wasn't warm by any means, but it seemed like the right thing to do. She didn't deserve to be cheated on, no matter how much of a cold-hearted bitch she was."

Another kiss on his shoulder. This time, he reached up, wound his hands into my hair, and held me against him. I closed my eyes against the relief that rolled through me at the evidence that he was still with me. That icy exterior was thawing ever so slightly.

I took the risk and rolled him over to face me, desperately wanting to see his face. He didn't resist, though that icy mask had melted and the pain I now saw in his eyes nearly broke me. As if he couldn't bear to look at me, he buried his face in my chest as he continued his story while I stroked his back, trying to offer comfort.

"A week after I caught him, I found my mom crying in her sitting room. She was just sitting in her chair, mascara running down her face, and I figured she must have found out about Dad's affair. I'd never seen her cry, not once, and it shocked me to see her like that. She sniffed a couple of times, then looked up, catching me standing there in shock. I asked her if she was okay, and she laughed. Just laughed like it was the funniest damn thing she'd ever heard."

He pulled back and looked at me once again. "I was so confused and kinda pissed, you know? I mean, I'd been worried about her for over a week, and there she was, laughing at me. I thought maybe she'd lost it, gone completely nuts, but I didn't know what to do, so I turned around and walked out. We didn't do *feelings* in my family, and I was thirteen. I didn't know anything about that kind of shit."

He tucked his face back into my chest as he continued, "Later that night, I heard them arguing in their bedroom. You'd think two narcissists would fight all the time, but they never did. Or at least, I never heard them. I stood outside their door, trying to figure out what the fuck was going on. I heard words like *pregnant* and *affair* and *abortion* and *tennis instructor* tossed around, and eventually, I pieced it all together." He laughed without any sort of humor. "Turns out, all that time I was worried about my dad fucking his secretary, or whoever she was, my mom had been screwing her tennis instructor. She'd gotten knocked up, and they were arguing about her getting an abortion. Not that one of them was in favor of it and the other wasn't, mind you. This wasn't any sort of moral or religious argument. No, they were arguing over whether my father should pay for it or whether Ken, the tennis pro, should."

Jesus. These people were *monsters.* Every time Finn revealed even a glimpse into his childhood, I marveled at how strong he was. There was no doubt he'd endured trauma and that it had affected all his relationships going forward, including ours, but he was so damn strong to get through it without breaking and even more, without turning into just as much of a cold-hearted, self-centered asshole as they were.

"These are the people who raised me, Jamie. I have their blood in my veins. Are you sure you want to be with someone who comes from *that*?"

My eyes blew wide at the unexpected direction of his question. "What? Baby...of *course* I want to be with you. What kind of a question is that?"

"They didn't love me, Jamie. I don't think they ever really even loved each other. Their entire marriage was a partnership based on what each of them could do for the other in terms of his career and her social standing. All my life, I couldn't figure out why they'd even bothered to have me. They clearly didn't want me. I was nothing but a burden and an inconvenience. But tonight...tonight I saw how much my father truly hated me. He'd always been cold and distant, but I suppose he'd felt it was his duty to become a father so he could portray that family man image. Tonight, though, instead of indifference, all I saw was disgust. He truly loathes me."

He swallowed hard, and I flinched at the depth of emotion I saw shimmering in his eyes. His face was contorted in anguish. "I just...all these years, I thought I didn't care. I was used to it. Numb. But tonight, the things he said to me...the way he looked at me... They really fucking hurt. And what if...what if I'm just like him? The blood running through my veins is poisoned, Jamie. It's contaminated with greed and ambition and ugliness." Tears were flowing down his face now and his words came faster and faster as he worked himself into a panic. "You're everything good and beautiful in the world, and I'm... I don't want to ruin you."

"Finn..." I started, trying to stop the flood of toxic thoughts spilling out of him. His words were tearing me apart, piece by piece, but I was helpless to stop the tide. I wanted to do something, anything to take away his pain, to reassure him that he was nothing like them. How could he not know how *amazing* he was?

"No, I'm serious." He sniffed, his eyes so earnest as he looked into mine. "Fuck my parents. I hope I never see them again. They deserve each other. But the fact is, I don't know what love looks like. I don't know how. And you deserve someone who does. You deserve someone who knows how to make you feel like you're the center of the universe. Who is kind and happy and isn't afraid to be with you. I'm none of those things. I'm a broody asshole who doesn't know how to let anyone in and is terrified of—"

"Okay, that's enough," I said, my tone harsher than intended. I sat up and raked my hands through my hair, pushing it off my face. For the last couple of months, I had eagerly awaited a time when I could finally break through all of Finn's barriers and truly get to the center of his heart. I had wanted to figure out what had hurt him and why he had buried himself underneath all those protective layers. Well, it looked like his parents had busted that all wide open for me tonight, and I couldn't take it anymore. I couldn't listen to him beat himself up over some misguided feelings of unworthiness.

I turned to face him, sitting cross-legged on the bed, and he sat up, mirroring my position. His eyes were wide, likely due to the tone I'd taken with him, and I took a deep breath, trying to calm my racing heart. I was angry, but not at him. No, I was pissed that the people who were supposed to love and support him had given him reason to doubt himself, to doubt his worthiness.

I took another breath, this time pulling his hand into mine as I tried to speak more calmly, though my voice shook with an intensity that I couldn't quite tamp down. "Listen to me. Like, really listen. Okay?" He nodded, and I saw his Adam's apple bob as he swallowed hard. I placed my other hand on the side of his face, cupping his cheek as I said, "There isn't anything or anyone in this world you don't deserve. You're a goddamn warrior. A survivor. Your parents kicked you out of the house, and you, what? You found not one but two jobs. You are completely financially independent of them because you work your ass off. How many kids from that rich-ass school of yours could have survived that?"

He shrugged. "I just did what I had to do. I didn't have any other choice," he said, his voice small.

I released him and raked my hands through my hair, my voice shaking in frustration. "Bullshit. You could still be living in Carmen's parents' basement right now. I haven't met them, but I'm willing to bet they wouldn't have kicked you out. You could have caved and gone crawling back to your parents. Fuck, you could be living in a homeless shelter. You did none of those things. You got your shit together, and you did what you needed to do. You're fucking amazing."

"Jesus, Jamie. Why are you so mad? You just said I'm amazing, but you sound like you want to kick my ass."

There was a fire in his eyes as he said it, his words laced with irritation. I was glad to see the fight back in him rather than the desolate shell he'd been when he got here, but I didn't want to be the cause of it. I felt like an ass. After everything he'd already been through, the last thing I wanted to do was make him think I was mad at him when nothing could be further from the truth.

I reached for his hands again, taking both of them in mine and tugging him forward until he was sitting on my lap with his legs wrapped around my waist. I wrapped my arms around him, holding him close, chest to chest. "I'm sorry," I said quietly. "I'm not mad at you. I'm mad at *them*." After a moment, I felt some of the tension drain from his body, and he laid his head on my shoulder as he brought his arms around me, squeezing me back.

"I just feel like I'm broken," he said, his voice choked with tears. "I don't know how...I don't know how to be—"

"Shh." I cut him off. "You're not broken, baby. And you don't need to be anything other than who you are right now. You, just as you are, are all I need." I rubbed his back as he fell apart, allowing the tears to fall once more. His body shook with the weight of it all as it poured out of him. The pain. The anger. The hurt. A lifetime of betrayal from the people who should have loved him. His parents hadn't abused him, at least not physically, but their callous disregard had left bruises on his soul that might never fade completely. All I could do as I held him through it all was hold on to the hope that my love would be enough to make up for it.

And I did love him. I think some part of me had known my heart was headed down this path nearly from the start. I'd been helpless to stop it, to stop myself from falling for this wounded, beautiful soul. I hadn't known the depth of him, the things that had hurt him, and the things that had made him strong, but as he let me in little by little, I was honored to be the one who got to love him now.

As his tears finally abated, I pulled back to look at him and said, "You know what I think?" He shrugged, his eyes dropping back down into his lap. I reached out, placing a finger under his chin, forcing him to look at me. "I think you have maybe one of the biggest hearts of anyone I know. I think you've been protecting it for a long, long time because those bastards who raised you taught you it was safer to bury it. But it's there, it's always been there, just waiting for the right person to come along and unlock it."

I moved my hands to either side of his face, swiping away his tears with my thumbs. "You've given me glimpses of that beautiful heart of yours. Will you trust me with all of it? Will you let me love you the way you deserve to be loved? Because I do, Finn. I love you."

More tears fell, landing on my thumbs where I still held his face, and as my vision blurred, I realized I was crying right along with him. I hadn't meant to say the words, had only just acknowledged that I felt them. But as it always was with Finn, I couldn't hold myself back. Something about him lit a fire inside me that roared to life anytime he was near, and it couldn't be contained.

Moments passed, my declaration hanging in the air between us. I refused to take it back. I hoped I hadn't scared him, but I didn't regret it. I still didn't know what his father had actually said to him, and I wasn't a violent person, but I wasn't above throwing punches if our paths ever crossed. But right now, I didn't need to know the specifics to know that what Finn needed, what he *deserved*, was to know that he was loved. That he was *worth* loving. I hoped he returned my feelings, but even if he didn't or if he wasn't there yet, it didn't matter. The only thing that mattered to me at that moment was *him*.

"You love me?" he asked, voice barely above a whisper.

I nodded, wiping away more tears. "Yeah, baby. I do."

He launched himself into my arms, throwing us back in a heap on my bed. I wrapped my arms around him, holding him tightly as if my arms could hold all his bruised and battered pieces together. "I love you too," he whispered, his voice shaking with emotion.

I held him there, heart bursting, just savoring the feel of him in my arms until, eventually, exhausted, we both fell asleep.

CHAPTER 25

I AWOKE in a tangled heap of arms, legs, and sheets. Jamie had his arms wrapped around me from behind and his leg thrown over my hip for good measure, as if he was afraid I would try to escape in the night. The room was infused with a soft glow in the predawn light, making me feel like we were trapped in our own little bubble, if only for just a little while longer.

My eyes felt gritty, both from all the tears I'd shed last night and the lack of sleep. If I had to guess, it had been close to three a.m. by the time we'd finally passed out, so we'd likely only been asleep for a few hours, but despite my exhaustion, I still found myself wide awake, my mind spinning.

My thoughts were bouncing all over the place between the things my father had said and the ensuing conversation I'd had with Jamie.

I was still angry and hurt by the things my father had said to me.

I didn't want to be. I didn't want to feel anything at all in regard to my parents, but I supposed it was human nature to seek your parents' love, no matter how much you convinced yourself you didn't need it. Although I had thought it was also human nature to love your children, but that instinct for loving and caring for your offspring must have skipped them.

The only silver lining I could find concerning that entire interaction was that I at least left feeling like I could forever close the door on that relationship. There could no longer be any doubt about how they felt about me, no more wishing things might have been different, no more hoping they would change.

I hadn't even realized I'd held out hope for any of that in all this time, honestly thinking their feelings about me simply hadn't mattered. In retrospect, I think I'd spent my whole life in a state of numb denial.

As a child, I'd not known there was anything different about the way my parents treated me. By the time I'd realized parents were supposed to not only love and care for you but actually play a central role in your life, I'd been so accustomed to the lack of those things that I hadn't bothered to wish for anything else.

Upon further reflection, I was starting to realize that those walls I'd built up over all these years weren't just a defense mechanism but a manifestation of my assumptions about my own worthiness to be loved. I hadn't just shut people out because I didn't want to get hurt or because I feared rejection, it went much deeper than that. I shut people out because I thought I wasn't worthy of opening myself up to those relationships, friendship or otherwise, because, at my core, I believed I was unlovable. If my own parents hadn't loved me, how could anyone else?

Yet, Carmen did. She'd proven that time and time again,

showing up for me, even when I pushed her away, even when I didn't deserve it.

And Jamie...his love felt like a miracle. A part of me struggled to believe him. My brain tried to tell me he was just a kind-hearted man who couldn't stand to see someone down and wanted to make me feel better.

But my heart...my heart knew that was bullshit.

I could *feel* his love in the way he held me while we slept. In the way he listened to me when I spoke. In the way he kept showing up, even when I made it difficult.

I'd never met anyone like him. Someone who was truly the best of humanity. He had a goodness inside of him that drew people in, that made us all want to be better. He could have had anyone. I saw the way people looked at him, the way someone would blush when he turned that beautiful smile on them, and the way others would eye-fuck him when they thought he wasn't looking.

I figured I could probably spend my entire life trying to figure out why he chose me. Despite his arguments to the contrary, I really was a broody asshole. But the fact of the matter was, he *had* chosen me. I could live in fear that he'd come to his senses, or I could do my damnedest to try to deserve him.

I felt a soft kiss on the back of my neck, and I sighed, pushing back into him. Jamie's leg tightened around me, pulling me impossibly closer to him as he continued trailing kisses across my shoulder. My ass was tucked against his groin, and I could feel his cock lengthen against me.

"This okay?" he asked, his lips continuing their path from my shoulder back to my neck and up, up, up to that sensitive spot just behind my ear.

"Mmm," I mumbled my assent as I ground my ass into his erection, eliciting a groan from him, which made me smile. As he pulled my earlobe between his teeth, his fingers trailed down my chest, tracing a path down my happy trail until he found my dick, tenting the front of my boxers. I whimpered as he squeezed me and then moved his hand up to the waistband, teasing the skin under the elastic before finally pushing his hand underneath the barrier. I felt his fingers move slowly through the hair at my groin before finally taking my length in his hand.

He gripped my shaft, sliding his hand in a slow upward stroke, his thumb finding the bead of precum at the tip and swirling it around the sensitive head of my cock. Goosebumps broke out on my skin as he teased my sensitive flesh, and I hissed in response.

I felt a puff of breath against my neck as he chuckled behind me. Taking him by surprise, I threw off the arm and leg he had wrapped around me and rolled over to face him. I swung my leg over his hip, grabbed his ass, and pulled him to me, thrusting my cock against his. "Something funny?" I asked as he let loose his own hiss at the feel of my cock rubbing against his.

"You feel amazing," he said as we thrust against each other.

"So do you," I said, but his eyes creased in confusion as I pulled away. I yanked my boxers down, my cock springing free, and threw them on the floor. Mirroring my actions, Jamie grinned and did the same. We both rolled back to our sides, and I pulled him into me once again.

He reached down, taking both of our cocks in his big hand, and stroked them together. We were both leaking precum like crazy, and he used that as lubricant as he stroked us.

Unable to help myself, I leaned forward and took his mouth in a sloppy, needy kiss. I licked into his mouth, stroking his tongue with mine. It was desperate and messy, but I didn't care. I tangled my hand into his long hair and held him to me as if kissing him was the answer to life's hardest questions. I was pretty sure it was the solution to every problem I'd ever had.

My mind bounced between the taste of him as we kissed and the feel of his cock against mine. My blood was on fire with need as he stroked us faster and faster. As my orgasm barreled down on me like a freight train, I tore my mouth away and grabbed his hand, stilling his movements.

"What? Are you okay?" he asked.

"I'm about to come."

His mouth curved up in a smug grin. "Isn't that the point?"

I didn't return his smile, instead staring intently into his eyes. "I want you to fuck me, Jamie."

His eyes burned with intensity as he felt the gravity of what I was saying. "Are you sure, baby?"

I nodded. "I love you, Jamie. I want to feel you inside me. I've been hollow for so long. I want you to fill me up. Please."

"I love you too. God, I love you so much." He kissed me again, hard and quick, before leaning back to grab supplies from his bedside table. "Lie on your back."

I moved to do as he asked, and he climbed over me, straddling my thighs. "You're so damn beautiful."

Something must have passed over my face because he shook his head and said it again. "You are, Finn. You're gorgeous. I hate that you don't know that, but I'm going to do my best to make sure you feel it every damn day."

He leaned forward and placed his lips on my forehead, letting them linger there for a moment before pulling away. I closed my eyes at the sweetness of the gesture, feeling them sting in response. Dammit, I'd cried enough tears last night. I didn't want any more of them today, so I squeezed them back before opening my eyes again to find his intense green ones trained on my face.

"Mine," he said before taking my mouth in a possessive kiss. I could taste his intensity as he fucked in and out of my mouth with his tongue, biting my lip before trailing kisses down my neck, nipping and licking his way down to my collarbone.

I wasn't sure what I had done to flip this switch but gone was the sweet Jamie of moments before, the caretaker who wanted to fix all my hurts and put me back together, whole and sound. This Jamie was feral in his desire to claim me, to make sure I knew I was his.

I was here for it. I was here for all of it: the light and sweet and the dark and demanding. I wanted every piece of him, and I wanted to give him every piece of me until our pieces reshaped us into something new and beautiful.

He sucked a hickey into my neck, causing me to arch my back, my hips seeking contact with his. I wasn't sure when he'd done it, but at some point, he must have lubed his fingers because I suddenly felt cool, wet contact with my hole and instinctively pressed into it, seeking more.

We hadn't gone this far, hadn't really even talked topping and bottoming, hadn't explored each other in this way, but it didn't matter. At this moment, I desperately wanted to feel him inside me. Filling me. Loving me in the purest form.

His fingers moved in circles around my rim, sending jolts through my body as I lost myself in sensation. He dipped one finger in to the first knuckle before pulling it out and repeating it a couple more times.

My cock was leaking, impossibly hard, as he teased my

entrance, and the next time he entered me, I clenched, trying to hold him there.

"More," I demanded, my voice guttural with need. "Dammit, Jamie. Give me more."

Eyes on mine, he sank his finger a little deeper. "Is this what you want?"

"Yes. No," I whimpered. "More, dammit."

He pushed his finger all the way in, and I groaned. "Like this?" he asked. "Or like this?"

Before I could respond, he bent over and took my cock to the back of his throat in one swift, hot-as-fuck motion. He pulled his head back, hollowing out his cheeks as he moved slowly, drawing out the torture. When only the tip was left in his mouth, he curled the finger still inside me and my entire body lit up like a Christmas tree.

"Fuuuck." I thrashed on the sheets, desperate to come, yet not ready for this to end. He added a finger, stretching me as he took my cock once again to the back of his throat. He continued this way, alternating deep-throating me with stretching my hole, adding a third finger, until I was a writhing, begging mess of sensation. I needed to come.

I needed to come now.

I reached down and grabbed hold of his hair, yanking him off me. "Fuck me, Jamie. Fuck me, now."

His moss-green eyes were blown wide with lust, his lips wet and red from sucking me off. And I knew at that moment that the image of him bent over my cock, red lips swollen, hair falling around his face in disarray, and eyes dilated would be burned into my memory as long as I lived.

Jamie reached over and grabbed the condom, making quick work of opening the package and rolling it on. He added more lube and then leaned forward and kissed me. Hard.

I could feel his tip nudging my entrance, and I pressed my ass into him, desperately wanting to complete the connection between us. Without breaking the kiss, he pressed forward, slowly sheathing himself in my body.

The feel of him moving inside me was everything I had hoped it could be and better than anything I could have possibly imagined.

He finally broke the kiss as he bottomed out and stared at me in wonder. He held himself still, allowing me to adjust to him, our eyes locked, lost in sensation. I was drowning in him, and I didn't want to come up for air.

"I love you," he breathed, barely a whisper, his voice filled with wonder.

I love you too seemed bland and gray compared to the myriad colors of emotion bursting forth inside me, but those were the only words I had. "I love you too. So damn much."

He seemed like he wanted to say more, but perhaps he also couldn't find bigger, more vibrant words, so instead, he began to move. His strokes were slow and sweet at first, but I wasn't having it. The drag of his cock in my tight hole felt amazing, but I wanted more. I wanted it down and dirty and raw. I wanted him to pound me so hard that I would remember for days that I belonged to him. That I was his.

I wrapped my legs around him, changing the angle and tugging him impossibly deeper as I leaned up and whispered in his ear, "Faster."

His breath caught, but then like a wildfire burning out of control, he picked up the pace, his hips pistoning in and out of me faster and faster, grunts and the slap of our skin the only soundtrack to our lovemaking.

A bead of sweat ran down his face, holding for a moment on the edge of his jawline before dropping down to land on my cheek near the corner of my mouth. My tongue darted out to lick it, the salty taste of him exploding on my tongue. His long hair hung loosely around his face, the strands mixing with his sweat, making him look just a little mad.

"God, I love you like this," I said, lust burning through my blood. "Wild and untamed."

"That's what you do to me," he said, his words coming out in stuttering grunts as he slammed into me over and over again, his pace relentless. "God, Finn. You make me lose control. I forget everything about who I am and who I'm supposed to be."

My orgasm was imminent. I could feel it building like a wave in a hurricane just about to crest. I was helpless to stop it, not that I wanted to. I reached up and threaded my hands in his hair, damp with sweat, and pulled him to me. "Good," I whispered before pulling him in for another heated kiss.

The slight change in angle had him pegging my prostate while my cock was trapped between our bodies, his abs rubbing against me, creating a delicious friction. That was it. I was done.

I exploded between us, hot, sticky warmth slicking our abdomens as I rode wave after wave. Moments later, he ripped his mouth from mine, threw his head back, and buried himself deep inside me. The sound he made was otherworldly as I felt him pulse inside me. His head was thrown back in ecstasy, sweaty hair falling around his face, sweat running down the column of his neck—he was beautiful.

As we both struggled to catch our breath, he carefully pulled out of me and dealt with the condom before pulling me against him, the little spoon to his bigger one. He reached for the blanket, throwing it over both of us, and we slept once again.

I woke just a couple of hours later, still exhausted but wide awake. My brain sometimes had a way of working through problems while I slept, and while I rarely remembered my dreams, I always knew I'd had one of those nights when I woke up and whatever problem I'd gone to bed with charged immediately to the forefront before I'd even had time to register I was awake. The second clue was usually a stiff jaw, meaning I'd been clenching it in my sleep.

It was incredibly annoying, especially when I was wrapped so cozily in Jamie's arms, but I knew there was nothing to be done about it. Despite my exhaustion, I wouldn't be able to go back to sleep. Still, I lay there for a moment, gently moving my jaw from side to side while examining which problem needed my attention the most.

My thoughts moved from the conversation with my father to the declarations Jamie and I had made to our intense lovemaking and back again, all in an unending kaleidoscope of thoughts and emotions.

But what I realized as I lay there, safe and warm in Jamie's arms, was that these weren't problems to be solved. I couldn't change my parents' feelings toward me, and it was time I stopped hoping for that. All these years, I'd closed myself off toward relationships with other people, and for what? I'd tried to protect myself, but Mom and Dad had still managed to hurt me, and in the meantime, what other aspects of life had I missed out on? Enough was enough. There was no problem to solve here—they would never love me the way I needed, but that didn't mean I was unlovable. It was time to invest my energy in those who would return it.

Jamie mumbled something in his sleep, the arm

wrapped over me squeezing before relaxing again as he settled back into sleep. It made me smile.

Something had shifted between us in the early hours of the morning. It was more than just declarations of love, more than just words anyone could utter in a moment of passion. It was a settling of souls, a recognition of completeness, wholeness. The threads of our souls had been braided together into something stronger and more beautiful. It was terrifying giving someone this much power to hurt me, but even more so in knowing that I could do the same to him, and because of that, I wanted, no needed, to do better. To meet him where he was rather than waiting for him to make the move. To offer my thoughts and feelings first rather than letting him take the lead. To do little things for him, just like he did for me. He deserved that. He deserved everything.

Right now, what he deserved most, was to sleep a little longer.

Quietly, I pulled myself from his arms and climbed out of bed. I found a pair of Jamie's sweats and a hoodie and pulled those on, cinching the drawstring to hold the joggers in place on my smaller waist. I tucked my nose into the neck of the hoodie and inhaled, my heart settling at his familiar scent.

After a stop in the bathroom, I made my way out to the kitchen to start a pot of coffee. I was surprised to find a mostly full pot that appeared to still be warm. I grabbed a mug and poured myself a cup, then took it out to the living room.

I was itching to write, to bleed out all these feelings on paper, but I didn't have a notebook with me. My iPad was out in my car, but I didn't want to run outside in the cold without shoes, and I preferred putting actual pen to paper anyway. There was something about knowing there was no backspace button. It made me choose words more carefully before I committed them to paper.

I pulled up short when I spotted Annie sitting on the couch. She had a colorful blanket pulled over her lap and a cup of coffee next to her on the side table. Her gaze was fixed on the Christmas tree, but I wasn't sure she was really seeing it. Her eyes appeared to be focused on something more distant, or maybe something internal, some memory only visible to her.

I started to back out of the room, not wishing to disturb her, but the motion must have caught her attention because she turned her head, her face lighting with a smile that warmed me. She was beautiful, even in the midst of her illness, her smile genuine and bright. It was evident that Jamie took after her in that way.

"Come sit with me," she said, patting the cushion next to her.

"I don't want to disturb you," I replied.

She gave me a look of exasperation. "Stop it. Come sit."

I gave her a small smile as I took the place she indicated next to her on the couch. We sat in companionable silence for a while, sipping our coffee and watching the colored lights twinkle on the Christmas tree.

The tree was a monstrous thing, huge and lopsided. Jamie had told me they'd always had live trees, and when he'd seen this one, that no one else seemed to want, he'd had to have it.

There didn't seem to be a cohesive design element to it. There was a hodgepodge of cutesy Hallmark ornaments mixed with colored balls and what looked to be handmade ornaments from Jamie's childhood. There was even a picture frame ornament that held an image of Jamie's first visit to Santa. Adorable in his *My 1st Christmas* onesie, he looked adoringly at Santa with a huge smile on his chubby face. I thought I'd heard most kids cried the first time they met Santa, but not Jamie. Not the one who made friends with everyone he met, even as a baby.

I was struck once again by the differences between our two families. We'd had no less than three Christmas trees in our house growing up. My mother had hired a professional decorator to set them up every year, each one with a different theme that suited the decor of the room it resided in. We'd also had poinsettias and elaborate flower arrangements that should have provided warmth to our space but instead made me feel like we were in some sort of Christmas-themed funeral.

There'd been no cozy traditions of our family decorating the tree and sipping cider while Christmas melodies played in the background. No, it was typical for me to come home from school one day to the decorations up with an admonishment not to touch anything.

Jamie and his mom, on the other hand, had spent a laughter-filled evening decorating with Bing Crosby playing in the background and hot chocolate warming on the stove. Aunt Cathy's family hadn't even participated, as this was something they'd always kept special just for themselves. The next day, Jamie had told me how he kept having to turn the lopsided tree in its stand until, eventually, he'd propped the heavier side against the wall in the hopes that it would keep it from tipping over. In his mom's weakened state, she had taken on more of a supervisory role, with Jamie doing most of the actual work, but I knew he'd been happy to have that time with her.

These were the kinds of things I wanted in my life going forward. I wanted mismatched picture frames on my walls and kitschy ornaments on a lopsided tree and cookie-decorating contests and car rides in pajamas to look at Christmas lights. I wanted laughter and warmth and family. I could see a life like that with Jamie, and despite his declarations of love, I was terrified to hope for it. It was too new and fragile, and I'd never had anything like it. I didn't know how to trust it.

But God, I wanted to try.

"You're good for him, you know," she said out of the blue. "Thank you for letting him in."

"What?" I turned to her, certain I hadn't heard her correctly. She was a kind woman, but I couldn't possibly be the type of boyfriend she wanted for her son. She'd want someone like Asher with the polished good looks and understated elegance. Someone educated and with a solid future. Not a broody barista who moonlighted as a jazz pianist.

"You're good for him. You challenge him. You make him want things for himself that he's never allowed himself to want."

"What do you mean?"

"You. He wants you. And I've never seen him work so hard to be with someone."

"He's had relationships before. Asher. I'm sure there were others." I wasn't sure what she was getting at. I wasn't sure how my making him work for it was good for him. Didn't that just mean I was a pain in the ass? Didn't he deserve someone who thought he hung the moon and the stars and treated him as such?

"Asher is a sweet, sweet boy. I love him like he's my own, and I will always be grateful that he was Jamie's first love, but Asher wouldn't have made Jamie happy long-term. He was too safe. Too comfortable. They loved each other in that tender way of young love, but there was no fire, no passion." She raised her eyebrows, a sarcastic twinkle in her eye. "Teenage lust, maybe, but that's just hormones. That's not the stuff that makes your heart skip a beat or sets a flutter in your belly. It's not what makes you laugh until you cry or carries you through the hard times."

A shadow crossed over her face, gone in a flash, but I knew I hadn't imagined it, and I wondered if she was thinking about her illness and what that meant for the future. I didn't want to contemplate it. I was just getting to know her, already caring for her in a way that surprised me. I didn't want to think about life without her, let alone what that would do to Jamie.

I rubbed my sternum, trying to soothe the ache that had built there. Turning back to the topic at hand, I said, "He's a people person, everyone loves him, and he's gorgeous. Surely he's had other relationships that challenged him, though I'm not sure why that's a good thing. I wouldn't think fighting with someone all the time is healthy."

"Is that what you two do? Fight?"

I thought back over the last couple of months and could only think of one instance that I would deem an actual argument. That was the weekend after Thanksgiving when I'd sort of shut down after Jamie brought Asher and Joshua to Ivory. Though I wasn't sure that qualified as a fight. I supposed we'd each challenged each other's perspective in that instance, and ultimately, the incident had pushed our relationship forward. We'd come to understand each other in ways we hadn't before. And there'd been some other times where we'd pushed each other too, but she was right. Those were each of us challenging the other's way of thinking, not fights.

"No, I suppose you have a point." I shrugged, not really sure where to go from here. I didn't want to argue with her, but I didn't fully get what she was saying either.

Seeming to sense my struggle, she turned toward me and took my hand. Her skin was soft and cool against mine, and I marveled at the feel of it. I couldn't remember ever holding a hand so small.

"Honey, Jamie has always worn his heart on his sleeve. He loves big and loud and bold. He's quick to trust and quick to forgive. He's fiercely loyal to his friends and family, which means pretty much everyone because he doesn't know a stranger. But despite all of that, he's never had a romantic relationship that lasted more than a few months besides Asher. Because while he's all those things I said before, he isn't interested in surface-level bullshit. He wants something meaningful. The physical isn't going to be enough for him. He's going to want someone he can talk to, have conversations with, someone who makes him laugh. Someone who *challenges* him. He saw what his dad and I had and isn't going to settle for anything less."

I looked down at our hands clasped between us, choking back some emotion I couldn't or didn't want to identify. "I um...I don't know what that looks like. My parents weren't exactly models of how to be in a healthy relationship. What if...?" I paused, swallowing past the knot in my throat. "What if I don't know how to love him the way he needs? The way he deserves?" I whispered.

"You already do. He doesn't need you to be anything other than who you are right now. The rest you'll figure out together."

A tear fell, then another, the drops landing side by side on my sleeve. "I just feel so broken," I admitted, my voice shaky.

"Oh, sweet boy," she said as she released my hand so she could place it around my shoulders and draw me in, placing my head on her shoulder as she hugged me to her.

"Wounded, maybe. Hurt. But not broken. The ones who raised you, they're the ones who are broken."

I thought I'd cried enough tears for a lifetime last night. I didn't want to shed any more tears for them, for the assholes who'd neglected me my entire life.

But these tears weren't for them. They were for me. For the child who'd closed his heart to everyone so he couldn't ever be disappointed. For the man I was now, who felt more love from this woman I'd only known a couple of months than from a lifetime with the people who'd raised me.

With each tear that fell, I released anger, hurt, and fear. I washed away regret and pain. No longer numb, I felt raw and exposed. But as the flow of tears began to ebb, I realized that as I released all of that shit I'd internalized for twenty-two years, I was allowing new feelings in. I felt hope. And as Annie held me tight to her, whispering nonsense in my ear like I was a small child in need of soothing, I felt cared for. Supported. Loved. And maybe even worthy.

Finally, I pulled away, wiping my face, feeling a little embarrassed at the way I'd lost it. She had a wet spot on her robe where my tears had landed, but as I looked at her, I realized that some of those tears had been hers as well. She, too, was wiping her face, her eyes red and a little puffy. "I'm sorry I upset you," I said, feeling terrible that I'd made her cry.

"Sweet boy, you have nothing to be sorry about. Not one thing," she said fiercely. "If you haven't noticed, we feel things big around here." Her mouth twitched in a sardonic grin. "Don't ever apologize for that. That's how we know we're alive."

I sat back against the cushions, resting my head on her shoulder. I wasn't one to seek out physical touch from anyone, but this felt right. "Well, thank you. For…I guess for making me feel like maybe I'm going to be okay."

"Of course you are. You're stronger than you think."

I smiled. "That's what Jamie said last night."

"He's not wrong. Now"—she patted my arm—"go look under the tree. Over there, toward the right, there's a small package wrapped in silver with your name on it."

I sat up and looked at her, eyebrows raised.

"Go on," she said. I did as she asked, retrieving the slender package and returning to sit beside her.

"I can't believe you got me something. Should we wait for Jamie to open it?" I asked.

"No, this one's just between you and me." Her eyes danced with excitement. "Go ahead and open it."

I carefully unwrapped it, simultaneously wanting to savor the moment and dying to know what was inside. Removing the paper, I lifted the lid to find a silver ornament picture frame. It held a picture of Jamie and me kissing in front of the tree. It had been taken earlier in the week when I'd dropped by for dinner. While Jamie was doing the dishes, he'd shooed me out of the kitchen, so I'd taken a moment to get a closer look at some of the ornaments on the tree.

Jamie had joined me after finishing the dishes, pulling me into him for a lingering kiss before sharing stories about some of his favorites. It had been a perfect evening in the middle of a hectic work week and holiday preparations when we'd barely had time to see each other. I had no idea his mom had caught us kissing, let alone snapped a picture.

I felt something textured on the back, and when I flipped the ornament over, I saw it had been engraved.

First Christmas

I smiled in wonder at such a simple yet meaningful gift. "*First Christmas* implies there will be more of them," I said.

"Won't there be?"

My heart flipped, then fluttered, before settling once again in my chest as I realized that I very much wanted there to be. "I hadn't even thought past this one. You seem so certain. How do you know?"

"I've seen the way you look at each other. And I know my son. He isn't letting you go anytime soon. He loves you."

I blushed all the way up to my ears. "I love him too. Thank you. This is beautiful."

"Why don't you go hang it up?"

I shook my head. "Oh, but this is *your* tree. Yours and Jamie's."

"And now it's yours too. You're stuck with us." She nodded encouragingly, so I crossed to the tree and found an empty branch to hang it on.

Arms wrapped around me from behind as I carefully placed the ornament on one of the branches, ensuring it was secure and wouldn't fall off. I hadn't heard him come in, but I'd recognize the feel of those strong arms anywhere. I leaned into Jamie's warmth, savoring the feeling of him holding me close.

"Merry Christmas, baby."

THE WEEKS FOLLOWING Christmas and New Year's were some of the happiest of my life. I was still working at The Daily Grind and Ivory, but Jamie's time was mostly free while he was on winter break, and we spent as much of it as we could together. When I was working, Jamie frequently came in to sit at a table. He said he just wanted to be near me. Sometimes he brought Asher or talked Carmen into meeting him, and sometimes he came by himself, toting along his laptop or a book.

He felt bad for leaving his mom, but she insisted he had his own life to live and couldn't spend all his time with her. Still, he'd frequently called on Aunt Cathy and her family to help out, insisting he wouldn't leave her without help, and if they weren't available, he made sure he could be.

In my free time, I'd found myself over at Jamie's house more often than not. After falling asleep at his house a couple of times, I'd taken to just spending the night there most nights, only stopping at home to change clothes. Carmen was still staying at my place. The last time I'd been there, I'd noticed the bathroom sink had been completely overtaken by her makeup and hair products, and the pile of clothes on the chair in the bedroom had been all hers. I didn't care.

Like someone stranded in the desert without any water, I'd been starved for affection my whole life, and now, I couldn't get enough. I savored every look, every touch, and the sound of every laugh. I worried that maybe I'd be too much now. I'd gone from aloof to stage-five clinger in record time, but Jamie never seemed to mind my neediness. He was so patient with me when I couldn't make sense of some emotion or feeling, allowing me the space to work through it, yet always nearby, so I knew he wasn't going anywhere.

If we were in the same room, we were always touching. Holding hands, thighs against each other, an arm wrapped around me, my hand resting on his thigh. It was as if I needed that connection to ground me, to reassure me that this was all real.

We often hung out with Annie, watching TV, doing a puzzle, or playing cards together. She tried to give us space, but Jamie assured her that we wanted her there. And we did. She was the closest thing to a mother I'd ever had, and I wanted to soak up as much of her love as I could. Jamie's family had become my family. It blew me away how seamlessly this shift had taken place. No one questioned my presence, and they all treated me as if I'd been a part of their unit for years rather than weeks.

Jamie was due to start student teaching the first full week of January, this week, in fact. His excitement was adorable. For Christmas, I'd given him a leather messenger bag which he'd packed with pens and pencils, his laptop, and several notebooks. I was currently sitting on his bed, giving him my opinion on several outfits he was contemplating wearing. His first day wasn't even with students, but he wanted to make a good impression on the staff despite already knowing quite a few of them through his mom. Though I thought that relationship might be driving this desire to impress. He wanted to be seen as his own person, not just little Jamie, Annie's kiddo.

I respected the hell out of him for his drive to do well, to make a difference, even as I felt a bit of jealousy at his success. We'd come from the same rich background, though he'd gone to public school and I'd gone to private, yet the outcome of our childhoods had been vastly different. Though I hadn't wanted the profession my parents had chosen for me, I'd still thought I'd have *some* profession. Was I really going to be a barista for the rest of my life? I loved the jazz musician aspect of my life, but that felt more like a hobby that happened to make me a little money. It didn't feel like a career. But then...what? What *did* I want?

"Finn?"

My eyes snapped up to Jamie's. "Yeah?"

"Where did you go just now? I asked what you think about this one?" He gestured to the button-down paired with a navy-blue sweater and dark-wash jeans.

"Oh, sorry. Just spaced out for a sec." I squashed the guilt at the existential crisis I'd been distracted by and focused on him. "I like this one. Professional on the top says you're taking it seriously, with jeans that say you're not trying too hard."

"That's what I was thinking too. Now which shoes should I wear?"

I suppressed the eye roll, knowing it was because he cared so much, and reached for his hand. "Come here," I said as I pulled him toward me.

"But I need to figure out my shoes, and I still need to pack my lunch and make sure my laptop is charged and—"

I pressed my lips to his, stopping the stream of consciousness he was about to embark on, until eventually, I felt him relax against me. He pulled back, resting his forehead against mine. "You're going to be amazing tomorrow."

"I'm just so nervous, and I don't know what to do with all this restless energy."

"I bet I can help you with that," I raised my eyebrows suggestively.

"Mmm...I know you can." He lowered his lips back down, but before they met mine, we heard a soft knock on the door.

"Come in," Jamie called out as we put some space between us.

"Hey, sweet boy. I have something for you." Annie walked into the room carrying a medium-sized gift bag.

"What's this?" he asked, taking it from her. I moved over so she could sit next to me on the bed.

"Open it and find out."

He dug into the bag, setting aside the tissue paper, and pulled forth a purple crewneck that said Swope Stags in bold white letters with an outline of a Stag mid-jump across the front. He looked up at her, his eyes bright. "When did you get this?"

"A couple of months ago. I called Jess in the front office and had her to set it aside for Cathy to pick up."

"But I just found out about the assignment a couple of weeks ago."

"I know." She shrugged, her delicate shoulders rising in her now oversized sweater. "I had a feeling you'd be placed there, and I wanted you to have something to wear on Fridays."

"Mom, this is so great. Thank you!" He leaned over and

wrapped her in a hug, his large frame enveloping her petite body.

"I'm proud of you, kiddo," she said, her voice muffled against his chest. "You've worked so hard for this."

He pulled back, releasing her, and fidgeted with the crewneck. "I'm nervous. I don't want to let you down."

"Impossible. What makes you think you could ever do that?" she asked, her eyes wide and eyebrows climbing up her forehead.

He sat on the bed on the other side of her, and she turned to face him. This seemed like a private moment, and I felt a little like a third wheel, but I figured leaving the room would only draw more attention to myself, so I stayed, trying to be invisible.

"You were an icon at that school, Mom. Everyone loved you...they still love you...students, staff, parents...I just don't know that I can ever live up to that."

It was odd to see Jamie so vulnerable. From the moment I'd met him, he'd exuded that rare combination of confidence and kindness. He never seemed to question a decision he made. Instead just walked through life carefree, as if he had all the answers. He was a caretaker and a problem solver. It had never occurred to me that he might experience self-doubt.

"Oh, honey, I've pissed off plenty of people in my day. You're never going to make everyone happy. And yeah, maybe people will have this idea that you're going to be a junior edition of me at first, but, sweetheart, they're also going to see how amazing you are in your own right. You are like me in many ways, but you have qualities of your father in you too. Things that will make you a better teacher than I was. You've always had a way with kids, and you're passionate about teaching. Those things will shine through.”

“Thanks, Mom. I love you so much.” He pulled her into him again, smothering her in a huge hug. At length, she pulled away. “Now, I’m going to head to bed. I need to get some sleep before my appointment tomorrow.”

Jamie’s eyebrows pinched together in worry. “Are you sure you’re okay going without me?”

“Yes,” she said, her tone exasperated. They’d been over this a hundred times. I was taking her to her appointment while he went to professional development with his cooperating teacher. I knew he trusted me to take her, but he couldn’t help feeling guilty. “Finn will take me, and I’m sure he’ll text you when we’re home. You can’t put your entire life on hold because of me.”

“You’re worth it, Mom. I would do it in a heartbeat if you’d let me.”

“I know, but I’d never be able to live with myself. Not when your Aunt Cathy or Finn can help.” I was honored, honestly. That Jamie trusted me. And that Annie felt comfortable enough with me to take her.

“I just don’t like it.” If I hadn’t known how conflicted he felt about the whole thing, I would have laughed at the way he crossed his arms and pouted at her.

“I know. But it will be fine, sweet boy.” She leaned over and kissed him on the cheek before rising from the bed and crossing to the door. She turned and looked back at him. “Goodnight.”

“‘Night, Mom,” he called out. After she shut the door, he scooted over on the bed, swinging around to lay his head in my lap. I pulled his hair from the tie and ran my fingers through the golden strands. “I’ll text you as soon as we’re home. You know I’ll take care of her.”

"I know," he said. "I know how much she means to you. It's just that...I don't know...I guess it's just that feeling of 'no one can take care of her like *I* take care of her.' I get that it's not rational, but it's hard not to feel that way."

I tried to think about what that might feel like, to have that strong connection with someone. I hadn't ever had anyone like that, but I supposed I could imagine I might feel that way if it was him. "You and your mom have had each other's backs for a long time. I can imagine it's hard to alter that dynamic."

He was quiet for a moment before responding. "Maybe. I just love her so much."

"I know."

MONDAY DAWNED COLD, the January sun reluctant to make its presence known, but Jamie beamed bright enough that it didn't matter. By the time I trudged into the kitchen, scratching my head and squinting at the brightness of the lights, Jamie was showered, dressed, and, if I had to guess by the restless energy rolling off him, on his third cup of coffee.

"Morning!" he said, his cheerful tone making me cringe in the early-morning light.

I grunted at him in response as I crossed over to grab a mug and pour myself a cup. I hadn't slept well, Jamie's restless energy somehow bleeding into my subconsciousness, preventing me from getting a good night's rest.

"For someone who tossed and turned all night, you're awfully chipper," I grumbled as I took a sip. He looked damn good too, despite his lack of sleep. I was pretty sure I looked like a skinny troll.

His face fell, and I immediately regretted my words. It

felt like I'd kicked a puppy. "Did I keep you from sleeping?" he asked, his eyebrows raised in concern.

I waved my hand in front of me, dismissing his worry. "Maybe a little, but that's okay. I'm off today, so I'll take a nap after we get back from Annie's appointment."

He took my mug and set it aside before pulling me into him so we were facing each other chest to chest. "I'm sorry, baby. I'm just so worked up about today."

I smiled as I pulled my head back to look at him. "I know. You're going to be great!" I wrapped my arms around his waist, squeezing him close. "It's nice to know you're human like the rest of us," I teased.

"What do you mean?" He was so legitimately confused that it was adorable.

"You just...like, you exude this confidence in pretty much everything you do. It's nice to see you get nervous, just like the rest of us."

He huffed out a breath of exasperation. "Of course I do!"

"Baby, don't take it personally. I love seeing you so excited about this. You're going to be amazing!"

His mouth stretched into a wide grin. "That's the first time you called me 'baby.'"

"So? You call me that all the time."

"Yeah, but it's a way bigger deal for you to do it, Mr. Relationship-phobe."

I rolled my eyes. "Good grief. I might never say it again, now."

"No, no, no! You have to say it now. It's like a rule!"

"A rule, huh?" I raised my eyebrow. "What other rules are you going to make up?"

"Well, let's see..." He pretended to think real hard.

"Oh my God, you're so full of shit." I laughed as I kissed

him, enjoying how easy it always was with him. I hated that I'd fought this so hard, but I would be forever grateful that he hadn't given up on me.

"All right, you two," Annie said as she entered the kitchen. "I need to get a picture of this one on his first day of school." She wore thick, mismatched socks, sweats, and an old Journey T-shirt, topped with a plaid flannel. Most days, she wore a headscarf, and today's was bright pink. My mother would have died before allowing anyone to see her in such a mismatched outfit, which made me love Annie even more.

I took the phone from her and snapped a couple of pictures, then gestured for her to join Jamie. Despite her appearance, she didn't hesitate to put her arm around him and lean in for the photo. The two of them beamed from ear to ear, their smiles turned up to full wattage, and I couldn't help but think that this type of love and pride and joy is what everyone should aspire to in all their relationships. Fathers and sons. Wives and Husbands. Friends. Lovers.

Jamie and me.

I handed her phone back, but not before sending the photos to myself.

Jamie looked at his watch, noting the time. "I better get going," he said as he dumped his coffee into a travel mug and grabbed the lunch he'd packed the night before out of the fridge. Annie gave him a hug, and then I walked him to the garage door. I leaned in for a lingering kiss, then pulled back, saying, "Knock 'em dead." He grinned, gave me one more quick kiss, and then he was off.

Annie's appointment wasn't until ten a.m., so I decided to treat her to breakfast at a little café just a few blocks from her oncologist's office. Her appetite had been hit or miss lately, but I knew this place had a good selection of lighter fare if she wasn't feeling up for anything heavy, and they generally weren't super busy, so there was less chance for her to come into contact with germs.

After being seated, we both pored over the menu for a moment, but in truth, I was frantically searching for something to say. This woman was coming to mean so much to me, yet I'd spent so much of my life avoiding conversation with pretty much everyone that I was awkward with it. I didn't know how to talk to her without Jamie as a buffer.

Our server arrived, giving me a few more moments to pull myself together. After placing our orders, we were left in silence with no menus to act as buffers. "So, Jamie was pretty excited this morning," I blurted, unable to think of anything else to say. *Lame. Way to state the obvious.*

Thankfully, she didn't seem to notice my awkwardness. Or at least she was kind enough to roll with it. A smile tugged at her lips as she said, "He's wanted to be a teacher for as long as I can remember."

"Yeah? I guess we never really talked about it. He told me he was studying to be a teacher, and it made sense for his personality, so I never really questioned it."

"Well, yeah, he's a natural caretaker. Always has been. But even when he was little, I'd take him up to school while I worked in my classroom, and he'd set up his own little pretend class in the back of the room. He could entertain himself for hours playing school."

I smiled at the thought of little Jamie pretending to teach an imaginary class of students. God, I bet that was adorable. Our server arrived with mugs and a carafe of coffee, which he poured out for us and then left us to ourselves once again.

"When he got older," she continued, "he taught swim lessons, tutored other kids, and was a camp counselor. In high school, he even babysat the neighbors' kids from time to time, when he wasn't busy with his other activities." I sipped my coffee as I listened to her talk and marveled at the fondness she held for Jamie. It warmed me to see the kind of love and pride she so clearly had for her son. That was how it should be. "He was always good with kids. Patient. Kind. He takes the time to really listen when they speak. He genuinely cares what they have to say, and they can feel it. Kids always know when you're faking it."

That was such a perfect description of who Jamie was at his core. In all the years I'd spent pushing people away, I'd learned that it was rare for someone to look past my prickly exterior and take the time to actually see *me*. It made it easy to push people away, to put my head down and go about unnoticed. It was the way I liked it. But Jamie was different. He'd looked just a little deeper, waited a little longer, and had seen something in me that was worth knowing.

His students would be so lucky to have him.

"Jamie's unlike anyone I've ever known," I managed past the lump that had formed in my throat. Her eyes, which had already gone soft as she spoke of him, glistened as she looked at me. "What about you?" she asked. "What dreams did you have for yourself as a child?"

I snorted in response, all sentimentality dissipating at the thought of my regimented childhood. Dreams were not something ever discussed. Ambition. Protocol. Expectation. Those were the tenets held above all else. Never anything so lofty as dreams. "It never occurred to me to have dreams of my own. I just did whatever my parents asked of me. My father wanted me to be a lawyer, to join his practice someday."

She raised her penciled-in eyebrows in question. She'd changed her clothes after Jamie left this morning, looking a little more put together, though she was still sporting that bright-pink head scarf. I couldn't help but think that she was beautiful. "And now? What dreams do you have for yourself now?"

Stunned, I realized I didn't know. My mind went utterly blank. In the last three and a half years, I hadn't looked any further into the future than about a month, and that was simply to make sure I was paying the bills. The first time I'd thought about anything beyond the present had been last night while Jamie was selecting his outfit, and that had been a glimmer of a thought, never fully formed.

"I don't know," I finally admitted. "In my heart, I think I always knew I didn't want to be a lawyer, but I never really figured out what I *did* want, and then after my parents kicked me out, I found myself without any choices in the matter."

She put her hand on the table, palm up, and I stared at it for a moment before tentatively placing my hand in hers. Her hand was so thin and small, but I loved the feel of her cool, soft skin against mine. It felt even better when she gave it a small squeeze. "So, what would you do if you could do anything you wanted?"

I shook my head. "I truly don't know. I have no clue."

"Okay. So what interests do you have? What about music?"

"I love playing the piano, but I don't know... Those gigs are like a stress relief for me. I'm afraid that if they're my only source of income, it will suck the joy out of it."

"Okay. That's fair. What do you do for enjoyment?"

"I write, I guess." The moment the words left my lips, I regretted it.

Annie, however, lit up like a sparkler on the Fourth of July. "What sorts of things do you write?"

I pulled my hand away and shifted uncomfortably in my seat. My eyes scanned the room, hoping our server would arrive with our food, anything to deflect from the question. My writing was deeply personal. It was how I processed all the shit life had handed me. No one, not Carmen or even Jamie, had ever seen my writing.

"It's okay, sweet boy," she said softly, her voice comforting me in a way no one else's ever had. "You don't have to share it with me. Sharing something you've created opens yourself up to a unique kind of vulnerability. It's like giving away pieces of your soul for someone else's scrutiny, knowing that those pieces might never be given back in quite the same way."

My eyes locked on hers, my heart hammering in my chest. That's exactly how it felt. How could she know?

Our server arrived at that moment, efficiently delivering plates of food, but I couldn't take my eyes off Annie's. The server asked if we needed anything else, and our eye contact was broken as Annie mumbled a response that I didn't bother to listen to.

"How did you—"

"—know?" she finished for me. She speared a strawberry with her fork and popped it into her mouth, contemplating her words as she chewed. My food sat untouched in front of me. "I didn't start my college career as an education major. I went for creative writing. I always enjoyed writing as a kid, making up stories and writing them down, but when I was in my teen years, I really fell in love with the art. My teachers always gave me high marks, so I decided to turn my passion into my major with the hopes that someday it would become my career. I wanted to be the next great novelist." She popped another strawberry into her mouth.

"What happened?" I asked, desperately wanting to know the rest of the story.

"Eat," she said.

"What?"

"Eat," she repeated, nodding toward my plate of what were likely now lukewarm pancakes. I sighed but reached for the syrup, knowing she wouldn't finish her story if I didn't dig in. She seemed satisfied after I took my first bite and finally continued.

"My first year of school was great. My grades were good, though there were a lot of non-major courses that first year, but still, I really enjoyed the one entry-level English course and made good grades there too." I shoveled in more pancakes as she continued.

"My second year was like a whole new ballgame. My classes were harder, the course load was more intense, and I had a misogynistic asshole of a professor for two of my required English classes. None of the work I submitted was good enough for him. His grading practices were completely unfair. Women consistently earned lower marks than the men in his classes, and he was known for favoring men when recommending internships with publishing houses and literary agents. I tried to go to the dean of the department but was shrugged off and dismissed from his office.

"By the end of the semester, I was so defeated that I began to look into options for changing my major. The department was small enough that if I kept on the same track, I'd likely have him for at least one more junior-level class, and I just couldn't stomach dealing with him again.

As it turned out, those classes he taught were required coursework for bachelor of arts students, but education students seeking an English endorsement had more flexibility in their course options. And with the coursework I'd already taken, I could change majors and still graduate on time as long as I took a couple of education courses over the summer."

"That's bullshit," I said, outraged. "That asshole should have been dismissed from his position."

She shrugged as she popped a grape into her mouth. "He had tenure and this was the nineties. Even now, women have an uphill battle when they make any sort of claim against a male professor. Thirty years ago, it was nearly impossible. And as a woman just barely out of her teens, I didn't have the fortitude or the tools to press the issue."

"Do you regret it? Changing majors?"

"No. If something like that happened today, I might handle it differently, but as it turned out, I fell in love with teaching. And because I'd had a professor like that, I strove to make sure I treated students fairly and with compassion. I never wanted any of my kids to feel like that in my classroom." She finished the last piece of her fruit and then started on her toast. I was happy to see her eating.

"What about your dream of becoming a writer?" I polished off my pancakes and started in on my bacon.

"Who says I don't write? Just because I'm not a published author doesn't mean I'm not a writer."

"Would you ever show me something you've written?" I asked. I was dying to see some of her work.

"I'll show you mine if you'll show me yours." Her eyes twinkled as she spread jam across her second piece of toast.

"Oh, that's low." I chuckled. "I didn't know you had it in you."

"You have no idea."

I shook my head, smiling at her sass. "I appreciate what you're saying, and up until recently, I hadn't given any thought to pursuing anything beyond my current job, but maybe I do want something more. I just don't know what that might be. I still don't have the money for college, and I have no idea what kind of writer I might be or if that's even something I'd want to do seriously." Even contemplating the idea of pursuing a career felt overwhelming. I felt like one of those colorblind people who'd been given special glasses and could now see all the vibrant colors around me. It was amazing and mind-boggling all at the same time. In some ways, it had been easier when everything was dull.

"You don't have to decide anything today, or even tomorrow, or next week. In fact, nothing ever has to change if you don't want it to. I'm not trying to pressure you into something you don't want. Jamie and I will love you no matter what you do." I swallowed past the lump in my throat. I didn't think I'd ever get used to how easily she threw out words like *love* when it came to me. "I just don't want you to settle because you never gave yourself a chance to think bigger. You deserve that, sweet boy."

I didn't know what to say, so I settled with, "Thank you. I'll, um, I'll give it some thought."

"Good. Now, what should we make for dinner to celebrate Jamie's first day?"

We finished breakfast, talking about dinner ideas for Jamie and speculating about how his first day was going, but the entire time my mind swirled with possibilities.

CHAPTER 27
JAMIE

THE FIRST DAY of my student-teaching assignment was... surreal. After all the coursework, a change in universities, and my mom's illness, I was finally living my dream.

The day had started with professional development revolving around combing through data and looking at which students needed more support to be successful. My student-teaching assignment was seventh-grade English, so I spent the morning with other seventh-grade teachers who all worked together on the same team.

Mitchell Davis, my cooperating teacher, had been at Swope for the last six years, though he'd been teaching for closer to twenty. I'd met him a few times through my mom, but since he'd come to Swope after I'd been through as a student, I didn't know him well.

Susan Lakes was the history teacher and was about the same age as my mom. She'd been hired at Swope the same year as Mom, and they'd been friends for just as long. She'd given me a sad smile when I'd walked in, and I'd caught her looking at me with pity a few times when she thought I wasn't looking.

Luis Lopez, Leslie Dawson, and Julie Stephens rounded out the rest of the team, teaching science, math, and reading. Those three were all in their first three to five years of teaching and closer to my age, which was nice. I hoped we'd get the chance to hang out. I'd had a lot of friends back at KU, but since I'd come home to help take care of Mom, I hadn't had time to form new friendships.

The morning was a blur of sifting through data until our eyes crossed, commiserating about problem behaviors from students and their parents, strategizing how to help students who were underperforming, all mixed in with talk about what everyone did over their break and flipping each other shit. I soaked up every bit of it. Despite the sarcasm and grumbling, I could tell these teachers really cared about their students and were dedicated to finding ways to help them achieve. I was eager to learn from all of them.

After running out for a quick lunch at Chipotle, Mitchell and I spent the afternoon working on lesson plans, making copies, and orienting me to the building. I knew my way around, of course, but he still took me around to introduce me to the staff and showed me the new gym addition that had been built a couple of years ago to replace the small, aging auditorium.

Back in the classroom, I sat at one of the student desks sorting out the poetry packets we would be giving the students tomorrow. Mitchell tossed his pen on his desk and leaned back in his chair behind his desk. "Your mom was one of the best. I was bummed to hear she wasn't coming back this year."

I looked up at him, pausing in the midst of counting out another stack of packets. My blood ran cold. She hadn't retired, she'd just taken a year's leave so she could fight her illness, and while I knew there was a very real possibility the cancer could take her from us, I wasn't yet willing to entertain the thought that she might not be back at Swope next year. "Is. She *is* one of the best."

"Shit," he muttered, running his hand through his hair. "I'm sorry. You're right." He let out a frustrated breath. "How is she doing?"

I let out my own breath, feeling the anger leave with it. He was my mom's friend and colleague, and he meant well. "She's stable. She had a scan today, and it looks like the tumors aren't shrinking as much as they'd hoped, but they aren't getting larger either, so that's somewhat promising. They are going to try a different combination of meds and see if they can push this thing in the right direction."

Finn had called earlier with the update, and while it wasn't the progress we'd been hoping for, anytime the tumors hadn't grown or spread was counted as a win with this kind of aggressive cancer.

"Good, good," he said, looking at me with a mixture of pity and sadness. I hated that look the most. He cleared his throat before saying, "You know, when I came to this school, I'd taught high school English for nearly fifteen years, and while I was smart enough to know that I didn't know everything about teaching, I thought I had a pretty good idea. Teaching seventh graders couldn't be that much different from teaching freshmen, right?" He chuckled, but I didn't respond, waiting for him to continue. "My first several weeks here were absolute hell. Kids made fun of my glasses, my haircut, my shoes... They were brutal. They hid my stapler, stole candy out of my desk drawer, ripped up worksheets and left them in tiny little pieces all over my floor. They refused to do their work, refused to put away their phones, refused to do pretty much anything I asked them to. I tried the dictator approach. I assigned detentions and sent office referrals. I sent emails home and scheduled parent meetings. Nothing helped. My classroom was out of control, and I had absolutely no idea what to do about it."

He took his glasses off and scrubbed his face before putting them back in place. I was rapt now. I wasn't sure where this story was leading, but he'd just described some of my biggest fears. I'd always been pretty good with kids at the camps I worked at, but teaching was different from being a camp counselor or swim instructor.

"I was sitting here at my desk after school one day, head in my hands, contemplating leaving the teaching profession altogether, though unsure how I was going to afford to break my contract, when your mom came in. She asked how things were going, and I just unloaded. All the bullshit I'd dealt with. Student behaviors. Parental accusations. All of it.

"Annie listened to me go off for probably twenty minutes straight, and when I finally stopped, she asked me who my worst student was. I didn't know how to choose when there were so many, but I settled on Johnny Jeffries. He'd called me 'Douchie Davis' right to my face, and despite being assigned in-school suspension, he continued to be a little shit in my class.

"Your mom looked right at me and said, 'Tell me one good thing about Johnny.' I couldn't think of anything. I just stared at her blankly. This kid had made my life a living hell for weeks, and I couldn't think of a single redeeming qual-ity. It kind of pissed me off, if I'm being honest. I wanted your mom to sympathize with me, not give me some guilt trip because I didn't like this kid." I smiled at him. That sounded just like Mom.

"Your mom, she wasn't going to let me off easy. She reminded me that he was a twelve-year-old kid, and I was the adult in the room. She told me his parents had separated over the summer, and it had gotten ugly. His mom was already seeing someone new who also had several kids, and his dad was fighting for full custody but had had a drug charge in his early twenties and courts tended to favor mothers in these situations. The point she made in all of that is that kids will be assholes for all sorts of reasons, but that's just the thing...there is always a reason. She taught me to look deeper."

She'd taught me that too. My dad and my mom both taught me to listen and look deeper. It's why I'd been so persistent with Finn. I knew there was depth behind the attitude he used as a front to keep the world out.

"I'm scared I won't live up to her," I admitted.

"You won't. No one will ever be quite like Annie. But that doesn't mean you won't be an amazing teacher. Don't worry about trying to emulate your mom or put a lot of pressure on yourself to live up to some impossibly high standard of what you think she'd want you to be. Just be the best teacher *you* can be. That's all any of us can do."

He was right. I'd never be the person my mom was. And there was a relief in that. There could never be another Annie Felton. So rather than trying to live up to some impossible standard of the teacher I thought I should be, I should embrace who I already was.

Something deep inside of me unknotted, and for the first time in days, I relaxed.

"Come on, kid," Mitchell said as he stood and grabbed his coat off the back of his chair. "Let's get out of here. We've done enough for today."

By the end of my first week, I was exhausted. Tuesday, the first day with students, I'd fallen asleep on the couch just after dinner, around seven-thirty. Finn had come home from his gig at Ivory later that evening and woken me up to drag me to my bedroom. He'd undressed me and helped me into bed like I was a drunk frat boy at a kegger. Wednesday hadn't been much better, although that night, I'd at least lasted an extra hour. I'd tried to cop a feel with Finn as we'd undressed, but by the time he'd gotten back to the bed from brushing his teeth, I'd already been asleep. Last night, he'd stayed at his own place, saying that he needed to spend some time with Carmen and get some chores done that he'd been putting off. I'd pouted, but the fact was, I'd been too tired to fight him. Aunt Cathy had been over that day and had stocked our fridge with more meals, so I'd heated up some pasta for Mom and me and then crashed.

I couldn't believe how tired I was, and I hadn't even done much actual teaching yet. Mostly, I'd spent time observing Mitchell in action and had helped grade papers. I hadn't even led any small-group instruction yet, let alone a full-blown class lesson. I couldn't imagine how tired I'd be then. Mom said it was normal. There's no tired like first-week-of-school teacher tired.

Friday night, though, I was determined to stay awake and spend some quality time with Finn. He'd spent the day with Mom, but Aunt Cathy was coming over to hang out with her while Finn and I doubled with Carmen and Isa, who was in town for the weekend.

We were getting ready in my room, but I kept getting distracted, watching as he swapped out an old pair of jeans for a newer pair of dark-washed denim. I watched as he slid those pants up his lean thighs and admired the way they hugged his ass. He moved his hips a little from side to side, and I looked up to see humor dancing in his eyes as he watched me in the mirror. Busted. I grinned at him shamelessly and walked over to hug him from behind.

He'd already shrugged on his button-down but had yet to do up the buttons, so I took the opportunity to slide my hands under the fabric and run my palms up his chest. I kept my eyes locked on his in the mirror as I flicked his nipple with my thumb. His breath caught, but he kept his eyes trained on mine, the humor there replaced with heat. I pressed my hips into his as I held him to me, my cock cradled in the cleft of his ass. Even through layers of cotton and denim, I could feel his heat as I thrust against him in suggestion.

It had been nearly a week since we'd done anything more intimate than kiss, and I wanted him desperately.

Our eyes finally broke contact when he dropped his head back on my shoulder, baring his neck to me in invitation. I licked a path up the column of his throat, where I then nipped along his jawline until he was forced to turn his body into mine so I could attack his mouth in a kiss.

I licked into his mouth, his tongue eagerly meeting mine as we kissed, hungry and desperate for each other. He turned all the way so he was facing me, chest pressed to mine, cocks grinding against each other. He hadn't done up the fly of his jeans, so I reached between us, shoving my hand roughly into his briefs to take his hard length in my hand.

His breath stuttered as I stroked him, rubbing my thumb over his tip, smearing the bead of precum around his head, using it as lubricant. "We're going to be late," he whispered against my lips.

"I hate to say it, but I don't think this is going to take long." I shoved the shirt off his shoulders and bent to pull a nipple into my mouth. He hissed in response. "God, I think you're right. Need you."

Without warning, he pulled out of my hands and dropped to his knees in front of me. He yanked open the front of my jeans and roughly shoved them, along with my briefs, down my thighs. My cock sprang free, jutting proudly from my body, eagerly awaiting the wet heat of his mouth.

"Jesus," I said, the sight of him on the floor in front of me nearly bringing me to my own knees. "Fuck, Finn. You are so goddamned beautiful like this. On your knees for me. Lips swollen and red. You gonna suck me down? Make me come? Make me lose my fucking mind?"

In answer, he leaned forward, wrapped his lips around my dick, and slid down my length until I hit the back of his throat. I gripped his hair, tangling my fingers in the strands, holding him to me for a moment. I was on a hair trigger. Any movement from him and this would be all over before it started. "Shit, baby. Damn. Go slow, or I'm going to lose it." Eyes locked on mine, he swallowed around me, and it was game over. I unloaded down his throat in an endless stream, and he swallowed every last drop. I pulled out of his mouth and yanked him to his feet, slamming my mouth down on his in a fierce kiss. The taste of myself on his lips drove me mad as I licked at him and he whimpered against me.

I pulled away and turned us so I could shove him down on the bed. I kicked the rest of the way out of my pants and briefs, watching while he did the same. I yanked open the drawer to my side table, pulling out lube and a condom. I lubed my fingers before tossing the supplies on the bed next to him. "Handle that," I said as I quickly worked myself open. By the time he had rolled the condom on and lubed himself, I was ready. Or at least ready enough.

I couldn't wait any longer. I needed him inside me. I needed to feel that connection to him. There were so many ways he'd supported me this week and made me feel loved, but nothing could replace the connection I felt with him when we were joined in this way, when he was inside me or I was inside him. When there was nothing but the two of us together, wrapped around each other, souls entwined.

I placed the blunt head of his cock at my entrance and slowly slid down his length until I was seated on him fully. I held myself there a moment, allowing the burn to ease as my body stretched to accommodate him. Finn's hands gripped my hips, holding me in place as we struggled to control our racing heartbeats.

I leaned forward, gasping at the feel of him inside me as the angle changed. I kissed his forehead, then pulled back to look into his eyes. His pupils were blown wide. Those blue pools held endless depths I could fall into forever. "Nothing feels as good or right as when we come together like this. I love you, Finn."

"Love you too. So much," he said, squeezing my hips again as I began to move. My cock hadn't fully recovered from my orgasm moments ago, but I didn't care. This wasn't about getting off again, not anymore. My initial actions had been motivated by lust, but now, I simply wanted to show him with every fiber of my being how good he made me feel. How important he was to me. How special he was in my life. I wanted him to feel good, wanted him to come, but I also wanted his soul to know without a doubt that it belonged to me and mine belonged to him.

I moved in slow-motion, pulling off almost to his tip before sliding back down. His eyes fluttered closed, his eyebrows pinching together as I moved up and down, maintaining that slow, delicious rhythm. Finn's hands moved from my hips back to my ass as he tried to pull me closer to him. "Faster, Jamie. Please."

His voice was needy and desperate, and I leaned forward and took his mouth in a kiss as I bowed to his demands. I picked up the pace, my half-hard cock trying valiantly to rally as it was trapped between us, his abs providing delicious friction as I moved up and down. Impatient, he thrust his hips up, and I gasped as he pegged my prostate, a delicious sensation shooting through my body like a jolt of electricity. "More, Jamie. Come on. I need more." His voice was whiny with need as I began to move in faster, more shallow strokes, but Finn decided to take matters into his own hands, rolling us so he was on top. He pushed my legs toward my chest as he set a rapid pace, his movements almost frantic as he chased his release.

While I hadn't cared moments ago about getting off a second time in favor of making sure Finn felt good, my cock had other ideas. As Finn pounded my prostate over and over again, my cock fully hardened between us, and I felt the telltale sign of my orgasm flutter along my spine.

The sight of Finn above me, eyebrows drawn together in fierce concentration, sweat running down his temples, frantic need in his eyes...I knew at that moment that I would remember that look on his face for the rest of my life. "Come on, baby. Let go. Come for me." His eyes popped open, boring into mine as he thrust one more time and held there, his cock jerking inside me. The sounds coming out of him were guttural as he pulsed, ripping my second orgasm from me. He leaned down and kissed me through it, sweat dripping from his face to mine, my release spreading between our bellies.

Sated, he collapsed on top of me, rolling over to his side and resting his head on my shoulder as we both struggled to catch our breath. His phone buzzed on the nightstand, and he reached over to grab it. He swiped open the screen, holding it in front of us where we could both see the incoming message from Carmen. He groaned as he read it.

CICI

We're here. Got a table in the back corner past the bar

He flipped open the camera and took a quick selfie of us, bare chests exposed, mussed-up hair, and sweaty faces. There would be no doubt about what we'd been up to. Quickly, he attached the picture and sent off a response.

FINN

We're going to be late

I looked at him and grinned. "I can't believe you just did that."

A shrug was his only response, along with a shit-eating grin. The phone buzzed with another incoming message.

CICI

Dick

You're buying the first round

FINN

Worth it

JANUARY MOVED INTO FEBRUARY, and Jamie and I grew closer despite our crazy schedules. I took turns with Aunt Cathy, taking Annie to appointments or just hanging out with her when I wasn't working at The Daily Grind. I treasured my time with her. She seemed happy to stand in as the mother figure my own mother should have been.

Jamie adjusted to a teacher's daily schedule and eventually figured out how to stay awake in the evenings, though he often brought papers home to grade or spent time reading whatever novel the kids were studying to stay ahead of the material.

I still kept my weekly gigs at Ivory but scaled them back to once a week so I could spend more time with Jamie. Carmen was helping out with rent since, let's face it, I barely lived there anyway, so financially, I was a little more comfortable. When Jamie wasn't grading papers, he and Annie found something to binge-watch on TV while I wrote.

I'd become more intentional with my writing, trying to determine whether I had something to say that anyone else would actually want to read. Over the years, my writing had been something I'd done for myself. All that time spent crafting sentences and paragraphs, lines and stanzas, had never been done with the intention that it would ever, ever be for anyone else's eyes. It had been a tool for processing my shitty excuse for an existence, something to help me bide my time as I moved through my life little more than a ghost of a human in a shell of a body.

But now...now I thought I might want to publish something. And that was terrifying. I labored over every word and turn of phrase, sometimes crippled with indecision, and I worried that perhaps trying to make a go at this might suck the enjoyment out of it for much the same reason I'd balked at the idea of making music my career.

But every so often, I got absolutely lost in the worlds I created on paper, and the words flowed on and on for hours until I looked up to realize I was alone on the couch with the TV off and a single lamp on next to me, not having noticed that Jamie and Annie had gone to bed.

In those moments, I thought I might actually be able to make a go at this.

Jamie must have noticed how much more time I spent with my pen pressed to paper, but he never said a word, just sat alongside me grading papers, his foot resting on my knee as I scratched out line after line.

Annie occasionally shot a knowing look in my direction, and I sometimes thought I might detect pride reflected there. I so badly wanted that to be the case. What would it be like to have someone actually be proud of something I'd done? The moment I gave it too much thought, I became crippled with the weight of the pressure, so I tried to push those thoughts aside. Most of the time, I was successful.

At the beginning of March, Annie developed a bit of a

cough. As it was the height of cold and flu season, we'd been careful not to take her out except to her appointments, but Jamie feared he'd brought some germs home from school. He took a day off from his teaching assignment so we could take her to the doctor.

The doctor listened to her lungs and then immediately ordered us to take her to the hospital for suspected pneumonia. Upon arrival, she was admitted and taken for an x-ray, where it was confirmed that she had pneumonia in both lungs.

Jamie was a wreck. He blamed himself and was terrified of what this could mean for his mom. She'd come so far in her treatments only to be set back with this complication.

She insisted he return to school the following day, saying he needed to keep up with his student teaching. He was so close to graduation, and she refused to be the reason he didn't graduate on time. He'd only relented when I promised to take some time off from The Daily Grind so I could stay with her during the day.

Jamie and I arrived at the hospital together first thing in the morning. He insisted on seeing her before heading to school for the day, so we took two cars. After visiting with her for a few moments and placing a gentle kiss on her forehead, he left reluctantly, assuring her he'd be back after school.

The worried look in his eyes as he turned at the door before leaving nearly broke me. I'd held him most of the night, neither of us sleeping much in the midst of our worry. As a result, he had deep circles under his eyes and his skin was pale. I tried to give him a reassuring smile before he turned to go, but I was fairly certain he saw right through it. He nodded once and then was gone.

"He didn't sleep last night, did he?" Annie asked, her

words stilted as she struggled to breathe. She had a nasal cannula in place to help with her oxygen and an IV in her arm to help fight the infection causing the pneumonia, and my eyes traveled along the length of several other wires traveling from underneath her gown to machines next to the bed, monitoring who knew what.

I forced my eyes back up, attempting to fix a smile on my face that I knew likely didn't reach my eyes. I wanted to lie, to reassure her so she wouldn't worry, but I knew she'd see right through the bullshit, so I didn't bother, opting for honesty instead. "No. Neither one of us slept well."

"He needs rest so he can focus on his student teaching."

I raised an eyebrow. "Would you be able to rest if it was him lying here in this bed and not you?"

"Pfft. We're not talking about me." She chuckled, but it turned into a cough. I started to panic when she continued to cough, but she finally got it under control and laid back, a bead of sweat on her brow from her exertions. I reached for the large cup and straw next to her and held it to her lips so she could take a drink.

"I'm okay, sweet boy. Sit." I set the oversized water cup on the tray beside her and did as she asked. I crossed my feet at my ankles and rubbed my sweaty palms up and down the legs of my jeans. Then I recrossed my ankles the other way. I didn't know what to say or how to act. I'd never been in a hospital before we'd brought her in last night. I felt anxious, like I should be doing something or like I was in the way. I didn't know. I felt uncomfortable in my skin, like there was a vibration just underneath the surface, and I thought I was going to lose my mind.

"Finn?"

My eyes snapped to hers. "Yeah?"

"I asked how your writing was going."

"You did?"

"Yeah, honey. I asked twice." There was sympathy in her eyes. I guessed she knew how uncomfortable I was. I certainly wasn't doing a good job of hiding it.

"I'm sorry. Um, it's fine, I guess."

"Just fine? What genre are you working on? Did you decide on poetry or one of your short stories?"

I felt heat rise up my neck, through my cheeks, all the way to my ears, and my eyes dropped to my lap.

"Erotica?" she asked. My eyes shot up, my eyebrows nearly meeting my hairline, and my mouth open in shock. "What?! No, why would you think—"

Her eyes twinkled in merriment. "It was the only thing I could think of that might make you blush like that."

I relaxed a bit. "Oh, um. No, it's nothing like that."

"Okay..." It wasn't a question, but her tone said she was waiting for more.

"It's just...I'm uh...I'm-writing-a-romance," I mumbled out in a rush of words.

"Romance?" she asked, her tone laced with surprise.

"Yeah. I've never been in a relationship before, um, before Jamie." I could feel myself flushing again, but I pushed through. "So I thought if I wrote a romance, it might help me process all these things I'm feeling."

"Oh, sweet boy. That's lovely." Her face softened into an emotion I wasn't sure I could identify.

"You don't think it's weird?" I asked.

"Why would I think that?"

"I don't know. I don't know what the hell I'm doing with this whole relationship thing. And I guess, well, I've never even read a romance. How the hell should I know how to write one?"

"Oh, honey. None of us knows what we're doing when

it comes to love. You make Jamie happy, so you must be doing something right." She winked at me, and I chuckled. "You just keep writing from the heart, and I've no doubt it will be beautiful."

I wasn't even remotely convinced, but she seemed so sure, so confident in my abilities, that I didn't want to ruin that notion for her.

Her eyes began to droop, so I suggested she get some rest while I pulled my notebook out and began to write.

***

JAMIE ARRIVED at the hospital in the afternoon after school, his eyes looking just as exhausted as they had this morning but also alight with something else. Excitement, maybe.

Annie was sleeping, as she had done off and on throughout the day between visits from Aunt Cathy and the various doctors who came in to run their tests and update her chart. At the sight of him coming through the door, I immediately hopped out of my seat on the small loveseat to give him my spot next to her while I took the spot on his other side. He sank into it gratefully, his eyes never leaving her face as he whispered, "How is she?"

"Tired, mostly. She has coughing spells from time to time, but the nurse says that's good because it helps her get all that junk out of her lungs." I placed my hand on his thigh, trying somehow to offer my support. "The coughing spells wear her out, though, so she's slept quite a bit in between."

He sat for a bit, her small hand clasped in his much larger one, watching her breathe in and out, the faint wheeze of her breathing mixed with the beeping of the machines and the soft whir of the filtered air pumping in and out of the room. At length, I broke the silence, quietly asking him how his day was.

"The morning was awful. I couldn't stop thinking about Mom and feeling guilty that I wasn't here, but Mitchell forced me to teach the afternoon lessons, which was a good distraction." He finally turned to look at me, and I could see the enthusiasm in his eyes. "I actually had a pretty good lesson with that last class. We had a great discussion about *The Outsiders*, and it was so awesome to see the kids making connections about social status and preconceived bias from a book written over sixty years ago to society today. Like they were asking questions and challenging each other's ideas in such a thoughtful way. It was amazing!"

I smiled at him. I couldn't help it. He was so earnest in his excitement. Jamie was already beautiful, but when he lit up like that, it was impossible not to fall in love with him just a little more. Those kids were so damn lucky to have him.

"That's amazing, baby." I leaned forward and gave him a quick kiss. "I love that for you."

"Thanks." The light in his eyes dimmed just a little, and he turned back to Annie. "I just wish I could do something for her, you know? I feel so damn helpless."

"I know. But I think the best thing you can do for her is to just keep your teaching commitment. I think she worries less when you're off doing your thing."

"But what if...?" His voice shook, and he struggled to speak. "What if I'm at school, and she...what if I'm spending her last moments at school when I could be spending them here with her?"

God, how did I answer that? I knew how much it meant to her that he was following his dream, following in her footsteps, but could I blame him for wanting to be here? I didn't think anything could keep me from his side if it was him lying in that bed.

Unable to come up with a suitable answer, I watched as a tear fell down his cheek, then another and another, each landing on the front of his sweater. He didn't bother to wipe them away, just let them fall quietly, a manifestation of the pain he couldn't hold inside.

I let my own tears fall along with him.

I SPENT every moment of visiting hours with Mom over the weekend. Aunt Cathy and her family stopped by again, this time with flowers and balloons, trying to add cheer to the dreary, impersonal space. Finn popped in for a brief visit on Saturday and again on Sunday, but he spent most of the weekend working at The Daily Grind and Ivory, trying to make up for the hours he'd missed during the week. He had a hard time walking out of the room each time, as he'd really grown quite attached to Mom, but he'd felt like he needed to work. I also suspected he wanted to give us some time alone. I was grateful for that, and as much as I missed him, there wasn't anything that could have taken me from her side.

When Mom was awake, we spent our time talking about how things were going at school and catching up on all the staff gossip. We talked about all the bizarre things middle school kids do and the things I never thought I'd say. I had actually told a kid not to lick the floor in the cafeteria last week. I shared the news of Julie's engagement to her longtime boyfriend. They were planning a destination wedding next winter in Jamaica. We talked about the girl who had come to school in the same outfit three days in a row and how Mitchell and I had worked with the counselors to get her some new clothes. Turns out her dad had lost his job, and they were bouncing between family members until they could get back on their feet. Things like that didn't often happen at a school in an affluent area like Swope, but it showed that homelessness could happen to anyone, anywhere.

And I told her about the little rubber duckies the students had randomly started bringing in to school and stashing all over the classroom. One had just appeared one day right next to the pencil sharpener, and since we found it amusing, we left it. The next day, we found another on a shelf between some extra textbooks we kept on hand when students forgot theirs. By the end of the week, we'd counted twenty-four ducks in various sizes and colors, all stashed about the room. We had no idea who was doing it, I suspected it was a group effort, but it was just the kind of silliness I needed right now in the midst of watching Mom's health decline.

And it *had* declined. Scans on Sunday had shown no change in her lungs, and in fact, her breathing seemed to be more and more labored. She slept more when I was there, so those times she was awake felt like priceless gifts, and I took advantage of them as much as possible.

It felt like she was slipping away right before my eyes. Each day, hour, moment, she seemed more frail than the last. Gone was the vibrant woman of my youth with an infectious laugh and a smile that drew everyone to her. In her place was someone I barely recognized. Cancer treatments had taken her hair and so much of her weight months ago. The pneumonia was taking the rest, taking every last bit of her vitality until she barely had the energy to open her eyes.

It was unbearable to watch, yet, I couldn't bring myself to leave her side.

Sunday evening, I walked into my house after spending the day with Mom and couldn't remember a bit of the drive home. I dropped my keys on the kitchen counter as I passed through and walked into the living room, unsure what I was doing there. I crossed over to the French doors that led to the backyard and stood staring out into the dark.

I hadn't even realized Finn was home until I felt his arms come around me from behind. He didn't say a word, simply held me as I continued to stare into the void, not really seeing anything beyond our reflection in the glass of the door. I thought I should cry, or perhaps scream, but I did none of those things. I was numb.

"Did you eat?" Finn asked. I felt the movement of his jaw as he asked his question with his face pressed against the back of my neck.

I shrugged. Had I eaten? I couldn't remember. It didn't matter. I wasn't hungry anyway.

"Baby, you have to eat." He let go of me only to grab my hand and tug me toward the kitchen. I took a few steps, following behind him, but then stopped, digging my feet into the carpet in protest.

He turned, concern etched into his features, though he didn't say anything.

"Take me to bed."

He took a step forward, brushing a stray hair off my cheek. "You need to eat," he repeated.

I shook my head. "No. I need you." I turned and pulled him in the other direction toward my bedroom. Really, my temporary bedroom since I'd moved in there when Mom got sick. Had I even shown Finn my real bedroom? The one upstairs that I grew up in with pictures and posters and perfect attendance certificates hanging on the walls? I couldn't remember.

We crossed the threshold, and I was hit with a wave of contradictory feelings. I wanted to hate this room. It served as a reminder of Mom's illness. But these walls also bore witness to the love Finn and I had professed for each other, both with our words and our bodies.

I wanted that again. I wanted to feel him. I wanted to feel anything besides this numb desolation.

"Make love to me, Finn. Please," I said as I took off my shirt.

"Jamie..."

I felt a flash of anger at his hesitation.

"Dammit, Finn. I need this. Make me forget." I pulled him into me, drawing our hands against my bare chest. "*Please.*"

He let go of whatever resistance he'd been holding on to, nodding once before stepping back and removing his shirt, followed by his sweats and briefs. I watched, unmoving, as he revealed each new sliver of skin, my cock lengthening at the sight of his body bared in front of me.

He stepped back toward me, reaching for the waistband of my joggers and drawing them down to the floor, where I stepped out of them, kicking them aside. As I stood, he palmed my erection through the fabric of my briefs, eliciting a groan from me.

He turned his face toward me, his lips millimeters away from mine, and said, "Tell me what you need, Jamie. You want it fast? Slow? Top? Bottom? Tell me."

I closed my eyes. "I don't know, Finn. Just...I just need to not think. Can you...?"

"Shh," he whispered against my lips. "I've got you."

Without warning, he shoved me roughly down on the bed. He yanked my briefs down, my cock slapping against my belly, red and aching. He climbed up to straddle me, roughly pressing his pelvis into mine. I hissed at the feel of his dick sliding against mine and thrust my hips up involuntarily in response.

He leaned forward and took my mouth in a bruising kiss as we rutted against each other. Relief rippled through me as I gave myself over to him. This was what I hadn't even known I wanted. I didn't want to think, only to feel. My hands reached around to his ass, grabbing a handful and pulling him into me, trying to control the rhythm and pace of our thrusting, but Finn wasn't having it. He yanked himself out of my hands and off my body.

I was instantly cold, the heat of his body taken from me, and I sat up, trying to reach for him. "No," he said, his voice firm. "You gave control over to me." My blood surged, white-hot in my veins at his display of dominance, heating my skin that had been cold only moments before. "Roll over, ass up," he said, his voice sharp and commanding. I hurried to comply.

The bed shifted, and I heard the sound of the drawer opening next to the bed as he pulled out the lube. We'd dispensed with condoms a couple of weeks ago after our tests came back negative. I heard the telltale click of the lube and pressed my ass up in anticipation.

His hands grasped my hips, pulling me toward him, and anticipating the press of his cockhead or his fingers, I was surprised to feel his hot breath against my hole moments before he licked a stripe up my crack from taint to tailbone. "Fuck," I ground out, arching my back as sensations rippled through my body. "You liked that, didn't you?" he asked. "The pretty boy likes it dirty, doesn't he?"

I couldn't even form words to respond before he went at me again, this time focusing his attention exclusively on my hole. "Again," I demanded. "Fuck, do that again!"

His tongue lapped at my entrance, wet and hot against my sensitive skin as he deftly ate my asshole like a fucking four-course meal. I writhed beneath him, tearing the bedding from the mattress and biting the pillow as every point of my being was centered on that one spot on my body. With one hand gripping my ass, the other reached under me to roll my balls between his fingers, and I nearly came on the spot.

I tried to pull away from him, not wanting to come until he'd buried himself inside me, but he only yanked me back to him, this time adding a finger in with his tongue. I could feel his saliva running down my crack and over my balls. "Please, Finn," I whined, not even recognizing the sound of my voice in this state.

Finn sat up, and I hissed as I felt the cool trickle of lube on my hole as he continued to deftly work me open, adding a second finger and then a third before I finally felt his dick at my entrance. "I'm ready, Finn. Just give it to me."

I felt the sharp crack of a slap against my ass, and I let loose a wail followed by a string of curses. "Fuuuuck. Shit. Goddamn." My eyes watered at the sting even as my dick jumped in response, and before I could decide whether I liked it or not, Finn slammed home, sheathing himself inside me in one deep stroke. The sound I made was feral as my body stretched to accommodate him. "Move, dammit," I ground out. I felt him every-fucking-where. I was being torn in two, so full of him that I thought he'd be permanently a part of me.

He pulled back, almost all the way out, and slammed home again. I grunted, clenching my ass around him, willing him to give me more. To give me the pounding I so desperately wanted. He pulled out again, but this time, he pulled me up with him, slamming up and into me, impaling me on his dick as I straddled his lap. He wrapped his arm around me, pulling my back to his chest, and began fucking into me in short, fast strokes.

"Yessss," I hissed, though I choked on it when he hit my prostate on the next stroke. And once he found that button, he hit it over and over again like it was the damn jackpot. I reached down to wrap my hand around my dick, not even bothering to find the lube or lick my palm. I didn't care if I was jerking myself dry. I just needed to get off like I needed my next breath.

Finn broke rhythm for a fraction of a second before batting my hand away and wrapping his slicked-up hand around me. He continued to pound me, stroking my erection in time with his thrusts. His breath was hot on my shoulder, our slick bodies sliding together. "Get there," he said, and for the first time, I heard the desperation in his voice. He'd been so commanding, which was hot as fuck, but the sound of his voice now, a little bit wrecked, was even hotter, and it sent me right over the goddamned edge. Hot white ropes of cum shot across the bed, over and over, as my dick pulsed in his hand.

Finn gave an almighty shout, and his entire body stiffened underneath mine as his orgasm detonated deep inside me. It felt like it might go on forever as he rode the waves, and we both struggled to catch our breath. Eventually, I pulled off him, collapsing forward onto the bed, avoiding the wet spot and curling into a ball. Finn followed me, pulling me into him, kissing my back and shoulder as he wrapped himself around me.

Without warning, my eyes flooded and tears began streaming down my cheeks. I couldn't have stopped the torrent if I'd tried. Big, painful sobs wracked my body while Finn continued to hold me, kiss me, and whisper words of comfort from behind.

It would seem I'd grossly miscalculated. I'd wanted to fuck away the numbness so I could feel something again. Or maybe I'd wanted to forget altogether. Just anything other than what I'd been feeling when I'd arrived home tonight.

Instead, I'd tapped into a raw nerve. I'd never been able to separate sex from emotion like some people, so I should have known that sex with Finn would never elicit anything other than *big* feelings. Pain and grief washed over me so deeply that I thought I might drown in it.

She hadn't even passed yet. What would this feel like when she had? Would I survive it?

"Shh," I heard Finn whisper between gentle kisses against my skin. And "I love you" and "I'm here." I heard those things, clung to those words over and over until I fell asleep.

THE CALL CAME in at three in the morning. Annie stopped breathing around two-thirty, and because she had a DNR on file, they hadn't attempted resuscitation or intubation. Jamie had been eerily stoic when the call came through, his responses to the person on the other end of the call terse and robotic.

I'd heard most of the other side of the conversation through the phone, and still, my stomach had dropped when Jamie disconnected the call, turned to me, and said, "She's gone." He'd then promptly gotten out of bed, dressed in his clothes from the evening before, and left the room without a word.

Despite the lump in my throat and the empty, hollow feeling in my chest, my most immediate concern was Jamie, so I got up and dressed and followed him out. I found him in the kitchen, staring at the coffee pot as if he'd never seen one before. Knowing sleep was likely finished for the night, I took the pod from his hand and gently nudged him aside to prepare the machine to make two cups. While the coffee pot did its thing, I turned to lean back against the counter while Jamie just...stood there.

He stood motionless in the middle of the darkened kitchen, looking off into the distance, his blond hair loose and hanging wild around his face. It was almost like he was catatonic, and it was scaring me.

"Jamie," I tried. Nothing. "Baby," I tried again. But there wasn't a flicker of motion or acknowledgment that he heard me.

The coffee finished, and I grabbed both mugs and crossed to him, setting his on the counter next to him. I reached out and gently touched his shoulder. He flinched, his eyes flicking to mine, almost as if he'd forgotten I was there.

I motioned toward the mug. "Coffee's ready." He looked at it as if it was the first time he'd ever seen coffee before, and then, without a word, he turned and left the kitchen, leaving his mug sitting on the counter, untouched.

Concerned by this behavior, I followed him as he moved down the hall, going past his room and turning left into the room Annie had been using for months. I stood in the doorway as I watched him move about the room, touching this and that and examining the couple of pictures he'd moved in here to help it feel more comfortable for her. I wasn't sure how much time he spent moving from item to item in the small room before he finally stepped over to the bed, pulled back the covers, slid under them, and closed his eyes.

CHAPTER 31

JAMIE

WHEN I WAS TWENTY-TWO, I became an orphan.

Having experienced the loss of a parent before, one would have thought I'd be prepared to handle the death of another.

Nothing could have prepared me for this utter desolation.

I was surrounded by people, and yet, I felt completely alone.

After my father's death, there had been an initial period of sadness, followed by anger and waves of grief. Eventually, those waves had become less intense and less frequent until they'd finally settled into a dull ache at the loss of the best man I'd ever known.

After that initial grieving period, I'd continued to move through life with an optimistic attitude. I'd felt lucky that I'd had the kind of father I had in my life. I'd clung to the memories I had of him and had done my best to try to be the man my father would have wanted me to be. I wasn't always successful, but I'd intuitively known that my father wouldn't have been disappointed as long as I always tried better the next time.

And for the next twelve years after my father's passing, I successfully carried myself through life with confidence and pride tempered with humor and kindness. I'd done my best to be patient with others around me, to listen just as much as I spoke, and to lead with compassion, always.

When Mom passed, the Technicolor bubble of my life burst. Like a fragile glass ornament landing on a ceramic tile floor, the explosion was magnificent. My life hadn't simply fractured. This hadn't been a spiderweb of cracks and fissures running through a pane of glass. This was a spectacular explosion of devastation, with shards of glass landing in places that quite possibly wouldn't be discovered for years.

And in the absence of that bubble that had allowed me to see life in beautiful, vibrant color, I now saw everything in shades of blues and grays like some kind of post-apocalyptic wasteland that stretched on for as far as the eye could see.

How was it possible that everything could hurt and I could be numb at the same time?

How could I be surrounded by Finn, Asher, and Aunt Cathy and her gang and still feel so utterly, deeply alone?

How could time pass and days go by, yet each day felt the same, one after the next, an endless stretch of nothingness?

Would I feel anything good ever again?

THE DAYS FOLLOWING Annie's passing flew by in a blur. Jamie seemed incapable of handling anything, so I'd taken care of notifying Aunt Cathy, who'd then worked through handling funeral arrangements and the notification of friends and family.

I'd gotten ahold of Mitchell at Swope and arranged for Jamie to take a leave of absence for the remainder of the week. They had spring break the following week, and I hoped that perhaps by the end of that time, Jamie might be able to push through the completion of his student teaching. He was so close, and I felt some sort of obligation to Annie to make sure he finished. Still, at the rate we were going, I wasn't sure two weeks off would be enough for Jamie. I knew grief looked different for everyone, but I was deeply concerned by the state Jamie was currently in. I could only hope I could love him through it, and he'd claw himself out of this depression he seemed to have fallen into.

Asher and Joshua had stopped by, bringing food and companionship. Jamie had barely spoken to them, and though he didn't show it outwardly, I hoped the visit had helped in some way.

Mitchell dropped off a care package from several teachers at Swope that also included a giant sympathy card from his and Jamie's students. The notes they'd written all over the poster-sized card had been really sweet, proving that seventh graders weren't complete heathens after all.

Jamie seemed uninterested in reading them.

He seemed uninterested in anything. He'd taken to sleeping in Annie's room across the hall, leaving me to sleep in the room we'd been sharing before her passing.

A part of me wondered if I should go back to my apartment. The man I loved was gone, and in his place was a shell of a human who seemed completely uninterested in my presence. But I couldn't leave him. In all the times I'd pushed him away, he'd never given up on me. He'd saved me from a miserable existence, showing me that life was beautiful when you truly allowed yourself to live it, and I was determined to do the same for him, no matter how long it might take.

On the morning of the funeral, the doorbell rang, and since Jamie seemed unable to deal with whoever it might be and Aunt Cathy was busy getting things ready for the service, I made my way to the door to answer it. The moment the door was opened, I found my arms full of Carmen. She wrapped herself around me, squeezing the life out of me in the open doorway.

I'd had no idea how touch-starved I was until that very moment.

It seemed like months since Jamie had touched me, rather than just a handful of days, and while I'd gone most of my life without hugs and those little day-to-day touches,

I'd become accustomed to them since I'd started my relationship with Jamie.

The feel of her wrapped around me did something to my insides, and for the first time in days, I felt like I could take a full breath.

At length, I pulled away, taking her hand and leading her into Jamie's room. She took the desk chair while I sat on the bed facing her.

"How are you?" she asked, her dark eyes full of concern.

"I'm...I don't know, CiCi. He's just so lost. I can barely get him to acknowledge me, let alone eat. And he spends most of his time lying in her bed, but I'm not sure how much he's actually sleeping. He has dark circles under his eyes, and—"

She held up her hand, stopping me mid-sentence. "You know I love Jamie, and I do want to know how he's doing, but I asked about *you*. How are *you*?"

"Me? I'm fine. I'm just trying to do whatever I can for him."

She leaned forward and took my hand. "But, honey, who's taking care of you?"

I looked at her, my face drawn up in confusion. "What do you mean? Jamie's the one hurting. He's the one who lost his mother. You should have seen him the night before she died. He was an absolute wreck. He loves her so much. And ever since then, he's just been a zombie. It's so unlike him, and I just feel so helpless." My voice caught on that last part. "I don't know how to bring him back," I whispered, a lump forming in my throat. "How do I bring him back?"

"Honey, I don't have the answers for you. I think you're probably already doing everything you can. He has to work through this in his own time." She squeezed my hand. "But what about you? You lost her too."

"Yeah, I guess, but I...I... Oh God, I miss her so much." My face crumpled, and the dam broke, letting loose a torrent of grief so strong it bowled me over. I pitched forward into Carmen's arms as sobs wracked my body. "She was the mom I always wanted my own mother to be, and I only got her for a few months. How can it hurt this bad to lose someone I only knew for so brief a time?"

"Some people are just like that. They're like magic. They come into our lives and make an impact so deep, so profound, it shifts something in our soul so that it never looks quite the same again."

Another sob ripped from my chest. "It's not fair. It's not fair that I just found them, and I've lost her, and now it feels like I'm losing Jamie too. I was perfectly fine living my life the way I was before."

She moved over to the bed, pulling my head into her lap, stroking my hair as I cried. "But you weren't living, Finn. You were existing. That's no way to go through life."

"Why not? It sure as shit didn't hurt as much."

"I know, honey, but we have to have the bad to appreciate the good. Would you have rather not known them at all? Never felt Jamie's or Annie's love? Never known your own worth?"

I snorted. "All that shit you went through with Amy... the lying, the cheating, the manipulation...you're telling me you'd go through all that again?"

"If it brought me to Isa? Yeah, absolutely. She's worth every moment of that shit I went through. But that's not really the point I'm making. The point is that life is about *all* of it, Finn. The good and the bad, the pain *and* the joy. When you let Jamie and his family in, you let in all that stuff. And it sucks so much right now, but the good will still be there on the other side. Just don't shut it out again."

Before I could respond, a knock sounded on the door, and I heard Aunt Cathy's voice from the other side. "Finn, honey, we need to be at the church in about an hour. Can you help Jamie get dressed?"

"Yeah," I called out.

"Thanks, sweetpea. I'm going to run home to change, and I'll meet you there, okay?"

"Yeah, see you in a bit," I responded, sitting up and wiping my face. I turned to Carmen. "Will you stay? Will you go with us?"

"Of course." My shoulders sagged in immediate relief. I hadn't realized how much of the burden I'd been carrying alone.

"Thanks, CiCi. Thanks for coming over today, for always being there for me, even when I didn't know I needed you."

She shrugged. "You don't need to thank me, sweets. I'll always be here when you need me."

WE ARRIVED TO A PACKED CHURCH. It wasn't a surprise, really, considering the kind of person Annie had been and all the lives she'd touched. There was a viewing prior to the service. The line of people who came to pay their respects—made up of friends, extended family, and former students—wound down the aisle and all the way into the social hall. The service started fifteen minutes late to ensure everyone got to say their goodbyes.

Through all of it, Jamie stood stoic in the receiving line, though he did find enough of his voice to politely respond to each guest's words of condolence and any anecdotes they wanted to share. Though the light was still missing from his eyes, it was the most animated I'd seen him in nearly a week.

Once the service started, we took our seats beside Aunt Cathy's family, with Carmen sitting behind me. I wasn't particularly religious, so I paid little mind to the pastor's words, instead letting the few memories I had with Annie wash over me. The conversations we'd had. The way she'd accepted and encouraged me, never once making me feel like I wasn't good enough for her son.

Midway through the service, I rose and made my way over to the piano. Earlier in the week, Aunt Cathy had shared with me that Annie had recently amended her funeral requests asking that I play *Claire de Lune*. I'd balked, feeling awkward about fulfilling such a request, despite how close I'd felt to her in the last month. Ultimately, I'd acquiesced after Aunt Cathy had assured me that Annie had specifically wanted *this* song performed by *me*. I played most of the song looking only at the piano, but as I played the hopeful strains of the final arpeggio, I chanced a look at Jamie. His eyes were locked on me, and I caught a single tear making its way down his cheek.

I returned to my seat beside him and felt his hand reach for mine and hold on in a fierce grip. I looked at him in surprise, but his eyes were resolutely locked on the pastor, who had moved on to the next part of the ceremony. Carmen handed me a tissue from behind, and only then did I realize I'd been crying as I played.

Later that evening, after the burial at the gravesite and after the last of the guests had left following the reception, I was in Jamie's room, changing out of my dress clothes into sweats and a T-shirt. Aunt Cathy had packed up the mountains of leftover food before heading home, and Carmen had placed a kiss on my cheek and admonished me to text her the following day. I was startled when I heard a soft knock at the door that could only be Jamie.

I opened it, thinking it odd that he had knocked on his own door, but I was relieved to know he was seeking me out.

"Um, can I sleep in here?" he asked, looking like a lost little boy rather than a twenty-two-year-old man.

"Of course," I responded, stepping aside so he could make his way past me. "Let me just go brush my teeth," I said before making my way across the hall to the bathroom.

Nighttime routine completed, I returned to the room to find Jamie sitting on the edge of the bed and staring at the floor, exactly as I'd left him. I crossed over and pulled him up to stand so I could pull back the covers. He slid in without a word, and I slid in behind him, wanting so desperately to touch him, hold him, and offer him comfort, but I didn't know what he needed.

"Will you hold me?" he asked, answering my unspoken question. I held my breath for a moment, suddenly nervous, but then cautiously moved closer, wrapping my arm around his chest and carefully pulling him to me.

A moment passed, and then two, and I finally released the breath I'd been holding, closing my eyes and savoring the feel of his body pressed to mine. There wasn't anything sexual about this moment, simply the rightness of one soul recognizing its mate in the other.

All the tension left my body as I struggled to grasp my emotions. His scent, the essence of him, wrapped around me, nearly making it impossible to breathe. I felt tears prick the corners of my eyes in gratitude for this chance to hold him once more. I didn't know when I'd have the opportunity to hold him again, or if maybe this was the last time, so I tried to live in that moment. That singular moment when the world felt a little broken around us, yet there wasn't anything so perfect as the feel of him in my arms.

"I don't want to be alone anymore," Jamie whispered, his breath a puff against my skin where he'd tucked his chin into my arm.

"I'm here, baby. I'm always here."

"I could feel her in that room. That's why I slept in there. I could feel her, but now I can't. She's gone, Finn." His voice broke. "I can't feel her anymore, and I'm alone. I don't want to be alone."

I squeezed tighter. "I've got you. I'm here, and I've got you."

"Don't let go, okay?" he asked, his voice choked with tears. "Don't let go."

"I won't. I promise," I said, trying to hold back my own tears.

I listened and held him as he wept, and when his breaths finally evened out and I was sure he was asleep, I let my own tears fall as well.

CHAPTER 33
FINN

JAMIE MANAGED to find it in himself to return to school after spring break. I think the knowledge that Annie had wanted him to finish was the only thing motivating him to continue.

He had also progressed from zombie to robot, though I wasn't sure robot could be counted as progress. At least now he spoke and interacted with others. Though those interactions were devoid of almost all emotion.

After the night he returned to his own bed, he shut the door to his mom's room, and it had remained closed ever since. He continued to sleep in bed with me, though he shied away from my touch.

It hurt to have him so close and be unable to touch him, but I took comfort in the fact that at least he allowed me in his bed at all. I tried to be patient. I knew grief was a winding, hilly path rather than a flat, straight line, and I needed to allow him the space to travel that path in his own time.

On a Saturday morning in early April, I came into the house through the garage and into the kitchen. I'd taken advantage of the beautiful spring day, running shirtless in the sun. I stood at the sink, chugging water from the tap and listening to the end of my podcast, when Jamie walked in.

"Jesus, can you put a damn shirt on? You're sweating all over the kitchen. This is where we prepare food, for Christ's sake." My mouth dropped open as he shook his head in disgust and walked back into the living room.

I continued standing there for a moment, debating how to react. Jamie had been snipping at me more and more lately, making passive-aggressive comments about how I loaded the dishwasher or about the socks on the floor that had missed the hamper, but this was the first comment where he'd outright called me out on something. I'd never seen him so aggressive.

The asshole in me wanted to follow him and push back on the way he'd been treating me, but these comments were so out of character for him, and I knew they were coming from a place of pain. I finished my water, allowing my heart rate to come down before I followed him into the living room.

I dragged my shirt over my sweaty torso as I walked. A month ago, Jamie would have made some sort of suggestive comment before licking the sweat off my body, maybe even joining me in the shower, but in the wake of his grief, this is what our relationship had come down to.

The physical manifestations of our love were a memory. And I wasn't just talking about sex. The little touches, forehead kisses, hugs, and even the brush of a hand against my arm were gone. In its place was a cold emptiness, a great divide I didn't know how to cross.

And despite it all, I hadn't stopped loving him. Hadn't given up on us.

So, when I approached him as he sat on the couch,

mindlessly flipping through Netflix on the TV, I kept my tone calm as I asked, "What's wrong?"

His eyes flicked to mine, then back to the TV. "Nothing. Is it too much to ask for you to wear a shirt in the kitchen? It's gross." I didn't remind him that he'd made me breakfast shirtless the first time he'd spent the night at my place in December. This wasn't about me being shirtless, not really.

"Okay, I'll wear a shirt in the kitchen from now on. I'm sorry that upset you," I said carefully.

"Whatever," he mumbled, continuing to scroll through the Netflix options. I wasn't convinced he was actually seeing them.

Essentially dismissed from the conversation, if you could really call it that, I made my way down the hall to shower. I didn't trust myself not to say something I'd regret, and I didn't want a fight. I thought the time and space my shower would provide might give us both time to calm down. When finished, my lower half wrapped in a towel, I returned to our room to get dressed, only to find Jamie pulling hanging clothes out of the closet. He was tossing them on the bed next to another pile of folded clothes that appeared to have come from his drawers.

"What are you doing?" I asked, surveying the assortment of clothes and personal items piled around the room.

"What's it look like I'm doing?" he threw back, not even bothering to hide the snark in his tone.

"I'm trying to figure that out. That's why I asked."

"Don't be a dick. I'm moving my shit out of here." He returned to the closet, coming out with another pile of hanging clothes.

"Why?" I was genuinely baffled at his behavior.

"I hate this fucking room. I don't want to be here anymore. I'm going back to my old room."

"Okay." Confused but not wanting to agitate him further, I crossed over to the dresser, where my clothes were still neatly folded and put away. I dressed quickly and hung my towel on the hook behind the door while Jamie continued to move items out of the closet.

Flummoxed and unsure of what else to do in the midst of this erratic behavior, I picked up a stack of hanging clothes. "I'll just start moving some of this stuff up there." I'd only been in Jamie's childhood bedroom once when Annie had taken me up to show me some of his childhood memorabilia. That had been shortly before she'd gone into the hospital. I didn't think I'd even mentioned it to Jamie.

Jamie crossed over to me and yanked the hangers out of my hands. "Look, I don't need your help. I can move my own stuff."

"Okay. I'll just grab some of my things then." I crossed back over to the drawers and began pulling out a stack of T-shirts.

"Stop."

I turned to look at him. "What?"

"I said, stop." He let out a frustrated sigh. "Listen, I'm not trying to be an asshole, but I need my own space, okay?"

Time slowed to a standstill. Moments were measured in the space between heartbeats as I tried to make sense of his words. With one sentence, he'd eviscerated me, and I'd never be the same. For the rest of my life, there would be a before and an after, and this was the moment delineating the two.

My devastation must have registered on my face as I stood there in stunned silence.

"Don't make that face. I never even asked you to move in here." He dragged his hair tie out of his hair before scooping it up and piling it back into a knot on his head, his movements efficient and businesslike as if he wasn't ripping my heart out piece by piece. "Look, I appreciate everything you did for my...for my mom, but she's gone, and I'm a big boy." He took a breath and let it out as if coming to some decision. "I think it's time for you to go home."

Go home.

For the second time in mere moments, the bottom dropped out. Everything inside of me sunk right into the floor. For months *this* had been my home. *He* had been my home.

"Are you...are you breaking up with me?" I finally managed to get out past the lump in my throat and the tightness in my chest. I was terrified of his answer.

He clenched his jaw before responding. "I don't know. I just...I can't think when you're here, Finn. And you're *always* here. I need some space. It's all just been too much."

Fuck.

I knew he was hurting. I wanted to believe this was coming from a place of pain. From some need he had to shut everything and everyone out. Some delusional method of self-preservation. I could certainly relate because I'd spent most of my life running on auto-pilot, trying to feel as little as possible. But that wasn't Jamie. Had never been Jamie.

Jamie was Big Feelings. Capital *B*. Capital *F*. He was sunshine and warmth and happiness. Compassion and kindness and humor.

He was *love*.

I wanted to believe that it was the grief talking. And maybe it was, but the words being said were Jamie's. They came out of *his* mouth, were said in *his* voice.

They fucking *hurt*.

How had everything come down to this? He'd been the

one to chase me. Relentlessly. Breaking down all my walls until I believed that maybe, just maybe, I had enough value that someone might actually want me.

And he *had* wanted me. He *had*. Jamie was the one who wore his heart on his sleeve, the one who didn't hold back. The one who felt everything so damn big, he couldn't hold it in. He didn't even want to. Just bared his soul for everyone to see.

And he'd done all of that for me. This beautiful human had shown me that love, brilliant, blindingly beautiful love, was worth fighting for. It was worth holding on to. *I* was worth holding on to.

Only he wasn't holding on to me. He was letting me go.

No. Not letting go. Fucking shoving me out the door.

Shit. My head was a mess. I had whiplash as I tried to process what he'd said to me. What he'd done.

And Jamie? While I was doing mental gymnastics trying to make sense of the bomb he'd just dropped on me, he stood silent with his brow raised, hands on his hips, impatience radiating off him in waves.

"Okay," was all I managed. It was all I could choke out past the lump in my throat and the roiling in my stomach. He wanted me gone, so I'd go.

Calmly, I put the T-shirts back in the drawer and closed it quietly, as if my entire world hadn't just been turned on its axis. As if my heart hadn't been torn out through my throat, leaving my chest empty where it had once beat for him.

"I love you, Jamie," I said, tears running down my face. When he didn't respond, just continued to sort through the pile of clothes on his bed without looking at me, I walked out.

After leaving Jamie's, I called out of my afternoon shift at The Daily Grind and, thankfully, already had the night off at Ivory. I wasn't in any condition to work. I numbly made my way over to Carmen's apartment—I guess it was still technically mine—not remembering how I got there.

I stood on the doorstep for a long moment, pondering what I'd even say to her. Technically, I didn't need to knock, but I hadn't really lived here for months, and it seemed weird to just barge in. Eventually, not knowing where else to go, I raised my hand and rapped on the door.

Carmen answered, her thick ebony hair pulled into a messy bun, wearing leggings and an old Royals T-shirt. Her brows immediately rose in concern.

"Finn? What happened?"

Without a word, I walked past her into the apartment and sat on the couch. She followed me, sat beside me, crowded into my space, and pulled me into her arms.

"He kicked me out," I finally said, hating how the words felt on my tongue. They were bitter and nasty. They fucking hurt.

"Who? Jamie?" Carmen asked, confusion evident in her voice.

"Yeah. He said he needed space."

"Carmen? Who's here? Did I hear the d—?" Isa glided into the room, somehow looking graceful, despite being dressed in an oversized T-shirt and an old pair of sweats. "Oh. Hi, Finn," she said, taking notice of my pathetic self sitting on the couch next to Carmen.

"I didn't realize Isa was here this weekend," I said, not wanting to unload my tragedy onto them when they should be enjoying their time with each other. "You don't need me bringing you down." I made a move to stand, but Carmen shoved me back down.

"Don't be ridiculous. You're not going anywhere."

"What's going on?" Isa asked, perching on the arm of the couch next to me and taking my hand in hers. Her face showed nothing but concern, and I was struck by how lucky Carmen was to finally have found someone worthy of her. Her previous girlfriends would have been pissed that someone was taking her attention away from *them*, but Isa only showed concern about *me*. I was important to Carmen, so, therefore, I had become important to her. We'd only met a handful of times, and each time had been pleasant, but at this moment, I knew she was the one Carmen had been waiting for. I was happy for her, even though my own life felt like it'd been decimated.

I let out a sigh, then spilled the whole story. Of how Jamie's behavior had been more and more erratic lately. How he'd snapped at me after my run this morning, his abrupt decision to move rooms, and the ensuing argument about how I hadn't given him any space.

The words poured out of me in choppy, stilted phrases. Reliving what had happened was brutal and painful, and I wasn't sure how much of what I was saying made sense, as jumbled up as it was. Hell, it didn't make much sense to me either.

All I knew was that Jamie had been hurting for a while now, and the poison of not allowing himself to feel and process what had happened had finally been forced to the surface. Had he really meant everything he'd said this morning, or had I merely been the easy target standing in front of him? Was he just transferring his own pain onto me?

I'd take it over and over again if it meant he didn't have to feel any of it himself.

God, that was unhealthy as fuck, but I loved him. I was helpless to do anything else.

Carmen and Isa listened, mostly without comment, until I finished the whole thing. "What are you going to do?" Isa asked.

"I don't know. What *can* I do? He said he needed space. I guess I have to give it to him." I choked back the tears at the thought of losing him for good. It all felt so hopeless.

"You don't think you should fight for him?" Carmen asked, ever the romantic. She'd always wanted a hero to swoop in and fight for her.

"Maybe. But not today." God, I *did* want to fight for him. I wanted to march over there and shake him until he—the Jamie I'd fallen in love with all those months ago—came back to me. "I think he needs time to cool off."

Carmen, who hadn't let go of me the entire time, squeezed her arms tight, hugging me to her. "He loves you, Finn. You know that, right? He's just hurting."

I pulled away a little so I could look at her. "Yeah, I think I know that. At least, I want to believe it. But it's taken me a long time to get to a point where I even felt anyone would think I was worth the effort. Hard not to feel like I'm right back to where I started." I swallowed as my eyes filled with tears. "Only now, I know what I was missing."

"Oh, sweets. He'll come around. I've seen you two together. No way will he let you go for good." Her words swept through me, leaving an achy, restless feeling in my soul. Hope was a dangerous thing.

"I want you to be right," I said, my voice dropping almost to a whisper. "I don't know what I'll do without him. He's my everything."

CHAPTER 34
JAMIE

A COUPLE of hours after Finn left, I lay on my bed in my old room, staring at the ceiling of my childhood, the cloak of righteous indignation wrapped around me like a blanket. When I closed my eyes, I could still see the look of pain and hurt on his face as he walked out the door.

I pulled that cloak a little higher, choking off any feelings of guilt that threatened to seep in.

It had been nearly a month since Mom had passed, and Finn had been there every single day. His constant presence was a weight on my existence, demanding I continue moving forward when all I really wanted was to be left alone to drown in my grief.

He was worried about you.

Didn't I have a right to grieve in peace without someone breathing down my neck?

He's grieving too.

Sleeping in my bed every night.

You said you didn't want to be alone.

Constantly asking if I'm okay. The little sideways

glances when he thought I wasn't looking. Never leaving me in a room by myself.

He's worried because he loves you.

I shoved out of bed, annoyed by the pesky voice in my head that wouldn't leave me alone. The one that kept whispering *now what?* The one that cried, *what have you done?*

I didn't want to give that voice my attention. I wanted the anger. Anger was so much better than numbness and pain and sadness. Anger was a fire in my blood that made me feel alive. Anger made me want to set the world on fire so I'd never have to feel anything else ever again.

A knock sounded at my bedroom door, and for a split second, I felt the irrational hope that it was Finn coming back to fight for me, despite the fact I'd been the one who'd asked him to go. A mixture of surprise and disappointment barreled through me as I turned to see it was Asher darkening my door. A lump formed in my throat at the sight of my oldest friend, but I pushed any sentimental feelings away, replacing them with annoyance and irritation.

"What are you doing here? How'd you get in?" I sneered.

Asher flinched as if I'd struck him but remained steadfast in his spot. "I've had the garage code for years."

"Well, you can show yourself out. I'm not in the mood for company." I turned away from him in dismissal, but the asshole didn't take the hint.

Quiet as a mouse, Asher stepped beside me as I stared out the window into the backyard. There was a bare patch in the middle of what was otherwise a pristine lawn where a play structure had once stood. Dad and Uncle Bob had built it the summer of my sixth birthday, and I'd spent hours and hours out there. So many summer nights had been spent with Asher and me swinging our hearts out, trying to best each other on how far we could fling ourselves off the swing while it was in motion, daring each other to cross the monkey bars naked during a sleepover, and pouring our hearts out to each other as we entered the teen years and navigated the social landmines of middle school. Mom had sold it sometime in my teens, and we'd never quite been able to get grass to grow there, no matter what we tried.

As if Asher had been watching the same highlight reel of our childhood, he reached out and wrapped my hand in his. A single tear rolled down my cheek, which just pissed me off. I yanked my hand out of his and swiped away the wetness, turning away from him and stepping away to put some distance between us.

"What are you doing here, Asher? Shouldn't you be in Columbia?"

He ignored my questions, instead asking one of his own. "Where's Finn?"

"He's gone."

"Why?"

"Why do you care?" I turned and scowled at him. "What's it fucking matter?"

I saw the muscles in his jaw tighten, just for a moment, before his face returned to calm impassivity. "I care about *you*, Jamie. Finn hasn't left your side since the funeral." I flinched at that word. Most people danced around it, like speaking about my mom's death might send me over the edge, but Asher hadn't hesitated. I didn't know whether I appreciated his forthrightness or whether his audacity pissed me off. "I don't think he'd leave you unless you sent him away."

"I needed a break."

"A break from what?"

No matter how much venom I spewed at him, he kept

the questions coming, his voice calm and steady like a damn therapist. It made me want to lash out. Push him. Hurt him until he pushed back. Then he could feel an ounce of the rage I felt. Then maybe he'd leave me alone.

"What do you mean 'from what?' He was here all the damn time. I couldn't breathe." Agitated, I crossed over to my dresser and started loading the clothes I'd brought from downstairs.

"He was here because he loves you, Jamie. Didn't you tell him you didn't want to be alone?"

"How do you know that?" I shoved the top drawer closed now that I'd loaded it with socks and underwear and began working on the next drawer down, piling in T-shirts. "Anyway, that was a month ago. I didn't mean I needed him here every second of the damn day."

"Okay. So you went from scared of being alone to feeling suffocated?"

"Basically." I tried to shove the drawer closed, but it wouldn't close all the way, so I yanked it open again, took all the shirts out, and started over.

"Did you give Finn any indication you needed space? Or have you been stomping around the house, snarling like a wild animal that's been cornered in a dark alley?"

I tried to close the drawer again, even more forcefully this time, as Asher's words struck a little too close to home, but the damn thing still wouldn't shut. "Fuck you, man. I don't need you coming up in here and judging me." I yanked the drawer back open and gave the shirts another shove before pushing the drawer closed again. It still wouldn't close all the way. "Goddammit!" I yelled, pounding my fist on the top of the dresser. "Why won't this fucking thing close?" I pounded the dresser twice more, but on the third time, Asher caught my fist mid-swing, pulling it instead into my midsection and wrapping me in a bear hug from behind. While he matched me in height, he'd always been much leaner, but at that moment, the difference didn't matter. All the fight went out of me, and I collapsed in his arms. He pulled me to the floor with him, wrapping his arms around me as I shook with full-bodied sobs.

"Why'd you really send him away, Jamie?" he whispered into my hair as I sat beside him with my head buried in his chest.

"Because having him here hurts."

"Why?"

"Because I love him so damn much."

"And that hurts?"

"Yes, dammit!" I hissed. "It's too intense." I took a gulping breath, trying to get my sobs under control. "Right before Mom...died"—I stumbled over the word, hating everything it represented—"I felt so empty, so numb. I didn't want to feel that way anymore, so I begged Finn to... to fuck me. I just wanted to feel alive again. Only it was too much. Too intense. Too raw. I felt *everything*. Fear. Pain. Grief. Sadness. Anger. Despair. It felt like I was drowning in all of it. Like I might never feel okay ever again."

I took a few more breaths, still struggling to get myself under control. The floodgates had opened, and it felt impossible to stem the tide of my tears and my words. "So the next morning, I buried it. Buried all of it. I pulled away. I thought he'd take the hint, that he'd give up, and then I could be alone."

"I thought you were afraid to be alone," he said as a statement rather than a question, his arm still wrapped around me, holding me tight.

I whispered, "As much as I was scared of being alone, that would be better than..."

"...better than feeling everything else," he finished for me.

I nodded, sniffling.

"But he didn't take the hint, did he? He stuck."

I nodded again. "It pissed me off. I kept pushing him away, but he kept coming back. I hurt him over and over, I could see it on his face, but he never wavered. Why would he let me do that to him?" I couldn't understand it. I'd been awful to him, and he never wavered. I didn't deserve his loyalty.

"Because he loves you."

"I love him too," I whispered, and I wondered if I'd spend the whole of my life aching with the pain of it. Of having him and hurting him and sending him away.

"Do you really want him gone? Out of your life?" He pulled back to look at me. "Do you really want to be alone?"

"I just don't want to hurt anymore."

"What about love? Joy? Happiness? Laughter? If you shut down all that other shit, you shut out the good stuff too."

"I don't know if I'm capable of those things anymore."

He sighed. "Look, I'm not going to tell you it's not going to hurt and that it's not going to be hard, but you *are* capable of those things. And shutting all that other shit down without properly dealing with it is only setting yourself up for something much worse later. Hurting Finn, pushing him away, doesn't change the fact that Annie died. Those feelings are just going to find their way out another way, whether Finn's here or not. But, Jamie"—at the sound of my name, I turned my head to look at him. The sadness, the empathy I saw in his eyes, nearly broke me open all over again—"if he *is* here, you don't have to do it alone."

The ramifications of what I'd done slammed into me

like a punch to the gut. I nearly doubled over with the realization of it. I'd pushed away the person who mattered more
than anyone else. The one who'd stuck by me through all
my bullshit. Who'd helped take care of Mom, no questions
asked. Who'd helped with the funeral arrangements. Who'd
played piano at her funeral. Who'd suffered my silence and
mood swings and the words I'd flung at him when I was
lashing out. He'd not once pushed back or called me on my
bullshit, instead absorbing every blow, pushing through the
silence, and holding me up every step of the way. All those
years his parents had neglected him, treated him like he was
nothing, and I'd done the same thing.

No.

Shit.

NO.

Asher let go of me, jostling me as he dug in his pocket
for something.

"Here," he said, holding out a sloppily folded piece of
paper that looked like it'd been pulled out of a spiral notebook. I could see little strips of paper on one edge where it
hadn't torn cleanly along the perforated line.

"What is it?" I asked, eyeing it skeptically.

"It's from Finn. He's the one who sent me over here."

"Finn sent you?"

He gave me a small smile. "You gutted him, Jamie." I
flinched, my body flooding with guilt. "But even in the
midst of his own pain, he still didn't want you to be alone."

"What does it say?" I was scared to read it.

"I don't know. It's between you and him. I'm just the
messenger." I gingerly took the paper from him, eyeing it
warily, barely noticing as he stood. He stuck his hand in my
face, offering to help me off the floor, and I took it,
unbending my frame and rising to stand facing him.

"You probably think I'm the world's biggest asshole," I said, but he only shook his head.

"I don't. I think you did an asshole thing because you're hurting, but that doesn't mean you *are* an asshole. You're my best friend, and I love you. Nothing's going to change that."

I threw my arms around him, nearly knocking him off balance as I pulled him into a massive hug. "I love you too," I said through another round of tears. "I'm sorry I was a dick when you got here."

"Forgiven," he said without hesitation, then a little softer, "I miss her too."

Those simple words were like a balm to my battered soul. They said *I'm with you* and *I feel it too* and *You're not alone.*

"Thank you," I whispered.

I SPENT a lot of time Saturday evening staring at the letter Asher had brought me. It had a water spot where one of my tears had landed. The wetness had caused the blue lines on the notebook paper to bleed ever so slightly, giving that spot a distorted look.

I wasn't sure what the letter contained, but I found myself paralyzed with indecision, torn between wanting to absorb every word Finn had written for me yet terrified it would reveal that the damage I'd done to our relationship was permanent. Irrevocable.

Not yet ready to open myself up to whatever fate the letter had in store for me, I set it aside and moved on with the task of reorganizing my bedroom. The dresser drawers were much more cooperative this time as I completed my task more calmly before moving on to the organization of my closet. I put fresh linens on my bed and changed the towels in the en suite bathroom.

Once finished, I stood in the center of the room and forced myself to take a couple of cleansing breaths. While I'd made a hasty decision to clear out the room downstairs, it had been the right one. Being in here, in the room of my childhood, felt right.

I had always loved this room growing up. As far as I was concerned, it was the best room in the house. On one end of the room sat my queen-sized bed with a side table on either side. Above my bed hung posters of my favorite teenage idols: an enlarged copy of the Sports Illustrated cover featuring Michael Phelps adorned with a stack of medals from the 2016 Olympics, Salvador Perez, catcher for the Royals giving Lorenzo Cain a 'Salvy Splash' after one of the games in the run-up to the 2015 World Series, and for the book nerd in me, a banned book poster that read "I'm With The Banned" and included covers of works like 1984, Fahrenheit 451, and To Kill A Mockingbird.

On the opposite end of my room was a sitting area, which held my dresser, a bookshelf filled to the brim with my childhood and teenage favorites, and an oversized bean bag chair badly in need of new filling. It hadn't been used in at least five years.

My favorite feature of the room was the padded bench which ran the length of the wall and sat beneath a row of windows. I had spent much of my youth curled up on the bench with my favorite book while daylight poured over me. Or, even better, were those chilly rainy days with a blanket tucked around me while I read, the pitter-patter of rain-drops hitting the window-panes a comforting soundtrack.

I grabbed a blanket off the foot of my bed and crossed over to sit on the bench with my back resting against the wall. The sun had long since gone down, but it didn't matter. I shut my eyes as I let my thoughts wander back over the events of the last couple of months.

Thinking about the last month was like looking at a mirror that had been smudged. I could tell it was me in the reflection, yet I couldn't see myself clearly. If I thought back on my actions since Mom's passing, I could honestly say I barely recognized myself. Gone was the optimistic, happy-go-lucky, confident guy, and in his place was a barely functioning human who had lost the ability to see any sort of light at the end of the tunnel. I'd been performing tasks at the most basic level, but anything past that had simply been beyond my capabilities.

I wasn't sure how I'd allowed myself to get to this point, but I knew I didn't want it to continue. I'd lost both of my parents by the age of twenty-two. Those were awful, gut-wrenching experiences that no one my age should have to go through, but was this how I was going to go on for the rest of my life? Pushing away everyone around me, angry and bitter and alone?

Was this the kind of teacher I wanted to be? Mitchell had barely allowed me to teach any lessons in our classes, and a part of me had been relieved because interacting with others was exhausting. But what kind of teacher would that make me? I wasn't getting the teaching experience I would need to be able to lead my own class, and I sure as shit wasn't making the kind of difference with my students that I had dreamed of.

And Finn.

I knew I'd hurt him deeply. I'd worked so hard to get him to open up to me, to convince him that life was worth living, not simply something to get through, and then I'd spent the last month doing just that, just getting through it.

Worse still, he'd finally learned to love out loud in full color, and I'd kicked him out. He'd trusted me with his heart, with the scars of his childhood and the most hidden pieces of himself, and with just a few harsh words, I'd brought it all crashing down.

But it wasn't just a few harsh words, was it? I'd been treating him carelessly for weeks. He'd peeled back all those layers, revealing a beautiful, courageous soul. One full of kindness and compassion and loyalty so fierce it took my breath away. He'd trusted me with his heart, and rather than treasuring it like the precious gift it was, I'd shredded it. I'd snuffed out his light, the light that had only just begun to shine.

Even if I could convince him to forgive me, I wasn't sure I could ever forgive myself.

CHAPTER 35

Jamie-

It kills me to watch you suffer so. To see your light diminished so profoundly that I fear I may never feel its warmth again. It's terrifying, really. A fear quite unlike anything I've ever felt before, to see someone I love so deeply, so fully, be so lost and there's not a goddamned thing I can do about it.

The depth of love you hold for your mother is a beautiful thing. Notice I said hold and not held because that love will be with you for the rest of your life. Annie didn't take that with her. It remains within you. And it must feel so heavy right now, holding all that love inside you without a person to bestow it on. Funny, isn't it, that the same love that can make you feel lighter than air can also feel like the heaviest of burdens? Can you give that burden to me to carry for a little while? I'd carry it for days, weeks, months, or even years if it would bring back your smile, even for a moment.

Sending me away today...that hurt. I won't lie or

pretend like it didn't. But perhaps you're right. Perhaps I haven't given you the space to breathe. The space to sit with your grief and feel it. To be angry and sad and the whole messy range of emotions between. You have a right to that time and that space.

I won't apologize for it though. For the need to hover and maybe to smother you a little bit. I did it because I was worried about you. You were so damn lost, Jamie. I thought maybe I could be your anchor. That maybe I could be your North Star when you were ready to find your way home. I can still be that for you if you'll let me.

I love you, Jamie. Wholly. Deeply. Eternally.

The day you walked into the coffee shop was the day you saved me. You saved me from a lifetime of loneliness. Of never letting anyone in and never taking a risk. You challenged me to dig deeper and be braver and to go after what I want. To figure out what the fuck I wanted in the first place.

And you know what I want most in the world? You. Just you. In your pain and your sorrow and your grief. I hope someday to have your smiles too, but for now, I want whatever pieces you're able to give me.

You loved me whole, Jamie, and I'm here, waiting, whenever you're ready to let me do the same for you.

Love always,
Finn

SUNDAY MORNING, I pulled into the cemetery, making my way slowly down the gravel path until I found the spot I was looking for. I pulled over to the side and turned the car off but remained sitting for a moment, contemplating what had possessed me to decide to come here today.

After unloading all my drama on Carmen and Isa, I'd contacted Asher. As upset as I was over everything that had taken place, I hadn't wanted Jamie to be alone. Feeling like I had to say *something*, I'd scratched out a letter to Jamie and asked Asher if he could deliver it. All I could do after that was wait.

I'd taken a nap after that, drained from the emotions of the day, and when I'd woken, Carmen had insisted on feeding me tacos, and then all three of us had crammed onto my tiny couch and watched horror movies until three in the morning.

I hadn't woken up with the idea of visiting Annie's gravesite. In fact, I hadn't visited this spot since the day we'd buried her, but after a sleepless night spent tossing and turning on the couch, worried about my uncertain future with Jamie, I'd risen early and had spent some time attempting to write. It had been a frustrating endeavor. Much of the time had been spent glaring at the page, trying to find the words that stubbornly refused to reveal themselves to me. When I finally did set the pen to paper, I ended up crossing most of it out, unsatisfied with the turn of phrase or word choice. I just couldn't quite get it right.

Perhaps attempting to write a love story while in the midst of a potential breakup with the love of my life hadn't been the best choice.

I got out of the car, glad I'd worn a hoodie to ward off the early springtime chill, and crossed to the gravesite.

Annie had been buried next to her husband, Howard, and though his headstone had borne the effects of weather over the years, the marble of Annie's still gleamed white in the morning sun. I knelt in the grass in front of her marker, ignoring the dampness that soaked through the knees of my jeans.

I wasn't sure what to say or what to do or even why I was here, really. I'd never visited anyone's gravesite before. I was pretty sure you were supposed to bring flowers, and I hadn't even thought to pick some up.

Feeling foolish, I contemplated getting up and returning to my car, but the sound of footsteps on the gravel behind me held me in place. A shadow fell over me from behind, and I knew without looking that it was Jamie.

We stayed like that for some time, with him standing and me kneeling in the wet grass, a tense silence looming between us. At length, he cleared his throat before speaking. "She loved you, you know," he said, his voice full of gravel. My eyes pricked with tears at his words. How desperately I hoped that was true. I wasn't sure how to respond, though, so I stayed quiet.

"She'd be so disappointed in the way I've been behaving," he started, "at the way I've treated you."

"I think she'd be willing to cut you some slack under the circumstances," I responded without turning around.

"Maybe." He fell silent. My heart raced as I sat there, quietly waiting. I wanted to fill the silence. Even with the way he'd hurt me yesterday, I wanted to tell him it was okay. To touch him. To hold him.

But I didn't know where things stood between us, so I did none of those things.

"Everything feels upside-down right now. My whole life, I've been an optimist. The one who could always find the silver lining. The person in the group who had a ready smile and a joke to cheer someone up. The one who never let anything ruffle his feathers. And it wasn't that I never had bad days or that bad things never happened to me. I mean, I lost my father when I was ten, for fuck's sake, but it's just that I've always bounced back. I've always been able to shake it off." He paused for a moment, and when he continued, I heard a quaver in his voice. "I don't know how to shake this off. I don't know how to bounce back. How do I recover from losing the person who's been everything to me?"

I stood and faced him, unable to stand the distance between us any longer. "I don't think this is something you ever recover from. Not really. I think you have to learn to live *with* it rather than try to pretend it doesn't exist."

"What if I can't?" he asked, his voice small. He leaned forward, resting his forehead against mine, closing his eyes against the tears threatening to fall. "What if I spend the rest of my life feeling like this? Like I'm drowning, and no matter how hard I try to kick myself to the surface, the weight of it all keeps bringing me down?"

I placed my hand on the back of his neck, squeezing gently, trying to give him whatever comfort I could. "Then I'll keep doing my best to pull you toward the surface."

He let out a stuttering breath. "God, Finn. I'm so fucking sorry. I didn't mean—"

"Shh. Baby, it's okay." I moved my hands from the back of his neck to the sides of his face, pulling back slightly so I could look at him.

"It's not okay," he said. I started to speak again, to reassure him, but he interrupted before I could get the words out. "It's not," he insisted. "You've done so much for me this past month, and I can't believe I lashed out at you like that. You didn't deserve it. I can't believe you're even speaking to me today. I just—"

I cut him off with a kiss. I couldn't remember the last time we'd kissed, the last time he'd even let me touch him, but I couldn't stand it anymore. I needed to feel his lips pressed to mine, and I needed him to feel me too.

It was like coming home.

We melted into each other, our bodies touching from our lips down to our toes. I wrapped my arms around him, trying to hold all his pieces together in much the same way he'd done for me all those months ago. The feel of him pressed up against me was *everything*. I never wanted it to end.

Eventually, he pulled back, again settling his forehead against mine as we both struggled to catch our breath. "I love you, Finn. I know I haven't shown it this last month, but—"

I pulled away to look at him. "Stop, Jamie. It's really okay."

"Just let me say this. Let me get it out."

The intensity in his eyes prevented me from saying anything more, so I nodded.

"You said in your letter that I saved you the day we met, but in the last month, I think it was *you* who saved *me*. I've felt so fucking lost, Finn, but like you said, you gave me an anchor. Something to tether me to my life."

"I didn't think I was helping at all. You barely even looked at me, Jamie."

He bowed his head. "I know, and I'm sorry. But you were there for me in all the ways I needed, even when I was pushing you away." He brought his eyes back up to meet mine, earnest and searching, like he was begging for my forgiveness. He didn't know that he already had it. Yet, after thinking I might have lost him, there was a part of me scared to trust this, and I needed to hear him out.

"You didn't ask anything of me," he continued. "You didn't serve up empty platitudes or tell me to get my shit together or push me when I wasn't ready. Even yesterday, when I was completely irrational, you took it in stride and tried to support me. I fucking kicked you out of my house, and you still sent Asher to me. You've been everything I needed you to be, and I don't deserve you, but I do love you so damn much."

"I love you too, Jamie. I don't think there's anything that could ever stop me from loving you." I pulled him into a tight hug, holding him to me in a fierce embrace.

"I feel so broken, Finn, and I don't know if I'll ever be okay again. I don't know if I'll ever be the man you deserve, but I'm too selfish to let you go."

I'd said something similar to him back in December, and I remembered all too well that feeling of thinking something was wrong with me and that I'd never be good enough for him. I shook my head in denial. "You never lost me in the first place. I'll always be here as long as you want me."

"I'll never stop wanting you. Never." He pulled away from my embrace, taking my hand in his, his eyes boring into mine. "Will you come home with me?"

"Are you sure? You said you wanted space..." My heart yearned for that, to go home with him, to spend the night—maybe all our nights—holding him, but I didn't want to push him. If he needed space and time, I'd give him that. I'd give him anything he wanted.

"I was so fucking stupid. I thought if I had space, I wouldn't have to feel the pain of losing her. If I shut down my feelings for you, I could shut down my feelings for everything else. But when Asher came over last night, he helped me see that all sending you away had done was make me feel double the loss." He squeezed my hands and pulled me closer so we were nearly nose to nose. "I don't have a choice in living without Mom, but it kills me knowing I might have ruined my chance to have you. Please tell me I haven't ruined it..."

"You haven't ruined anything. I love you, baby. I'd be happy to go home with you."

"Thank God," he said as he pulled me into his arms, crushing me in his embrace.

We stood just like that, locked in each others' arms for a long while, and I didn't know what was going through his head, but I knew I was savoring the feel of him, his scent, his warmth, his heartbeat pounding against my chest...had it been just an hour ago that I thought I might never have the privilege of holding him ever again? I never wanted to let go.

Eventually, we turned to face Annie's grave as if we'd only

just remembered where we were. I watched as Jamie took a couple of steps forward and fell to his knees in front of her headstone. I expected tears, and when none came, when he remained still and solemn, I feared he'd retreated into himself again. But when he turned and gestured for me to join him on the ground beside him, it wasn't with a blank, empty stare but rather one of immense sadness. And as weird as it sounded, I was relieved because he was allowing himself to feel it.

I sank to the ground next to him, pulling my knees up in front of me and wrapping my arms around them. He resituated himself so he was sitting by my side in the same position, hips and shoulders touching, sharing our warmth in the crisp April-morning air.

"You know, the day I met you was the first day I'd ever gone into that coffee shop. I typically made coffee at home, but we'd run out, so despite the fact I was running late, I decided to pull into The Daily Grind on my way to campus. I'd driven by it almost every day since the start of the semester, but for whatever reason, I hadn't come in."

I could feel his eyes on me, so I turned to look at him. He reached up, brushing a hand gently down my cheek. "From the moment I laid eyes on you, I was captivated. I had to rush out of there to get to class, but I came back later that day because I couldn't get you out of my head, and I just knew that I had to see you again."

"I remember." My lips turned up in a small smile. "You were kind of a creeper that day."

"And you shut me down cold." He returned my smile and then reached into his pocket and pulled out his wallet. He slipped his fingers inside and came out with a scrap of paper, which he handed me. I unfolded it, immediately recognizing my slanted scrawl on the page. My eyes darted to his in confusion before returning to the words I'd written there.

Darkness falls on my descent into madness
The flavor of him lingers on my lips

I remembered writing this, playing with the words, trying to get them just right. I'd finally been frustrated and torn the paper out of my notebook and given up. I hadn't written it for anyone in particular. I'd just been toying with different thoughts and ideas and playing around with words. I was surprised he'd kept it all this time.

"I can't believe you saved this," I said, dumbfounded.

He shrugged. "Like I said, I was captivated from the moment I saw you. But this...this called to me on a deeper level. I wanted to know the person who wrote those words. I wanted to know *you*." He paused for a moment as if contemplating his next words before continuing, "You came into my life at the worst possible time. I was in the middle of the semester at a new school trying to finish my credits so I could student teach while juggling taking care of Mom. With all the madness going on in my life, I had absolutely no business pursuing a relationship with anyone. But almost from that first day, it was like I didn't have a choice. Something compelled me to stop in that particular coffee shop on that particular day. And even after you shut me down and called me a rich pretty boy a few days later"—I grimaced at that memory—"I don't think it's a coincidence that I happened upon you stranded with a flat tire."

He grabbed my hand, rubbing his thumb in circles against my skin. "I think you were always meant to be mine. And I don't know, looking back, maybe the timing was exactly right. I'm glad Mom got to meet you and love on you." My eyes pricked with tears. Some days I felt angry that my time with her had been so brief, and other times, I felt blessed to have known her at all, to know what it was like to feel a mother's love. "I think in the end, it helped her to know that even after she was gone, someone would be here to love me. Someone who'd make sure I didn't have to go through this alone." He laid his head on my shoulder and sighed.

"I'm glad for that too," I said as I pressed my lips to the top of his head before resting my head on top of his. We sat like that for a long time, staring at Annie's grave as the sun rose higher in the sky, burning off the dew on the grass.

I thought about everything that had happened in the last six months. All the steps we'd taken. Forward. Backward. Sometimes sideways.

The path we'd traveled had been anything but straight, and there'd been moments one of us had supported the other when our steps had faltered, but it had been the path meant for both of us to take together. And it dawned on me finally that this was what love was really about. All that time, I'd been so concerned I didn't know how to do this, that I didn't know how to be in a relationship, that I didn't know what love looked like...it looked just like this. It was picking up the pieces when the one you loved fell apart. It was comfort and laughter and patience and lust. It didn't mean there weren't hard times. It didn't mean there weren't fights and angry words and sadness. Love didn't make you immune to any of that. But it made all of that shit worth it. It made the joy that much sweeter. The make-up sex that much hotter. The hugs that much warmer. It was tiny moments and big life-changing events.

It was him saving me and me saving him right back.

It was ours.

Only ours. Not anyone else's. I didn't need to have a good example of what love looked like because *our* love, mine and Jamie's, was as unique and extraordinary as a single snowflake falling in the midst of a blizzard. No one could define what that looked like but us.

It turned out all I had needed all along was *him*. We could figure the rest of it out together.

EPILOGUE
JAMIE

September

The late summer sun beat down on us as we loaded up the U-Haul we'd rented over the Labor Day weekend. In early June, I realized I couldn't stay in my childhood home any longer. Everywhere I turned were reminders of the parents I'd lost and the family I'd once had. I couldn't move forward, always stuck in memories of the past and wishing for things that would never be. It'd been an absolutely heart-wrenching decision, one made after spending the first week of summer vacation sliding deeper and deeper into a depression I couldn't shake myself out of.

After that day at the cemetery, Finn and I became closer than ever, and while things had gotten marginally better, I'd still struggled in my day-to-day life. I'd finished my student teaching, and though I was sure I hadn't given it my best effort, I'd managed to do well enough to be offered a permanent position this fall. I had to credit Finn and Mitchell for getting me through it. Without Mitchell guiding and supporting me at school and Finn holding me together at home, I wasn't sure I would have made it.

Still, I'd crossed the stage in early May and received my diploma. It had been a proud moment after everything I'd been through, but there'd still been a shadow hanging over the day because my parents hadn't been there to witness it. Aunt Cathy and her family had done their best to fill that void, but after all the friends and family had left my small celebration, I'd laid my head in Finn's lap and cried myself to sleep.

Once school released for the summer, I found myself adrift once again. This time without the distraction of teaching to keep my mind off all I'd lost. Finn came home from a shift at The Daily Grind one day to find me sitting in Mom's chair in her bedroom. Not the room she'd used before she passed, but the one she'd shared with my father as I was growing up. She had often used that chair to read or have a quiet moment when life was moving too fast. And sometimes, when I was little, I'd find her there and climb up on her lap to cuddle or have her read me a story.

When Finn had found me, I'd been sitting in the chair, staring into space. It had taken him three attempts to get my attention. He'd finally had to shake me to get me to look at him, and when my eyes had landed on his, he'd looked terrified. At that moment, I'd known I couldn't stay in that house anymore. I would never be able to move on.

Shortly thereafter, Finn urged me to start seeing a therapist. It didn't take much convincing, as I'd been contemplating seeing one on my own anyway, but I talked Finn into seeing one too. We both had plenty of issues we needed to work through, and it was past time we got started.

I also took a job as a lifeguard at a nearby pool for the summer. It proved to be a nice distraction during all those empty summer days, and I took to arriving early so I could swim laps before starting my shift. I'd forgotten how good it felt to work my body this way. I could lose myself in the rhythm of each breath and stroke and feel the power in my body's ability to move through the water. It had been almost as good for my mental health as the therapy.

Finn continued to work at The Daily Grind and Ivory, though he'd cut back his hours to focus more on writing. He'd balked at that at first, worried about how it would affect his bank account, and though he wouldn't take any help from me financially, he did agree to move in with me while Carmen took over the lease on his apartment.

The changes in him over the last couple of months had been a bright spot in my world where I'd lost so much. He had become more and more open with me, allowing me to see all the beautiful sides of him. My favorite was how often he smiled now. He'd always been beautiful, but when he smiled, it positively lit my soul on fire. It made me want to earn those smiles as often as I could, just so I could bask in his glow.

"You ready to roll?" Finn asked as he loaded the last box into the backseat of his Jeep. He whipped off his T-shirt, using it to mop sweat off his face before tucking it into the waistband in the back of his shorts. I watched as a single bead of sweat made its way down the center of his abs before being absorbed by the elastic waistband of his athletic shorts.

I blinked, shaking myself out of the lust-filled haze that image had evoked, and adjusted myself, trying to remember what he had asked me. The smirk on his face told me he'd totally caught me staring, but I just shrugged. My boyfriend was hot.

Remembering he was waiting for an answer to his questions, I sobered. "Yeah, give me just a minute." I pressed a kiss to his temple, then turned to head back into the house.

"You want me to come with you?" he called out as I walked away from him.

I paused, knowing even before I turned to look at him that I'd see worry etched into his features. "Nah, I just need a moment to myself." I offered him a small smile. "I'm okay. I promise." The worry on his face eased some, but not completely. Still, he simply nodded, then turned back toward the U-Haul, ostensibly to make sure everything was secure, though I knew he was likely just giving me the space I'd asked for.

I made my way into the living room and stood a moment, my head on a swivel as I surveyed the empty space. Memories swept over me of a lifetime spent in this room. Despite having vacuumed, you could still see the indentations in the carpet from the furniture that hadn't been moved in years. We'd sold or donated most of it. Our new two-bedroom apartment in the Crossroads District was much smaller and wouldn't hold it all. Much of it was dated and didn't really fit our needs anyway. Still, as I played through the highlight reel of my childhood, I imagined all of it as it used to be. The recliner where my dad had watched the evening news almost nightly. The area rug that was placed strategically to cover the Kool-Aid stain I'd left when I'd accidentally spilled my cup when I was seven. The coffee table where I'd raced my Hot Wheels, and then later, when I was older, where I'd sometimes done my homework while sitting on the floor. Where Finn, Mom, and I had shared a pizza the first time he'd come over to hang out with her.

My eyes traveled over the shelves of the built-ins. Once

filled with pictures, they were now empty. They looked a little sad without all those memories filling them.

Then there was the corner where we'd always placed the Christmas tree. I had years and years of happy memories decorating a tree with Mom and Dad, then later, just Mom and me. This year, it would be Finn and me. And while I knew I would be sad that it was the first year I would do so without Mom, it would also be Finn's first year decorating a tree at all. It would be nice to start a new tradition with him in a new home. One that I hoped we'd be able to repeat for years to come.

I continued my good-bye tour of the house, going room by room, allowing memories to wash over me as I stopped in each one. My heart hurt, but it was a sweet kind of ache. Since school had started a couple of weeks ago, I'd realized that it was getting easier to find the happy moments even in the midst of my sadness. Between the therapy, my relationship with Finn, and the space to truly process the loss of my mom over the summer months, I'd finally started to heal. It had taken the start of the school year and establishing a routine in my new role in the classroom for me to finally be able to look back and see the progress I'd made over the last couple of months. I was no longer simply surviving but was actually starting to thrive once again.

And so now, as I stood in my childhood bedroom, once again looking out over the yard, I was able to look back and see all the ways in which I'd been lucky as hell to have the kind of childhood I'd had. I was able to acknowledge the pain of the loss of the best people I'd ever known but also treasure the fact I'd had them in my life for as long as I had.

Arms came around me, and Finn pressed a kiss to the back of my neck before resting his chin on my shoulder. "I know you said you wanted to do this alone, but I couldn't stand the wait any longer. I hope this is okay," he said softly.

I grabbed his hand and brought it to my lips, then held it clasped against my chest. "Yeah, it's fine. Thank you."

"Why are you thanking me?"

"For knowing when to give me space. And knowing when to love on me."

"You do the same for me." I turned and pulled him around so we stood side by side, arms wrapped around each other's waists, his head tucked under my chin. A feeling of contentment washed over me, one that I hadn't felt in a long time, and I knew in that moment that I was ready.

I turned to face Finn, placing my hands on either side of his face, and drew his lips to mine. I poured all the love and gratitude I felt for him into that kiss, wanting him to feel just how very glad I was, not only that he'd come into my life but that he'd stuck by my side through the darkest parts of it.

I pulled away ever so slightly and whispered into his lips, "Let's go home." Then, with one more quick kiss, I pulled back and smiled, happiness radiating through me. He returned my smile, and grasping my hand, we turned and walked out.

Out of my old room and my old house and into a new life filled with new challenges and new beginnings. One filled with hope.

And so much love.

The End

Want more Jamie and Finn? Click here for a Bonus Epilogue!

Want to interact with me and other readers to discuss the book, learn more about my inspiration, and see what I'm working on next? Join my readers group on facebook: Melody's Lane.

My mom passed away from cancer in 2021. It was the third type of cancer she'd battled, and her body had simply had enough. And while her story is completely different from Annie's, and mine from Jamie's, many of the emotions and feelings evoked here are the same.

The feelings around the death of a parent are complicated and unique to each individual. We all work through grief differently. I didn't set out to write a book so that I could process my mother's death, but perhaps my subconscious knew that was what I needed. There were moments in writing I knew would be challenging, and others that completely took me by surprise, and I learned that I have a lot of work still to do in this regard.

I hope you weren't too mad at me for letting Annie go. I had thought early on in the writing stages that I might need to write it this way, but I put it off, trying to find other ways around it. In the end, this was the only way the characters would let me tell their story. I sobbed while writing it. And again several times after that.

The flashback scenes...these are always controversial.

Some readers love them, while others hate them. I tried to find a good balance in offering a few, but not too many, and deliberately kept them shorter in length. And while each vignette doesn't always have a specific bearing on the plot in present day, my hope was to show the differences in Jamie and Finn's childhoods, and how the events of their past, and the way they were raised, have shaped them into who they are today. These events frame how they interact with others and how they perceive the world and, I think, give some insight into their internal conflict and motivations. Thank you for humoring me in including those glimpses of their past into the story.

ACKNOWLEDGMENTS

I wrote a book! Thank you for taking a chance on a new author! This has been an amazing experience, and one which I could not have done without some key people.

To my husband - you are my biggest cheerleader and supporter! You have listened to me babble endlessly about all the ins and outs of the actual writing, and the business side of authoring, and never batted an eye when I said I needed to purchase just one more thing to get this book to publish. I adore you endlessly.

To my daughters - you inspire me in ways you will likely never understand.

To Kayla, Francesca, Aiden, Brenda, and Nicole - Your feedback was invaluable in shaping Jamie and Finn's story. This book wouldn't be the same without you! Thank you for allowing me to pop into your DMs with random questions and for talking me off the ledge when need be!

To Abbie - Commas are dumb. The end. Just kidding - your editing was fabulous! Thank you for helping me polish my words!

To Melanie Harlow and the Harlot Authors Group, and A.M. Johnson - every author needs mentors and you are mine! I couldn't have navigated this path without your leadership and support!

ABOUT THE AUTHOR

Melody Claire writes emotional contemporary MM romance stories with moderate heat and a whole lot of heart. She hails from Kansas City but resides in Omaha and loves setting her stories in the Midwest. She is married with two almost grown kiddos, a dog, and a kitty. By day, she teaches middle school, and by night can be found writing on her laptop or curled up with her kindle. She's addicted to Pink Drinks and the sound of her husband's laugh, and loves nothing more than to escape into a love story.

Connect With Me!

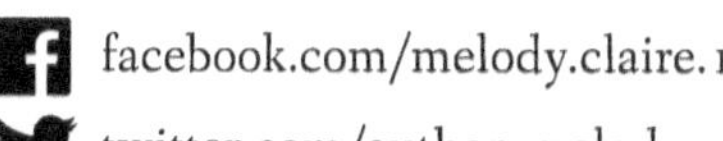

facebook.com/melody.claire.1

twitter.com/author_melody

instagram.com/melody.claire.author